Dandelion Days

By the same author

Wuthering Depths

Silver Riding

Dandelion Days

Bette Howell

CHAPMANS
1991

Chapmans Publishers Ltd
141–143 Drury Lane
London WC2B 5TB

BRITISH LIBRARY CATALOGUING IN PUBLICATION DATA

Howell, Bette
Dandelion days
I. Title
823.914

ISBN 1-85592-009-3

Copyright © 1991 by Bette Howell

The right of Bette Howell to be identified as the author of this work has been asserted by her in accordance with the Copyright, Designs and Patents Act 1988.

Photoset by Rowland Phototypesetting Ltd
Bury St Edmunds, Suffolk

Printed and bound in Great Britain by
Bookcraft (Bath) Ltd

For Richard and Edyta

One

It all started with the letter. It was a bright, sunny morning and Otley, my husband, was just tearing up his income tax forms.

'If they want me they can come and get me,' he said, when the letter-box clanked and in flew a purple envelope smelling of mildew and Parma violets.

'It's from Napoleon,' he said. 'I knew he wasn't dead.'

It was in a bold, passionate hand and addressed to Mr Craven but I'm used to that because I'm only the backroom boy. He turned away to read it and I looked over his shoulder.

Claro
by the light of the moon

Dear Otley,
Help! The roof's leaking and they're digging the meadow up for a car-park. Swire Sugden's behind it, he's got the council in his pocket. I can't stand it any longer. I'm going back to come again as Princess Di. Don't tell anybody I'm dead because they don't know I'm alive.
Your devoted cousin,
Elinor Mydnite
PS Aunt Bedelia gets on my wick.

Trossachs! I thought to myself as I sat down to finish my fibre-filled, cholesterol-free breakfast. Not another mad relation!

'"Devoted cousin",' I said. 'You haven't seen her for ten years or more, not since that time she fell in the sheep-dip up at Jimmy One Eye's.'

'Blood's thicker than time,' Otley said darkly.

'Well, what can we do?' I inquired. 'We've got no clout. Us peasants have to do as we're told.'

'We can't refuse a cry for help, moral support an' all that,' he said. ''E's after building a holiday camp as well – Scandinavian chalets, saunas. He's got to be stopped.'

'Frolicking in the snow?' I murmured.

'Whippin' each other up an' that,' he said.

'Whatever next!' I exclaimed through my jumbo oats.

'And not only that,' he went on, 'the Orient-Express want to buy the Settle-Carlisle line. Bloody cheek!'

'To be honest,' I said recklessly, 'I don't care who runs it as long as they get that viaduct mended first.'

His face began to take on the aspect of a mad beetroot and I transferred the bread knife over to my side of the table.

'You'd sell your birthright for a mess of pottage, wouldn't you?' he challenged as we glowered at each other across the marmalade. It's funny how you can love somebody and hate them at the same time.

'Yes,' I said, 'if I was hungry. British Rail don't want it, anyway,' I reminded him.

'Well, we don't want that lot up here with their fancy lamps, how much are they going to charge?'

'It'll close the trade gap,' I informed him. 'Direct link with the Chunnel. All Europe shall be as one.'

'We shan't be able to get on it when we want to go camping – it'll be full of Japs going up to Glasgow for a bit of oshi dashi,' he said grabbing a spoon and bashing in his boiled egg as if it were the bald head of an oriental gentleman. 'You'll not be able to get a bacon sandwich. It'll be all prawn cocktails an' flamin' Filofaxes.'

'There'll always be an England,' I said.

'If we can stop it being ravaged by the fast buck brigade first.'

'It'll be all right now that Maggie's gone green,' I assured him. 'She's already mending the hole in the ozone layer.'

'Hope the Orient-Express don't buy British water,' he mused, 'coming here dumping their unwanted concubines when they've clogged up the Bosphorus.'

I should say here that my husband, Otley Craven, is a war hero battling with the male menopause and as such tends to go off on mad forays in preference to tidying his room and emptying his wastepaper basket. I'm the serf, May, obliged to act as his runner, but I don't mind as I'm trying to keep my weight down. The Bible says we can have carnal knowledge but we're too tired when we've done everything else. I think he's looking for a wise virgin with some oil in her lamp. Our son, Mike, is away at college and has made a lot of hermaphrodite friends with interchangeable clothes.

'... and charity begins at home,' Otley was saying. 'You've got to put your own patch in order first before setting the world to rights.'

He went round the house like a whirlwind throwing things into holdalls, and before you could say Nicholas Ridley we were off down the road in our old banger.

It's hard to find Claro on the map. It's a secret place, a hidden relic of the old wapentake from which the name derives. You go upalong, downalong and roundalong to where the river stops rushing down from the moors and broadens out lapping the water meadows. Fat black and white cows stand knee-deep in the water on hot, sunny days; in the distant haze are blue hills speckled with sheep, and lower down the valley the hay meadows, nodding with flowers waiting to be executed to provide munching material for our fat friends.

'Might get a bit of fishing in while I'm here,' said Otley, his green eyes echoing the woods and fields. In his corduroys and army-surplus camouflage jacket stuffed with gadgets, squashed headgear to match, he was well on the way to being a woodiwiss. I was wearing my lambs-wool sweater that I got for twenty-five pence at a car-boot sale, over a cotton shirt from Open Sesame, my walking boots and Italian army trousers.

'I'm not staying long,' I said. 'I've got to do the oven with Mr Muscle. It's disgusting.'

'You've got no soul,' he said.

'I don't get the chance with all that drudgery stuff,' I complained to deaf ears.

We spluttered round a bend and came to a stop in front of a crazy house built by a yeoman at the end of the Civil War, neglected by a follower of John Wesley who roamed the country on horseback, improved by a Victorian industrialist who added the Jubilee Tower and prettified by an Edwardian plant collector who added a dinky little conservatory on to the bathroom so as not to waste the steam. 'Claro' it said.

The site itself was ancient. Roman coins had been found there and on certain days you could see the playing-card outline of a Roman marching camp on a level bit half-way up the hillside. Last year we went to a WEA history class about Roman Britain. I stuck up for Cartimandua, our local lass, who did a deal with the invaders and Otley said no wonder her husband left her and tried to join up with Boudicca; we all love her but it takes all sorts, and anybody can go on the rampage with a battleaxe. He kept on about messes of pottage and then went off to learn dry-stone walling up at Mallerstang for a week.

We knocked and pushed open the door just as Aunt Bedelia came billowing towards us and enfolded me in a warm embrace like a feather eiderdown. She had been left the house by its previous owner, an old bachelor, and could never quite cope with the outside. Inside was a mad mix of Edwardiana, Swinging Sixties and MFI.

'You're just in time to help me do my dandelions,' she said. A star turn at the WI, Aunt Bedelia can do anything with dandelions: wine for the winter, beer for the summer, young leaves for the salad bowl, coffee for the coffee morning, a tea for the dropsy and a gummy goo for curing warts.

'It's a grand little flower,' she went on. 'If they were a pound apiece you'd all want one.'

Standing in the scullery knee-deep in foliage we learned that Swire Sugden had got planning permission for a holiday complex with chalets, a supermarket and a car-park, which would shut us off from our favourite stretch of the Wharfe. The Hon. Mrs Grindlewood-Gryke, lady bountiful of Claro and commanding officer of the WI, wanted to establish a theme park and living history museum in the same place. Furthermore, the archaeology class at the WEA had found evidence of a civilian settlement connected with the Roman camp and wanted to investigate, and a chap known as Tumbleweed from Friends of the Earth was guarding a bog asphodel in an adjacent swamp. Nobody had actually spoken to him but he could be spotted at times rolling across the landscape covered in sphagnum moss and lousewort.

'Sugden's threatening to dig up the meadow when nobody's looking,' Bedelia said. 'Like they did with the old chapel, he sent the bulldozers in the middle of the night and when we got up next morning there it was – gone!'

'The scurvy, conniving skink!' I exploded.

'And what about my dandelions?' Bedelia wailed. 'My little moppets, my little rays of sunshine fallen from the sky, I can't live without them.' She gathered an armful and hugged them to her pink nylon overall giving the impression of a dish of rhubarb and custard.

'We'll do what we can,' Otley assured her in his best war hero voice.

My heart sank into my boots at this. Bang goes sitting by the river with Dorothy Wordsworth's *Journals* and a muesli bar.

'Where's Elinor?' I asked.

'She lives at the top of the tower like Rapunzel,' Bedelia scoffed. 'Only comes down here when she's hungry.'

'What does she do all day?'

'She studies continuum with relation to reincarnation,' she replied unable to conceal a snigger.

'Oh!' I said.

'Granny always used to say she'd been here before,' Otley put in.

'I think there's something in it,' I ventured. 'Haven't you ever had the feeling that you know what's going to happen, what somebody's going to say next and what happened in history that it doesn't tell you in the history books?'

'No.'

We pulled all the petals off the dandelions and Bedelia put them in a bucket to start the wine. A smaller amount in a pan with some ginger and lemon peel for the beer all stirred up with a big wooden spoon. Then we chopped up the roots and put them in the oven for coffee.

'Wine'll be ready for Christmas,' she assured us. 'Beer only takes a week.'

I couldn't help thinking that a supermarket in the vicinity would come in very handy. If it wasn't for people like Swire Sugden we'd still be living in the Stone Age.

'Smells delicious,' I lied as I washed the gungy mess off my hands.

We sat in front of the magic lantern to have our midday snack of bubble and squeak made with dandelion leaves, semolina pudding and jam and tea made with Morrison's tea-bags.

'They're only sixty-odd pee,' said Aunt Bedelia. 'Them at Co-op's nearly a pound now.'

The messenger on the box informed us that Europe was trying to get Britain to join the snake but she wasn't having any. The spectre rose before me of a line of Brussels bureaucrats doing the conga, growing into a gigantic boa constrictor and gobbling us all up. I edged closer to Otley and caught hold of his hand for reassurance.

'When they build the Chunnel it'll come over and get us,' I said.

'It isn't a real snake you nit,' he replied. 'Anyway they'll never get that tunnel finished, they've been trying for about two hundred years.'

'Have they?' inquired Auntie between mouthsful of semolina.

'Yes,' he went on. 'There's holes all over the place and they once found an underground train with fifty skeletons sitting in it going to work.'

'I'll show you round and then we'll go and see Elinor,' Bedelia said clearing the table hurriedly. 'She does get in a stew at times.'

The kitchen was furnished with DIY flat-pack Formica, lopsided doors that wouldn't shut and gaps that let in the draughts, beetles and slugs. Clusters of tiny, blue pellets were placed strategically in this corner and that, and holes bunged up with putty or covered over with sticky tape.

'I phoned the pest control people once,' she explained. 'But they said they didn't come out for slugs.'

'Where do you cook?' I asked, fearful of the answer.

'We use the dining-room now – only put junk in here.'

An ancient gas oven, cavernous sink, a Stephenson's Rocket sewing machine, an oak davenport, china cabinet crammed with bric-à-brac and various cupboards and tables smothering a Turkey carpet filled the dining-room. Assorted chairs huddled together like a rugger scrum.

'It's cosy,' I said.

The parlour was similarly furnished but with the addition of tinkling glass lamps and a three-piece suite in red dralon from Kingsway. The bathroom was on the ground floor and used to be the buttery until an iron bath was put in and then French windows and a conservatory.

'It'll be handy,' said Otley, looking round, 'when you want to cut your toenails and water the plants at the same time.'

'I'll show you upstairs later,' Bedelia said as she ushered us out into the garden – herbs and cabbages at the back with clumps of cottage garden annuals rollicking in algae-covered stone troughs, chimney-pots and wheelbarrows; at the front a lawn rampant with buttercups and daisies and a rambling rose fighting for space with a belligerent bindweed. The letters of 'Claro' hung drunkenly from a gate made out of an old cartwheel.

'That's where the water comes in,' said Bedelia pointing to some missing slates. 'You'll have to put a bucket in your bedroom.'

The Jubilee Tower was a field away on a grassy knoll and we made our way thorough bush, thorough brier, like the fairy in *A Midsummer-Night's Dream*; goose grass clutching at our legs and brambles at our hair.

'We were worried when we got the letter,' I said as we puffed and panted up the hill. 'Said something – about – doing away with – herself.'

'Take no notice,' Bedelia said, sitting down suddenly. 'That's just the way she talks; next minute she'll be dancing a fandango. She fair gets on my wick.'

The river lay below us and in a lazy bend snuggled a few houses and a farm. To the east loomed Swire Sugden's hacienda-type residence, white stucco and curling red tiles. To the west Grindlewood Park, laid out on a grand scale in the Age of Enlightenment by the first of the slave-driving mill owners, Sir Mauger Grindlewood. An army camp during the war, it mushroomed with Nissen huts and later welcomed the remnants of General Anders' Polish Army who could be heard on a Sunday cracking their whips at the water-lilies and surrounding statuary. Between them on the river bank lay the disputed ground. Who it really belonged to was a secret hidden in the mists of time. Legend has it that the rightful owner is the son and heir of Lord Chatwin of Spignel Meu, if he can only be found. He was lost by a careless nanny and is thought to be living with the gypsies, his father, taking to drink, burned down Chatwin Hall and himself with it.

'That's the Roman camp,' Bedelia said, waving her arm at a flat piece of land to the side of us and slightly below. 'It leads down to the ford where the WEA class is digging.'

'They were here a long time,' I said. 'Four hundred years, was it?'

'An' it was a long way to walk in those sandals,' said Bedelia.

Two

The West Riding hills are alive with towers and obelisks commemorating this battle or that jubilee and nobody can remember which. Regarded with curiosity and called at on a day out after the information centre and the public convenience, they are nothing more than places for children and dogs to play hide-and-seek round.

Elinor thought the Jubilee Tower might have something to do with Napoleon and the Battle of Waterloo and she was hoping to see him one day, which is why she kept a pot of Parma violets handy – his favourite flower.

'If anybody's going to come back here it's Julius Caesar,' said Aunt Bedelia, clinging to a rope going up the spiral staircase.

'He didn't get so far, Mr Firth told us at school,' I said, casting my mind a long way back.

'Him!' said Bedelia in disgust. 'Snotty-nosed kid from Monkey Park, his mother used to wear a man's cap and get drunk every Friday, what does he know about it?'

We leaned on the heavy, oak door and it creaked open slowly to reveal a sorcerer's apprentice of a girl turning the pages of a dusty, old book. A flurry of red silk, sapphire glance and raven's wing locks.

'Otley!' she squealed leaping at him and winding her arms and legs round him like the tentacles of an amorous octopus. I recalled that she had had a crush on him when she was at school.

'What's all this about then?' he asked, producing the letter and not in too much of a hurry to detach himself from her stranglehold.

'We've only got a month, then they're going to dig the place up,' she told us. 'There's a public meeting tomorrow. We're not letting them do it. We shall fling ourselves in front of the bulldozers – chain ourselves to the trees – throw ourselves into the whirlpool – anything to stop them.'

'You can carry things too far,' said Aunt Bedelia.

'If we can trace that little boy, Lord Whatsisname, we can pull a fast one on old Sugden,' said Otley, gazing into Elinor's eyes.

'I know,' she replied eagerly. 'If you'll run me over to the archives in Bradford – '

'I will,' he said before she'd finished talking.

'And if there's nothing there we'll try Leeds – '

'We will.'

'And then Wakefield – '

'Harrogate.'

'And surely there'll be something in the Records Office or Somerset House,' she pressed on, reluctant to let him go.

'We can have an Awayday,' said Otley, smiling at the prospect.

The afternoon sun slanted through the stained glass cupola lighting up the pair like a Burne-Jones idyll. Was she the wise virgin he was looking for – and right here on his doorstep? But we must remember Mike, our first duty is to him. He's taken to wearing a pearl in his left ear like Shakespeare and a codpiece over his Levis when he's on stage with his group from the tech – Jilly's Jazz Band. Children don't realize what a worry they are to conscientious parents. He keeps telling us to have a few weeks in Majorca but we don't want to let him down.

'Excuse me,' I said, coughing politely. 'I've got a headache. I think I'll go and get some aspirins.'

'An' I'll go and get some dinner ready,' said Aunt Bedelia as we all tumbled higgledy-piggledy down the steps after her.

We had macaroni cheese and stewed apples for quickness; plum cake, Wensleydale cheese and a pot of strong tea to finish. No *petits fours* for us – there'll be enough of that when the Orient-Express comes rampaging through the Chunnel, Otley says.

Bedelia passed round some dandelion wine while the man on the box told us that the pound was holding its own against another basket of currencies. Then suddenly it all went quiet as a man on a white horse came riding through the wall and went out through the window. He was wearing a plumed helmet, what appeared to be horse brasses on his chest, and a short sword in his belt. His lower half was hidden in a mist but I thought I could see a natty little skirt and leather-thonged calves before he vanished.

'Are you all right?' Otley was shaking me. 'You look as if you've seen a ghost.'

'He came through that wall. Didn't you see him?' I babbled. 'It looked like that bloke on the *Sunday Times* wallchart.'

'Which one – there's millions of 'em?'

'The one on the white horse.'

'With the spear?'

'No.'

'With the three fellas following him like Wilson, Keppel and Betty?'

'No.'

'Well, which one, then?'

'Him with the feathers in his hat on the right-hand side.'

'That miserable-looking sod!'

'That wine's a bit potent this time,' Bedelia said, looking at the label. 'I picked the dandelions up by the Roman camp last year. They were huge – as big as sunflowers, some of them.'

'What you've experienced is a time slip,' Elinor said excitedly.

'What's that?' I said, still in a daze.

'Clock time's only man-made and irrelevant unless you want to catch a bus; real time is continuous, unbroken, and if the conditions are right we can get a glimpse of past lives, sometimes our own.'

'How d'you mean?' asked Otley while Aunt Bedelia snorted.

'Most phenomena occur in places of high electromagnetic activity such as geological faults, especially on sites of great antiquity,' Elinor explained, walking over to the window. 'We're on the edge of the Craven fault here, with the Roman road from Elslack to Tadcaster running east and west, another road from Manchester to Aldborough and the marching camp virtually on the crossing point.'

'Balderdash,' exploded Bedelia, getting out her mint humbugs.

'There's something here – I can feel it,' I said.

'And what then?' Otley asked, hypnotized by the mellow tones that fell over us like folds of brown satin.

'It only needs a trigger factor to set it all in motion.'

'The wine – the dandelions from the camp!' I exclaimed.

'Exactly,' said Elinor. 'And it could be another life you're living.'

'Don't encourage her,' cautioned Otley.

'It is, it is. I know where he was going. He was looking for her – I mean me – Carrie that is,' I stammered.

'Carrie?'

'Cartimandua, you know the Queen of the Brigantes, our Yorkshire lass,' I said in a rush.

'Oh, her!' said Otley. 'You're not starting that again, are you?'

'I wasn't a traitor – I did my best – history books have got it all wrong – clever dicks with their scratchy pens – writing history in their own image.'

'I think you need a good night's rest, my dear,' Aunt Bedelia said. 'There's nothing on the box, only a documentary about computer viruses.'

'Keep a record of your time slips,' Elinor urged. 'It'll come in handy for the living museum.'

We were shown to different bedrooms as Otley snores and I fidget, but we don't mind being torn asunder as we get to live like royalty that way. Still drowsy with the wine, I watched the figures flickering before me like an old black and white movie. Soon I was part of it and I picked up my pen and began to write.

At the Villa Claro
AD 51

Dear Boudicca,

Salute! that's Roman for wotchercock. Jupiter be praised! I've got rid of that hooligan Caractacus at last. My husband Nutty – that bow-legged chap with the ginger beard and tartan long johns – well he went off and took his smelly old Brits with him. Good riddance to bad rubbish, I can get the place cleaned up now. I expect he'll turn up at bedtime blind drunk as usual.

It's a thankless task being a queen innit luv? I've worked my fingers to the bone getting orders for the common market now we are one, but d'you think they'll learn the language? not they!

Tony's coming over with his marinated meatballs and I'm knitting him a British warm, them stupid togas are no good when the wind gets up.

Like the sound of your new battleaxe with the easy-grip handle, shame the old one's still stuck in the centurion's helmet, they're not cheap.

Druids coming round with their begging bowls again, I'm off! they're always on the cadge. Arrivederci! That's Roman for mindowyergo. Regards to all in Iceniland.

Your fellow monarch,
Carrie Brigantum

PS Do try and keep your temper luv, if they want spaghetti let 'em have it but not smack in the face.

The scene faded and I crept into bed and lay wondering what Mike was up to. They're planning to break into the mayor's parlour on Bastille Day and tip a dish of custard on his regalia. Now I know what the Queen felt like when Andy went and squirted everybody with that squidgy stuff. It's no joke being a monarch and a matriarch.

Elinor presided at the meeting supported by Jack Bolland, shop steward at an old nail works mouldering in a scrapyard by the railway. His mates formed a rusty phalanx in the front row and shook their fists every time he spoke.

''Ave yer noticed who's missin'?' he asked.

'Aye!' they chorused.

'Yer, Swire Sugden – '

'I'll smash 'is face in!'

'An' the Honourable Mrs hoity-toity Grindlewood-Gryke,' he concluded.

'Honourable my arse!'

'Language, language!' Elinor admonished, hitting the table with a ruler. 'Please curb your tongues – there are ladies present.'

'Where?' inquired a rusty one in feigned surprise.

'Point of order,' interjected Cyril Gibbs, a clerk at the council offices in Bradford and a stickler for detail.

'Shut yer gob!' replied the rusty one.

A sensitive soul at the back got up as if to depart but was soon persuaded to stay and sat down again with a loud tut-tutting.

'There's room for us all,' Elinor counselled. 'Yorkshire loves its baddies as well as its goodies – '

'Hear! hear!'

' – Our Guy Fawkeses and Arthur Scargills as well as our Captain Cooks.'

'That's right.'

'So let's get on with the meeting.'

We had come up against a brick wall it seemed. Jeremiah Scrape of the planning department was never in when we phoned, so it was decided to present a petition and beard him in his den. Swire Sugden threatened to horsewhip anyone found on his premises. Volunteers were required. The Hon. Mrs Grindlewood-Gryke wanted to distance herself from any scrimmaging and was anxious to be getting on with a pageant for the theme park. Once our living history was under way and the visitors flocking in we would have something to fight Swire Sugden with. But we would have to get a move on before the bulldozers came.

It was the two hundredth anniversary of the building of Grindlewood Park and the nail factory. A double jubilee was called for and the Hon. Mrs Grindlewood-Gryke would spare no expense. Ox-roasting, Punch and Judy, knobbly knees competition, ham rolls and sticky buns, the lot.

'In view of our close connection with the Roman era I propose to set up a military patrol – like the Ermine Street Guard – that sort of thing, if anybody's interested.' The speaker was a fungus-faced young man in musty drill and soil clinging to his boots. Keen dark eyes and an aquiline nose put me in mind of the patrician entering the dining-room on our wallchart.

'That's him from the WEA,' said Bedelia, digging me in the ribs. 'Nigel Nidd – he'll be coming to tea on Sunday.'

'Looks as if he knows a thing or two,' I replied, all agog.

A forest of arms went up from the front row wanting to be in the Roman patrol providing their shop steward could be the guard commander.

'That's fine,' said Nigel, looking round. 'Any objections?'

'What about the Ancient Britons?' shouted Otley.

'I'm coming to that,' said Nigel. 'If we have twelve of each that'll make it even for the fighting, and dustbin lids make very good shields.'

'The ladies will be divided up into housewives and camp followers,' Elinor added. 'Use a bit of imagination with your costumes – we don't want everybody turning up in old hearthrugs.'

'Can I be Julius Caesar?' implored Jack Bolland.

'He was a bit before our time,' Nigel told him as gently as he could. 'We're dealing with the Claudian invasion of AD 43.'

'Oh yes! I saw it on the telly – it was good. I'll be him then.'

'You'll have to walk with a limp,' Nigel warned him, 'and stutter.'

'I'll not bother then,' Jack said.

'We're very lucky to have Mrs Craven with us,' Elinor announced. 'She's sensitive to this area and is able to regress into her past life. Time is an enigma . . .'

Groans issued from those who had heard all this before.

' . . . a continuum, an unbroken mass of past, present and future and it is given to some of us to travel at will unravelling the past like a ball of string.'

'She does go on,' Aunt Bedelia complained.

'Stand up, May,' Elinor commanded and at once I was aware of Nigel's piercing gaze. If he's not that tribune on the wallchart I'm a Dutchman.

'I'll do what I can to help,' I said and promptly sat down.

It was decided that Elinor and I would go and see Jeremiah Scrape, and then Otley would accompany us to Grindlewood Park. Volunteers to petition Swire Sugden were difficult to come by and in a rush of blood to the head I said I'd go. A rustle of papers and the meeting was ended.

'You're mad!' said Otley as we separated into groups.

'Now then,' said Nigel, 'Romans to the left, Ancient Britons to the right.'

I followed Nigel to the left while Otley glowered at us from the opposing side. Aunt Bedelia went round with tea and biscuits, trying to remain impartial.

'It'll be a pity if you've got to stop digging,' I said to Nigel. 'Have you found anything yet?'

'The usual kitchen midden stuff – broken pots, burnt porridge, that sort of thing,' he said, a trifle dejected.

'Sounds exciting,' I lied in an attempt to cheer him up.

'A few coins of the Claudio-Neronian era which indicates early occupation of this territory,' he went on absentmindedly. 'We thought we'd got down to the foundations of a villa but it's not possible at that date – '

'It is a villa,' I broke in. 'I lived – I mean Cartimandua lived there. Ossy built it for her.'

'Ossy?' he inquired.

'Sorry, the governor Ostorius Scapula, nice bloke,' I told him.

'If only it were so,' he said with a wry smile.

'Keep digging,' I said.

Elinor could not make up her mind who to align herself with. In her past lives, she said, she had been a Silurian slave, a mistress of the Merry Monarch and possibly the Empress Josephine, which was why she was anxious to contact himself to settle the question once and for all. Her crystal cupola was an open sesame to the stars, sliding back on a bright, moonlit night for her to re-charge her electromagnetic batteries.

'Sometimes,' Aunt Bedelia said, 'you'd go up with a mug of cocoa and she wouldn't be there.'

Well, she was here all right now, all over Otley. A pang of jealousy stabbed at me which I decided to ignore. I'm a queen now, after all.

Three

Elinor knew where to find Jeremiah Scrape and we set out with our petition of five hundred names. You can never get hold of these people in their offices; you have to go and throw a brick through their window at home. I had one in my shopping bag in case he wouldn't let us into his Victorian semi.

We were shown into a dim, dusty room by a tall, thin gentleman with a wisp of white hair and steel-rimmed spectacles perched on the end of a large, sniffing nose. One wall was lined with ancient volumes to do with highway surveys, tithe maps and land drainage. An arrangement of dried foliage crackled in the empty fireplace and an ashtray full of stale cigarette ends overflowed onto the carpet. The general decor was that of a waiting-room at a disused railway station.

'Now ladies, what can I do for you?' Jeremiah queried, wheezing into a big, khaki handkerchief.

'Well, it's like this . . .' Elinor began the narrative.

' . . . we shall be cut off from the river,' I concluded, handing him the petition. 'It's a right of way as well – bloomin' cheek!'

The land was in fact owned by trustees of the late Lord Chatwin, he informed us, and the general public allowed access for exercise. Nothing mentioned about the river. If Swire Sugden let us walk through his holiday camp the law would be complied with. Funds had run out and consideration had to be given to other usage. Sorry and all that.

'I'm just stating the facts,' he sniffed. 'I don't care one way or t'other, but the law's the law.'

'Is there no other way?'

'Only if you get orders slapped on it,' he said, waving us out.

'What sort of orders?'

'SSSI.'

'What's that?' I asked.

'Site of Special Scientific Interest.'

'Anything else?' I asked, not being a scientist.

'There's the AGLV,' he replied impatiently. 'Area of Great Landscape Value.'

'It's just a nice little river,' I apologized.

'AONB, Area of Outstanding Natural Beauty?'

'We like it,' Elinor said, 'but I can't speak for anybody else.'

'NNR, National Nature Reserve?' he tried next.

'It's only meadows and a footpath,' I said, shamefaced.

'But there is a bog and a bluebell wood,' Elinor added.

'Hardly the thing for a National Nature Reserve,' observed Jeremiah. 'But there's the LNR – the Local Nature Reserve.'

'That sounds more like it,' I said, cheering up.

'Or the TPO,' he said finally.

'What's that, then?'

'It's a Tree Preservation Order,' he said, showing us out.

'We've got a lovely old oak about twenty feet thick and it's got a seat all round it,' Elinor said looking at me to add my voice.

'Yes, the crows moved in when their elm was taken ill and died.'

'If he chops that down I'll murder him,' she said.

'We will,' I agreed.

'Nothing to do with me, you understand,' Jeremiah said hastily. 'As far as I'm concerned it's going to be a holiday camp.'

'But you'll give our petition to the trustees, won't you?'

'I'll do that,' he said with a sniff and a wheeze.

'Thank you, Mr Scrape,' I said.

'You know that's not his real name, don't you?' Elinor said when we were out of earshot.

'No, I didn't.'

'They call him that because he's so stingy. You know the yellow bags that Oxfam and Spastics push through your letter-box for jumble? Well he keeps them and cuts them up for wrapping his sandwiches in.'

'Crikey! Why didn't you tell me?' I said, blushing.

'I thought you knew,' she said. 'His name's Millington-Smythe.'

Before getting the bus back to Claro, we looked round the market, bought some fudge for Bedelia and then stood bedazzled at the waterfalls of gold, turquoise, crimson and emerald in the Open Sesame Emporium.

'Don't you wish you were an Indian princess?' I joked.

'I was once,' Elinor said. 'It brings it all back to me.'

The buses have gone mad these days with all manner of things blazoned on the sides – adverts for condoms, local radio stations, all done up in reticulated patterns like giant, pregnant giraffes. The one before us had 'Jorvik Viking Centre' on each side in two-foot-high letters. A party of tourists alighted grumbling that all they had seen was the sewage works. They had thought they were going to York. They were not to know that the number seventy-nine only goes to Boggle Brow and turns round at Oggy's Corner.

'You should have said,' the driver reprimanded them, as they stumbled out clutching cameras, Pac-a-macs and West Riding Explorers, Metro Saverstrips, Roses Runabouts and Discovery Guides.

'It's a diabolical liberty,' fumed a disappointed sight-seer.

Our double-decker rumbled us out of the dusty metropolis and into the fresh, green country lanes; dropping us at the river and turning back as if it had arrived at the Great Wall of China. We crossed an ugly iron bridge that resembled a ship's boilerhouse with an inscription on its stone foundation telling us it had been laid by Alderman Bob Cartwright, forgetting to add 'in a moment of madness'. A blurred figure came into view on the horizon and vanished again.

'Have you set about tracing the Chatwin heir?' I said.

'Not yet. Do you mind if I take Otley with me?' Elinor inquired. 'It's a bit creepy hanging around old churches.'

'No,' I assured her. 'I'll stick to the Roman camp and see what vibes I can pick up.'

'Take a flask of dandelion wine with you and keep a bottle in your bedroom,' she went on as we toiled up the hill towards Claro.

'That's a good idea – in case I hit a blind spot,' I panted.

We called in at The Bluebell for a breather and sat down at an upturned barrel near a mullioned window set with roundels. Haughty ladies and arrogant gentlemen looked down on us over the top of an impressive blazon.

'That's the Chatwin coat of arms,' Elinor explained, 'chequy a bend or and three martlets sable . . .' she droned on as I studied what appeared to be three pigeons on a draughtboard pecking at a giant apple dumpling.

Suddenly the peace was shattered by the juke-box playing 'The Locomotion' and a tiny tot in a pink jogging suit danced over to us.

'That's Kylie Minogue,' she said copying the movements she'd seen on *Top of the Pops* – a shake of the head here, a bend of the elbow there, a lift of the knee and a waggle of the small behind.

'I like *Neighbours*,' she said dancing over to her baby brother strapped in a push-chair, who was gnawing on a chicken nugget. Their grandad got up to have a dance as well and baby let out a shriek, flinging his chewed tit-bit to the floor.

'Where's Michael Jackson?' he screamed.

Another coin went into the metal maw and the tune changed but the dancers pressed on regardless. I finished my tomato juice and looked in my handbag for an aspirin to no avail.

'I shall have to go, I've got a splitting headache,' I said.

Otley had been fishing and found one of those old, noisy dustbin lids, which he was very pleased about. The others all had black plastic ones and you wouldn't know whether they were fighting or shuffling a pack of cards, he said. Bedelia said he could have her imitation goatskin rug and a false beard and wig that she had got from the joke shop in Leeds when she played King Lear with the amateur dramatics.

Elinor and I rummaged in the dressing-up chest in the tower and found heather tweeds from the Edinburgh Woollen Mill, chunky knits from Marks & Spencer and an old fur coat that could be cut up for body-warmers. But supposing it was hot, what did the Ancient Britons wear in a heatwave? We delved further and came up with silks and muslins from the days of the Raj and mellow shantungs from China.

'This one's classy,' I said holding up a shantung tea-gown.

'You can't wear that,' said Elinor snatching it away.

'I can,' I said snatching it back again, 'Nero sent me it.'

'Nero?'

'I mean – it's possible Cartimandua had a silk frock for best. It was arriving in Rome along the silk road from the first century BC.'

'All right then, if you say so.'

'I think we've got enough stuff here,' I said, piling up an armful of goodies. 'When are we going to practise?'

'When we've seen Mrs Grindlewood-Gryke.'

'That's not till next Monday.'

'Well, I want to speak to Nigel Nidd first.'

A shiver went up and down my spine. Soon it would be Sunday:

salmon salad, tinned peaches and cream and a Victoria sandwich. A stroll in the woods in the hour of limbo, then back to watch *That's Life*. I hope to be able to tell Nigel more about my villa; I'll nip off to the Roman camp with a cheese roll and some dandelion wine and see what happens.

We skittered down the spiral staircase into the round parlour for some artificial mistletoe in with a box of old Christmas cards waiting to go to the boy scouts.

'That'll do for the Druids,' Elinor said.

Down into the round kitchen for an artificial ham hanging on a hook on the black iron range; making a dizzy circle and out again, picking up a cudgel on the way.

'Adds a note of realism,' she gasped.

We struggled down to Aunt Bedelia's with our treasure, promising Otley a bit of fur for a loincloth. He gripped my arm when I tried the tea-gown on and drew me to one side.

'No muckin' about with that Nigel,' he warned.

'It's just an academic exercise,' I told him. 'I'm anxious to find out about the villa – do what I can to help – nice chap.'

'Whatever happens, I'll never let you go.'

'I don't want to go.'

'Well then – ' he began.

'And anyway, you'll be off with Elinor,' I reminded him.

'Well, we don't want her throwing herself in the whirlpool, do we?'

I had to agree. As always we swore our allegiance and vowed that nobody would part us except at bedtime. Our little flirtations added a pinch of spice to what was an everyday pudding; and we went to bed to sleep anyway; *that* was much better under a haystack.

'See you in the morning,' I said as Otley and Elinor went off to the pub.

It was a golden evening and when Aunt Bedelia settled down to watch the snooker I put up two cheese rolls and an apple and filled an empty medicine bottle with dandelion wine, picked up my notebook and pencil and made my way up the hillside.

Orange sky to the west turned Grindlewood Park into gingerbread and the river below curled round the houses as if to devour them like a stream of red-hot lava. I ate my picnic, drank the wine and made myself comfortable against a tree trunk. I was just nodding off when a clanging noise woke me up and a foreign-looking chap staggered past pursued by a fella with a ginger beard.

'Izza no my fault,' the dark one was saying. ' 'E senda me 'ere. I no lika, I go 'ome to mamma – izza too cold.'

'Clearoffahdovit yer poncin' poltroon,' the ginger one shouted. 'If I catch yer round here again I'll skewer ye through yer collops.'

The Roman stumbled and his moneybag flew open scattering coins as he fled. They will keep doing that. They'll never be able to save the fare to get back home. They won't listen to me any of them, I might as well talk to a brick wall. I'm fed up with men, they're more trouble than they're worth. I wonder how Boudicca's getting on with them.

At the Villa Claro
AD 52

Dear Buddy,

Salute again! Looking through your last letter I see you've been having a bit of trouble. I bet they were surprised at the way you got stuck in there slogging it out with the best of them. But sorry to hear you've bent your new battleaxe already. I have to confess I'm a bit of a coward myself. I've got this nice little tree-house and I sit up there with my knitting till they've done. Do you knit at all?

Witch hazel's good for bruises and you can strap your broken leg to a piece of wood till it mends. Can't you go on holiday next time war breaks out? Come up here for a few weeks as soon as you can move about; I'll introduce you to Tony, he's full of admiration for you as indeed we all are, but be careful with that new chariot, luv – if you go slicing the legs off the legions they're not going to like it are they? What are they going to march with?

Uncle Claud's ordered another lot of sheepskins and we hope to get into leather next year. Do you remember his stepson Nero? well he's going to be the emperor one day. That greedy fat boy with his thumbs turned down who hit your little girl with a cattle prod and gave her the rinderpest. Have you thought of him for a son-in-law? They say he's quietened down now and plays the fiddle.

Have to go now Tony's here. Oh dear! he's lost his money again.

Best wishes to all.
Carrie Brigantum

PS No, you've got that the wrong way round. You knit the wool and eat the spaghetti. Yes, peppermint's good for belly-ache.

I watched the comings and goings for a while longer. The ginger one belaboured his missus and told her to get on with the dinner, then a Roman patrol came and ate it all up and made off with the female.

'Ye scurvy scampullions!' ginger beard bellowed after them. 'I'll teach yer to eat my vittles.'

The next thing I knew was Otley pulling me to my feet but his voice seemed far away as if coming from the bottom of a swimming pool.

'Three o'clock in the morning . . . looking all over . . . thought you'd got knocked down . . . no consideration . . .'

'. . . ever since the pub closed,' Elinor joined in. 'Bluebell wood, scrapyard, Saxon's alley, Hepper's ginnel . . .'

It was getting lighter now and the voices changed. Where are we?

' . . . worried to death . . . fire brigade . . . police . . . didn't know what to think.'

That was Aunt Bedelia. We must be home. I opened my eyes to the red, dralon sofa in the parlour, my head resting on the embroidered cushions where a lady in a purple crinoline was gathering red and yellow hollyhocks underneath a bright green pergola rampant with blue and orange roses. A sharp pain went through my head like a screwdriver.

'Have you got any aspirins?' I asked.

I had only taken a picnic up there to take in the vibes, I tried to explain. Leaned up against a tree trunk to watch the sunset. Waiting for the show to begin. They said they found me in a hole, covered with bracken and clutching a piece of wood as if about to hit somebody with it. I might have been there all week if they hadn't seen a hedgehog emerge with an apple core impaled on its prickles.

'I told you that wine was good,' said Bedelia.

It was good all right, and my other life was becoming more real to me with every sip, but where would it end?

'Don't overdo it, May,' Otley said, slipping his arm round my shoulders. 'You could have gone and sat on that hedgehog.'

'And vaccinated yourself against all known germs,' laughed Elinor.

They exchanged glances and for some reason I found myself wondering what they were up to.

Four

The church bells woke me up the next morning and I reached for my aspirins. I love the sound, especially when they play 'Oranges and Lemons', but it sets off my migraine. It's my husband who's passed his war nerves on to me. He's a lot better now and the doctor says I have to be careful not to give them back.

'Wakey wakey!' Otley called as he burst in with a cup of tea.

He said he'd been on a five-mile hike, mended Aunt Bedelia's sit-up-and-beg and read the tabloids. He likes the headlines: 'GOTCHA!' – 'GAZZA!' – 'YOU'RE A LIAR, MAGGIE' – 'DROP DEAD, ROBBO'. He's mad. On our honeymoon he got up at six o'clock to clean the windows; he said he couldn't see the sea. We went roller-skating every day and dancing every night. One day I'll have a real honeymoon with palm trees and violins. He can please himself whether he comes with me or not.

'Come on, you lazy good-for-nothing,' he scolded, dragging the bed-clothes off me. 'Let's see how many press-ups you can do.'

'Leave me alone. I've got headache. I'll just lie here and do deep breathing exercises till it's gone.'

'I'm off down the pub then with Elinor,' he said. 'See what we can find out about the Chatwins.'

'Good luck!' I mumbled.

He patted me on the head as if I were a pet poodle with distemper, and was gone. I drank my tea, took another aspirin and lay taking in the scenery to the call of the carillon.

The effects of the wine, the clanging and clashing and the red peonies on the wallpaper sparked off a daymare in which I found myself on honeymoon with Julius Caesar. Oh dear, it was tiring! Roller-skating from one legion to another doing kit inspections, all across North Africa, round the Middle East and back to Rome. Muggins had to make the tea and do the washing-up.

'You said you'd do it when we got back home,' I complained.

'I want to get my head down after all that, don't I?' said Caesar.

When we'd had our conjugal rights he studied his map of the world and looked very pleased with himself until he came to the triangle in the top left-hand corner with 'Britannia' across it.

'I'll get those buggers one day,' he said.

'I shall want some new roller-skates,' I told him. 'The wheels are coming off these.'

'Come on, get your skates on, it's nearly tea-time,' Otley scolded, shaking me like a rag doll. 'That WEA chap's here. Make yourself look respectable.'

Suddenly I was aware that the air was clear, the bells had stopped and the peonies on the wall were back to their normal proportions. I leapt out of bed and took a deep breath at the open window. The afternoon sun rode piggy-back on a fluffy, white cloud and a little breeze riffled the countryside into differing shades of green.

'Have you been having a nightmare?' Otley asked.

'Why?'

'Because when I came in you were shouting "Take your bloody toga and clear off back to Calpurnia" and something about fed up of having sand in everything.'

'It must be that wine,' I said. 'I'm seeing Romans everywhere.'

A flight of crazy stone steps ran from my bedroom window to the garden and bathroom. It was originally a door through which bales of cloth were brought down from the weavers to be loaded onto the pack-horses waiting below. A quick look round to make sure I would not be sitting on that prickly cactus, a hasty plunge into the iron monster's innards and I could emerge from the bathroom-conservatory as if I had never been dishevelled. Rinse my hair with camomile, a smooth of cream and a dab of lipstick, my champagne sandals and my cross-your-heart bra under the shantung tea-gown and I was ready for anything.

Don't misunderstand me. I love my husband. But there are times when you want to pour a drop of brandy over the Yorkshire pudding, set fire to it and turn it into a crêpe Suzette.

I decided to wander about looking at the roses until the sun had dried my hair into spun gold. But then a door slammed and footsteps were heard on the garden path. Could be Nigel wondering where I've got to. Hope my hair looks all right.

'What the devil are you playing at?' Otley inquired. 'We're waiting to get our tea when you've done mucking about.'

'I'm coming as quick as I can,' I lied.

'And what's that you've got on?'

'Nero sent me it,' I said without thinking.

'I hope you've not gone doolally again. I had enough last time, you telling everybody you went on a flying saucer.'

'Mayeee, Otleee!' Aunt Bedelia called. 'Tea's ready!'

When we got in Nigel and Elinor were dancing a tango to Aunt Bedelia's battered, old seventy-eights. Bomp, bomp, bomp, bomp – dip – tara, ra, ra, ra they went, with their legs entangled and a serious look on their faces. Nigel had Brilliantined his hair and with a sliver of a moustache was more of a Rudolf Valentino than an archaeologist. Life's full of surprises. Bomp, bomp, bomp, bomp – he was breathing heavy now and Elinor had a wild gleam in her eye.

'It's her hormones,' said Bedelia, 'they'll get her into trouble.'

They were wearing something out of the dead box: Elinor a black lace frock over a pink body-stocking that looked like skin, hair scraped back and secured with a diamanté comb and a red rose between her teeth; Nigel a white satin shirt with a bootlace tie, flared velvet trousers and shiny boots with Cuban heels.

Glued together as if they were dancing a secret they were not willing to share, backwards and forwards they went not taking their eyes off each other.

'Look out!' said Otley. 'You nearly knocked the teapot over.'

'Tarra rarra bomp jealousee,' went the record in a change of tune as they trampled the carpet and bent over the sink in a blind passion.

'Tea's ready,' Aunt Bedelia called again.

'Tarra rarra weez jealousee. Tara – rara – rara – pompom!'

A final dip, Elinor spat the rose out and suddenly they were in a clinch, mouths clamped. I didn't know where to look so I sat down at the table and picked up a cucumber sandwich pretending I hadn't noticed. Soon they parted with a squelching sound like when you unblock the sink with a suction thing. Elinor patted her hair into place and sat down next to me smiling apologetically.

'There's nothing on the telly this time on a Sunday,' she said, 'only Harry Secombe in *Highway* an' that.'

Nigel sat opposite and gave an embarrassed cough.

'It's Latin,' he said. 'Near enough to Roman, I think.'

'Have you found anything yet?' Otley inquired, nodding his head in the direction of the river.

'No.'

'What a shame,' said Bedelia, handing round the sandwiches.

'How d'you think they danced then?' I asked conversationally.

'Maybe leaping about like satyrs,' suggested Elinor.

'We shall have to find out for the living museum,' I said. 'People won't want to come and watch us just sat eating porridge.'

'Actually,' said Nigel, 'I don't think they danced as such – they fought, speechified and had an orgy now and then.'

'We can do that,' said Elinor and Otley in unison.

'They do Latin American dancing at night school,' said Bedelia. 'It'll fill a gap.'

'Yes, yes,' said Elinor glancing at Nigel, in the grip of hormones more than enough for two and she was still looking for Napoleon, but Nigel was going to be busy finding the villa and getting the patrol off the ground. It was to be called the Watling Street Guard.

'That's a fair way off,' said Otley.

'Doesn't matter. We may have to range far and wide,' said Nigel, 'and you don't think the Ermine Street Guard live on Ermine Street, do you?'

'And what about the Brits?'

'I'll leave that to you.'

'Right then.'

So much to do we hardly knew where to start. Find Lord Chatwin's heir. See the Hon. Mrs Grindlewood-Gryke. Confront Swire Sugden. Get the theme park going. Raise the political awareness of the masses, said Elinor, and wean them off *Dallas* and *EastEnders*. Make a start by obtaining a TPO.

The church bells were clanging the faithful into evening service and I felt a megrim coming on as I picked up my Biro to write.

Claro
29th May 1988, Royal Oak Day

Dear Tree Officer,
   We've got this old oak with a seat round it. Lads and lasses kiss under it and old men talk about the war. We stick notices on it and the crows nest in it now all the elms are dead, it wouldn't be the same not seeing them going round cawing when the sun goes down. Kids want the acorns for their nature table.
   Swire Sugden's going to chop it down to build a car-park. We're not violent people but we'll murder him if he does. In the meantime it would help if you could give it a TPO. Mr Scrape said you would. He's got our petition.
           Yours faithfully,
           May Craven
           for the people of Claro
PS Cromwell hid in it during the Civil War. There's a pair of his boots in the pub.

We went for our stroll in the woods after posting my letter down the lane. A smell of wild garlic and damp fern, a few late bluebells, red campion and starry stitchwort embroidered the green cover at our feet. A rustle of leaves as someone made off away from us.
   'What's that?' said Aunt Bedelia, feeling for a mint humbug.
   'It's only Tumbleweed,' said Elinor. 'Let's follow him.'
   'I'm going back to do my dandelions,' Bedelia said, wheeling round.
   'Did you bring your wine?' asked Elinor at the mention of dandelions.
   'Always do – in an old iodine bottle,' I assured her, fishing it out of my handbag.
   'You'd better put a label on it in case anybody thinks it's poison.'
   We turned off the track in the direction of the rustling leaves. Down into a gully with a rushing stream, through shoulder-high ferns and nodding foxgloves. Off to the right to a soggy patch surrounding a shady pool rampant with sphagnum moss. The ground began to give and make smacking noises as we put our feet down and lifted them up again.
   'They're all here somewhere,' said Elinor.
   'Who?'
   'Bog asphodel, bog myrtle, sundew, lousewort – it's what he's guarding.'
   I looked hard but couldn't see anything except what appeared to be thousands of little green starfish. I trod on them and water squirted up my legs.

'It'll be nice on a hot day,' I said.

'We want his signature,' Elinor continued. 'As a Friend of the Earth it will carry weight.'

'Wonder where he hangs out,' Otley said, poking about in the bushes with a stick.

'Might have got a tree-house like me,' I said, 'I mean like her – Cartimandua.'

'That's something I want to talk to you about,' said Nigel, suddenly alert. 'You said there was a villa – '

'Her mind wanders,' Otley broke in, 'she's at a funny age.'

'If we go down there you can show us where it is,' Nigel said, all trace of the Latin lover hidden under a layer of fossil-hunting dust.

'Are you going to go to the dancing class?' Elinor asked.

'Let's all go, it'll be fun,' I said, grabbing Otley's arm.

'Julius Caesar didn't do the cha-cha-cha,' he said.

'We can do the paso doble, though. That's a march.'

'Aunt Bedelia hasn't got any paso dobles.'

'She's got "Viva España", hasn't she?' asked Otley.

'Yes, but – '

'Well, what's wrong with that? Everybody goes to Spain for their holidays – they'll like that.'

'Ooh yes!' I said. 'They can all join in and have a good old knees-up.'

We made our way down to the river and on to the dig where Nigel showed us a few bits of broken pots with burnt porridge sticking to them. I knew the villa was here somewhere so I left them in the hut looking at maps and walked along to the ford. I've got to be on my own to pick up the vibes. Other people make crossed lines and you end up with interference like when it 'snows' on the television. I sat down near a disused culvert, drank some wine, took a deep breath and it was not long before the show started.

A clash of metal, a whinnying of horses as they splashed through the ford. It's him again. Him on the *Sunday Times* wallchart. Bloke with him wearing funny bloomers. That's an auxiliary – they don't wear skirts. Same lot that comes through the wall in the Treasurer's House in York. What's he saying?

'That's the second pair of trousers cut to shreds. If I get my hands on that bloody Boudicca, I'll give her a right lathering.'

'Yessir,' said the one in bloomers dabbing woad all over his master's legs to heal the cuts.

'Now I know why they put this bloody stuff all over them – ouch!' the officer yelled.

Oh dear! I'll have to write and tell her to watch out. I warned her about that chariot. She will not be told. Lucky it's only his trousers.

At the Villa Claro
AD 53

Dear Buddy,

Salute! I told you. You've ruined his best trousers. He'll have your guts for garters. You know what men are!

Nutty turned up drunk again with his smelly Brits (present company excepted) I pray to Jupiter he'll stay up at Malham for good and fall down Windy Pike. The place was a pigsty! I went on my rounds getting stuff for Uncle Claud. Ten river pearls in exchange for fifty horses, he must be mad, but it's a nice day out. I like a good paddle.

How's your bad leg? It's no use trying to run up the shaft and stand on the horse's head until it's better, you'll go and break the other one. I hear you've been practising the new Barbarian Chop, mind you don't go and put your shoulder out.

They're at it again – hammer and tongs. I'm off to get my knitting.

Luv and kisses to all
Carrie Brigantum

PS Tony's sending you some ice-cream. I think you'll like it luv. You can either eat it or put it on your black eye.

The Romans had gone now and two bearded giants appeared carrying cudgels. They seemed to be looking for somebody.

'I saw 'em, the poncing poltroons.' It was our ginger friend.

'They'll not get far,' said his blond comrade-in-arms. 'They'll have to stop for a bath and a shave.'

'Put a clean frock on an' that and titivate their hair,' the red one sniggered and off they went laughing into the woods.

'Come on, you've not been seeing things again?' Otley said, as I got to my feet in a daze. I'll ignore him and tell Nigel when we get home. We went back the long way round to read the notices on the oak tree. Ours about the theme park had gone and one stuck in its place with a dagger.

KEEP OUT OF IT OR ELSE
S. S.

Five

The next morning there was a letter from Mike saying could the band practise at home for Bastille Day as they'd been thrown out of their digs. What can you do? I didn't want him sleeping in a cardboard box. God knows what they're up to! Eating junk, sniffing glue, gang-banging. No good cleaning the oven now till they've gone.

'As long as he doesn't want any money,' said Otley.

Elinor slept at Bedelia's. She was afraid to go up to the tower alone in case Swire Sugden was hiding in the bushes, so Nigel said he could stay there as it would be handy for his digging. And they could practise the tango in their spare time.

'Don't forget we've got to look in the archives today,' she reminded Otley at breakfast, 'and the social services – see if they know what happened to that Chatwin kid.'

'They won't tell us anything,' he replied. 'We live in a secret society, you have to break in to see your own medical records.'

The day was a complete contrast to the previous one – dull, grey and humid, the land veiled in a white vapour. Like living inside a steaming kettle. I was supposed to be going to Grindlewood Park but it was a good day for spying on Swire Sugden without being caught. We would have to confront him sooner or later.

'Take your bleeper in case you're attacked,' said Otley.

'Hang it round your neck,' Aunt Bedelia advised.

I put it in my handbag to please them but really, do they think a murderer is going to stand there while I bleep? He'd either stuff it down my throat or strangle me with the cord. Try a few wiles. Show him your holiday snaps, and would he like half of your Kit Kat. Then when he's lighting up his fag smash his face in with that brick you've got in your shopping bag. If that doesn't work bleep your bleeper.

I put my army trousers and walking boots on, cotton shirt and anorak, rucksack. Check the contents – sardine sandwiches, sticky bun, apple, pot of banana yoghurt and a plastic spoon, notebook and pencil, stick of eau de Cologne, aspirins, bus pass, Dorothy Wordsworth's *Journals*, nuts and raisins, Kendal Mint Cake that I could eat waiting for the helicopter to come and rescue me, sticking plasters, safety pins – I'm glad I'm not going to the North Pole – piece of cheese in the pocket where the map is, piece of plum cake in the other pocket, bleeper, whistle, knitting needle – the law says you can stab somebody to death with a knitting needle but not with a knife – Sainsbury's carrier bag and a ball of string. Think I've got everything.

'No muckin' about now,' Otley cautioned as he went off the other way with Elinor. 'Remember who you belong to.'

The fug was beginning to disperse and Swire Sugden's rancho-villa gleamed in the distance like a pearl in a newly opened oyster. It was further than it looked. Through the scrapyard and past the nail factory where the lads grimaced and gestured from the open windows.

'Hey up, can anybody come?'

'Quick march, quick march!'

Whistles, stamping, cheering, guffawing, crashing and banging.

'Gerremoff!'

Over the boilerhouse bridge and past the Help the Aged place where little, white-haired, old ladies played bingo. I shall be glad of that one day. Along the riverside through a froth of Queen Anne's lace and up on to the moor. I'm hungry so I think I'll have a sandwich. The mist rose and I sat there like a theatre-goer watching the curtain go up.

The Pennine Way is somewhere on the horizon with walkers coming down from the bogs of Kinder Scout to leafy Wharfedale. Black Victorian semis scowling back at the crags. Pink and white 'Shangri-Las' hiding in the trees. Rows of stone terraces running alongside the railway trying to keep up with the trains. It was getting hot now and my head started to spin in the dazzling sun. There seemed to be a gang of urchins running down the hill after a gentleman in a mini-skirt and a Beatle hair-cut. What's that they're shouting?

Julius Caesar,
Big, fat geezer,
Squashed his wife
In a lemon squeezer.

I shook my head and they vanished into thin air. I haven't got time for all that now. I've got to get to where Swire Sugden lives.

Down through a wooded ravine and out on to the open moor again. A ram blocked the path and we stood and stared each other out, he stamped his feet when I tried to get past and in the end I had to give him a sardine sandwich.

Presently I arrived at a sprawling, white-stuccoed building with fancy bits here and there in green and blue as if they hadn't enough stucco to go round. Curly, red tiles on the roof, white fencing and 'Rio Grande' on a signpost by the gate.

At the back, where most people keep their dustbins and grow cabbages, there was a tennis court, a neat lawn with round flowerbeds full of geraniums, and in the middle an oblong bit with Queen Elizabeth roses just like in the crematorium. A white BMW and a black Mercedes stood in a paved courtyard. I didn't think he'd be worried about our oak tree.

Round the side there was an iron gate hidden in the trees and I pushed it open and crept inside. Suddenly all hell was let loose as a black Doberman flew at me barking and rattling his chains in a mad frenzy to get at me. I screamed as he fastened his slavering jaws on my ankle.

'What you doin' with my dog?' a sleek fat man with a shotgun wanted to know. Three blue chins cascaded over a stiff, white collar.

'He's got hold of my leg,' I gasped.

'He lives 'ere, you don't. Lucky you didn't get your behind peppered an' all,' he said as he pulled the dog off. 'Quiet, Buster.'

'I was just walking by – ' I began.

'Snoopin' I expect; clear off and don't let me see yer up here again. There's enough things gone missing already.'

'I know, they even take your washing off the line,' I sympathized.

'Be off wi' yer.'

'I can't, my leg hurts,' I said, sitting down and rubbing it.

'Serves yer right.' He fondled the dog and walked away towards the front of the house.

'Sorry, Mr – er . . .' I called after him.

'Sugden,' he said. 'What yer waiting for? Be off.'

'Can I have a drink of water?' I asked.

'No you bloody well can't,' he snapped.

I struggled to my feet, hobbled over to the gate and was about to close it behind me when a female voice said, 'Give the poor soul a drink before she goes.' I looked back to see an anxious, little body with a sharp nose, mousy hair and an apron mincing across the yard like Mrs Tiggy-winkle.

'Thanks.'

'Come in and sit down a minute.'

I limped after her into what might have been a Butlin's bierkeller furnished by the madam of an Al Capone bordello. Red plush and crystal chandeliers, paper roses and hunting horns, satin hangings and tassels, sliding doors behind velvet curtains, pine bar with a brass rail and an alpenhorn, a collection of steins and a Tyrolean hat on the wall behind. It does seem that he was either a corporal in the Hitler Youth or a street soldier in the Cosa Nostra before he became a property developer.

'Let's have a look at that leg,' said Mrs Tiggy-winkle, rolling up my trousers. My left ankle was bruised and there were teethmarks all round it like a bracelet.

'He was only playin',' Swire Sugden said. 'He could 'ave bitten it off if he'd wanted.'

'You'd better go in the jacuzzi for a bit,' she said.

'Don't fuss, Millie. Yer get on my nerves.'

'Well, we don't want him putting down, do we? If she goes and reports it – you know what they said last time.'

'Please yerself.'

'Don't mind my brother,' she said leading me to the bathroom. 'His bark's worse than his bite.'

'Same as Buster?'

'They're very much alike.'

'I thought you were – '

'No,' she cut in as we entered a large marble room with gold taps, 'came up here to do for him when his wife died. I used to live down in Claro – glad to get away from there.'

'Why's that?'

'They're still living in the Middle Ages, right lot o' Luddites, won't countenance any sort of change at all.'

'Won't they?' I said trying to look surprised.

'He could do a lot for them but they block every move he makes. They always want something for nothing – everything costs and somebody's gotta make the money to pay for it.'

'They don't like to see the old things go,' I explained.

'The old things were new once, they forget that.'

She set the water swizzing and handed me some towels from a hot rail. I limped over to a padded bench and sat down to take my boots off.

'How stupid can you get,' I said.

'Those black houses they get all sentimental about and won't have stone-cleaned, they weren't that colour when they were built, they were white, yellow, bluish and pinkish,' she went on.

'I know,' I agreed, although I hadn't considered it before.

'And that nailery – it was the eighth wonder of the world when it was new – and what d'you think they'd say when they built the pyramids? They'd say "We're not having them here, it's our sand" wouldn't they?'

'They would.'

'They'd say "It's a right of way. My camel goes through there every Friday" wouldn't they?'

'I know.'

It was like when I'm listening to the party political broadcasts on the telly. They all sound so reasonable and sensible, I agree with all of them. Don't know why the world's in such a pickle.

I grasped the gold handles at the side of the jacuzzi and closed my eyes, letting my swollen ankle float to the surface. I could think I was in paradise.

There's a merry sound of splashing and skylarking. It's the noble Roman again with a Silurian slave. She's rubbing him with olive oil and he's whispering sweet nothings in her ear. If I get a bit closer I can catch what he's saying.

'A bit further down – that's where it itches.'

Now he's chased her into the Turkish bath and they come out steaming. Then the Brit with the ginger beard comes in doing his nut.

'Ye maulevering mouldywarp, I'll bongle ye in the balearics.' He brandished his cudgel to do the bongling and fell with a stiletto between the ribs. They won't be told. They think I'm always nagging.

They're annoucing something in the forum: 'Patricians United 12 – Barbarians nil.' Bad luck lads!

Aquae Sulis
AD 54

Dear Nero,

Hail Mighty Caesar! Sorry to hear Uncle Claud has gone to that Great Marching Camp in the Sky.

Yes, we've got plenty of walking boots and there's a free gift with every fifty pairs ordered:

a) tartan socks
b) sheepskin sporran
c) shaving mug with 'A Present From Brigantia' on it
Please tick one and return before Saturnalia.

It's nice here in our new leisure centre and they say they can cure anything. Have you got rid of your spots yet? Could I remind you to wear gloves when you write to me?

Boudicca sends her luv. Take no notice of gossip. Keep on the right side of her and she's got a heart of gold. Gets a bit touchy at certain times of the moon. Know what I mean?

Your IXth Legion marched into a bog last week. Have a word with Diddy about it.

Tony's here with his tutti-frutti. Arrivederci Roma!
Carrie Brigantum
PS No, I wouldn't dance in the marketplace wearing a see-through nightie and a Phrygian cap just yet. Let them get used to you first.

Somebody's banging on the door. It's not Julius Caesar, is it?

'Are you all right in there?' It's Mrs Tiggy-winkle.

'Coming - I must have dozed off,' I called back as I dressed hurriedly. My ankle was feeling better already. With a spot of Germolene and an elastic bandage round it I could have jumped over a five-bar gate.

'Have a bite to eat before you go.'

I was about to refuse until I watched Mrs Tiggy-winkle bustle about the kitchen setting the table. Freshly baked bread and scones, homemade strawberry jam and clotted cream. I thought of my wilting sandwiches and wilted in sympathy.

I strained my ears to listen to the conversation on the patio outside. Sugden was putting his foot down about something. His audience, a red-faced young Viking in dungarees, nodded his agreement.

'When they're all pissed on Saturday night,' he said.

'Which Saturday's that then?'

Mrs Tiggy-winkle dropped the cutlery and the reply was lost.

'How many JCBs d'you want?' the Viking asked, getting out a notebook.

'Three if yer can get 'em.'

'How many blokes?'

'As many as yer can get,' Sugden said, waving his hand in an arc to describe the universe. 'Make sure yer get the job done.'

Mrs Tiggy-winkle was bustling about the kitchen again oblivious to what was taking place a few yards away. Perhaps she'd learned not to interfere in case she got a thick ear. Same as the Mafia's madonnas.

'Have a piece of cake,' she said, pushing an iced chocolate gâteau across to me on a doilied plate. She must be lonely up here and it seemed as if she didn't want me to go.

Or did she know what she was doing after all? Maybe they were in the white-slave traffic as well, keeping me here until dark, then bundling me off to Buenos Aires in a JCB.

The Viking has an honest, open face, but sometimes they're the worst. That double glazing salesman with the big, blue eyes took Mrs Wagstaff's money and she never saw him again until he appeared in a punch-up on *Crimewatch UK*.

'I'll have to be going now – it's been nice meeting you,' I said getting up from the table.

The Viking had gone now and Swire Sugden came into the kitchen and grabbed a piece of chocolate cake, stuffing it into his predatory mouth like a foraging grouper.

'Eat your bread and butter first,' his sister scolded.

'Shurrup!' he said.

'You can run Mrs Craven down. She can't walk all that way with her ankle, can she?'

'Where's she live?'

'Down Claro.'

'Is she one o' them?'

'I'm only staying at Claro,' I assured him, 'I'm from Low Riding.'

'They're just as barmy there,' he said.

We drank more tea and ate more cake and the evening sky changed from red, purple and orange to a sliver of green and night black. Presently Sugden got up, straightened his black tie and put on a black jacket over his white silk shirt. That's how the godfathers dress when they've got an assignment. He picked up his shotgun.

'Come on then,' he said nodding towards the door.

I followed him out to the black Mercedes. Was he going to shoot me and put me in the boot? Buster was rattling his chains. I was in a trap.

I rummaged in my rucksack for the bleeper and hung the whistle round my neck. That was stupid: he could shoot me, choke me and strangle me all at the same time.

'Cheerio,' waved Mrs Tiggy-winkle. 'Mindowyergo.'

I sat clutching the door handle ready to leap out.

'I'll drop yer at bottom o' Claro,' Sugden said.

It was an eerie ride, like being on the ghost train and I held my breath. Up hill and down dale we went. We should be at Claro by now. Hope they haven't eaten my supper. We passed the bottom of Crag Woods and I was desperate to get out.

'You can drop me here, Mr Sugden,' I said.

The car screeched to a halt and I tumbled out.

'Just watch it you lot!' he called after me as I ran away.

Not much to report to Otley, just that Sugden is collecting JCBs. If only I could find Tumbleweed that would be something.

Six

The full moon hung like a Christmas bauble in the trees of Crag Woods and the day's warmth still lingered in the undergrowth. I sat down to rest my ankle before tackling the hill to Claro. I still had some food left and I could have a midnight picnic if I waited long enough.

Otley had always promised me a holiday that was different. We would stay in bed all day and go out all night. We never see the countryside when it's silver – only when it's in gold; and you can't get anybody to go for a moonlight walk because they're frightened of treading in something.

I ate my banana yoghurt putting the empty carton back into my rucksack as I didn't want a hedgehog getting stuck in it. I'll save the other stuff for later. What a lot of time we waste in bed!

I hoisted up my pack and began to make my way slowly through the sleeping bluebells. I'd be able to sneak in the back way up the steps to my bedroom and pretend I'd been there all the time.

Little feet scurried through the silvered foliage, a squeak here, a rustle there. Then a cracking of twigs as a dark shape emerged, I held my breath as it crossed the path ahead of me and disappeared leaving behind a brackish odour of stagnant pools and compost heaps. A clump of pondweed lay in a damp heap on the ground. It was him!

'Mr Tumbleweed,' I called.

Another stirring of the leaves and then silence. He couldn't have got far but I didn't know my way about these woods. Then I remembered the string in my pocket. I tied the end to a blackberry bush and followed him. Ball of string in my left hand, bleeper in my right hand, whistle in my mouth and the cord round my neck. Four ways to kill me if I'm not careful.

'Mr Tumbleweed,' I half whistled and half sang.

More rustling, now faint, now loud. He wasn't following me, was he? The ball of string was running out, it was only a twenty-pence one from the junk shop and I expect they'd been using it. The terrain started to make a different sound and I felt water getting into my boots. Squidge – squelch – squirt – smack – squeege – shlock – glupp – slurp. It must be where the bog asphodel lives.

'Gotcha!'

Suddenly I was clasped in a slimy embrace with my whistle and bleeper immobilized, and nothing I could do with my knitting needle and string except perhaps knit a dishcloth.

'Mr Tumbleweed, I presume,' I said, trying to sound nonchalant.

He turned out my pockets and emptied my rucksack before he got round to explaining himself.

'Sorry,' he said, 'but they sneak out at night digging things up for their gardens.'

'What things?'

'This sphagnum moss for instance – it's nearly four pounds a bag in Smith's Do It All.'

'Is it?'

'They're denuding the planet.'

'I know – ' I began.

'They dug out all the lady's slipper orchids in Victorian times,' he broke in. 'There's only one left now and my mate's guarding that.'

'Where is it?' I asked foolishly.

'Not allowed to say.'

'I won't pinch it,' I assured him.

'They're draining all the bog areas like this. There'll soon be no bog asphodels,' he went on as he handed my rucksack back to me.

'Would you like a sandwich?' I asked him. They were a bit limp by now but then he seemed to like sog.

We finished the plum cake and cheese and I learned that he had a hut in the quarry as an office, with a camp-bed, where he stayed in the summer months. In the winter he went back home to Bingley. At a guess he looked thirty-ninish but it's hard to tell with these David Attenborough types as they never grow old. A trace of designer stubble, keen eyes, dark curls and a sensitive mouth meant for kissing rather than bog watching.

'We've got a problem as well,' I told him, 'and we'd like to enlist your help.'

'It's a full-time job doing this.'

'We've got this oak tree . . .' I started off. He ate the apple and poked about with a stick in the spongy ground.

' . . . and Swire Sugden's going to bulldoze the lot,' I concluded.

'I've already written to the CC, and Prince Charles for a grant to establish a nature trail and a woodland management scheme here,' he said. 'I'm still waiting for an answer.'

'You're in Friends of the Earth, aren't you?' I pleaded. 'You know what to do.'

'I'll give you a copy of the letter I wrote the Countryside Commission – you can use that,' he said.

'Thanks but – '

'You say the same thing to all these people,' he butted in. 'So many of 'em you can't write to 'em all – NCC, WSAC, CPRE, HDRA – you can go on forever – NCVC, IDB, RSNC – might as well try SWAPO and the African National Congress as well, see what they can do.'

'And Bob Geldof.'

He plunged into the undergrowth and returned a short time later holding a piece of paper which he handed to me.

'Thanks.'

I began to follow my piece of string back hoping he hadn't noticed.

'You won't need that,' he said. 'Just keep by the stream till you come to a clearing and you'll see the path going at right angles.'

Feeling embarrassed I dropped the remaining bit of string into the nearest bush and made for the sound of water.

They would be pleased when I told them. I was just creeping up the steps to my bedroom when the window opened and Otley stuck his head out.

'Where the devil have you been to?' he demanded to know.

'Picnicking,' I said.

'At this time of night?' he said, pointing to his wristwatch.

'I'll tell you in the morning. I've got a headache,' I said.

'We've been looking all over for you. D'you know what time it is?'

'What time is it then?'

'Three o'clock in the morning. We were very worried about you. Aunt Bedelia's very upset.'

'It's such a lovely night and I had some sandwiches left. You keep saying we'll have an upside-down holiday and stay out all night but we never do,' I said, rummaging for my aspirins.

'We will,' he promised again. 'But where on earth have you been?'

'Don't shout at me, I've got a bad leg,' I said. 'Don't you want to know how I got it?'

'You know we've got to go to Grindlewood Park today,' he reminded me. 'You'll never get up.'

'I won't if you don't let me get to sleep.'

'Good night, then,' he said. 'Are you sure you're all right?'

'This big dog bit me,' I started to tell him, 'and . . .'

'Oh dearie dearie me!' he tutted in mock sympathy.

Bother! I wanted a rest day tomorrow. Everybody rushing about like headless chickens. Do this, do that, do the other! Izzy wizzy, let's get bizzy! Figaro here, Figaro there! I haven't had a chance to open Dorothy Wordsworth's *Journals* yet. But I expect it's right what that bloke said: 'For evil to triumph it is only necessary for good men to do nothing' – or something. I'd write to the Queen but we'd only get a letter from her lady-in-waiting: 'Dear Mrs Craven, Her Majesty wishes me to inform you that we have passed your letter on to the appropriate department.' Big deal. I'll drop a line to the President of the United States. There's an action man if ever there was one.

Dear Ronnie,

Hiya pard! Gee! you were great in Hong Kong, *guess you showed them commies a thing or two. My old man's a war hero too. 'Bust 'em in the guts,' he always says.*

You sure have earned yourself a li'l time to mosey around the old corral with Nancy. Mighty glad you got her away from Ol' Blue Eyes. The reason I'm writing, Mr President Sir, you remember that bomb you dropped on Colonel Gaddafi a while back? Well there's this guy Swire Sugden lives up on the moors, would you mind dropping one on him? Thanks ever so.

Your devoted fan,
May Craven,
Ancient Briton

PS Mrs Pickersgill's dog loved Bedtime for Bonzo.

I showed them Tumbleweed's letter the next day. There were a lot of 'aforesaids' and 'notwithstandings' in it – he must have been watching *Rumpole of the Bailey* – but at least we knew his name now: Spiggy Lee.

'Or is it Spider Man?' asked Otley.

'Anyway, I'll send it to Mr Scrape.'

'His name's Millington-Smythe,' reminded Elinor.

I told them about my adventures up at the Rio Grande while we helped Aunt Bedelia to dead-head the dandelions and set them seething in a pot. Elinor fetched up another bottle of last year's vintage for me as I was running out. I'm getting addicted to it and quite enjoying my other life.

'Are you writing your vibes down?' Elinor asked.

'It's all here in my notebook.'

'What are they up to now then?'

'Nero's the Emperor.'

'I'll be him,' said Nigel, setting off for the dig.

'You'll just be right,' said Elinor, 'tall, dark and handsome.'

'That's Rudolf Valentino,' I reminded them, 'Nero was fair-haired, with a spotty face and a big fat belly.'

There was a stunned silence at this bombshell but I saw him when he came over here to fetch Uncle Claud's elephants back.

'It doesn't matter,' said Elinor, 'they won't know.'

Nigel said they had found some tesserae near the culvert and there were indications that it could have been a bathhouse.

'It's too early to say but there are grounds for optimism,' he told us. 'We shall renew our efforts until we can achieve a result.'

'There was a black and white floor with swastikas round it,' I said.

'Greek key design – first century – could be,' said Nigel.

'A garden with roses and pinks – '

'They put them in their wine,' he interrupted eagerly.

'I lost my ring when I was weeding. Tony gave me it – '

'Are we going to Grindlewood today or aren't we?' Otley butted in.

'I can't walk all that way with this leg,' I complained.

'Tell you what,' said Elinor firmly, 'I'll go to the Social Services and you and Otley can go over to Grindlewood in the car.'

Otley agreed reluctantly.

'Don't bring any sandwiches,' he said. 'We'll have a pub lunch.'

Down the lane to the boilerhouse bridge. In and out and downalong and roundalong. These places are awkward to get to. When you sit up on the hillside it seems as if you can just put your hand out and touch them.

The road unwound like a toilet roll, the one that goes on forever. Dark, silent conifers marched in rows up the hillside.

Soon they were transformed into legions of marching men and I was back in my other life.

'Have you seen her?' the centurion barked.

'Who?' asked the men.

'Her with the yellow hair and the bent battleaxe.'

'She was 'ere yesterday rantin' and ravin', she can't have got far in these woods,' a soldier replied.

'Well, get after her then; she's wanted for murder, grievous bodily harm and tax evasion.'

'We can't,' the men wailed. 'She's chopped all our legs off.'

'What a shame,' said the officer. 'Now you'll have to do sliding drill instead of marching drill.'

At the Villa Claro
AD 54

Dear Buddy,

Salute! I gave Nero your luv. He's coming over for a holiday when they've sent him all the taxes. What with them and the Druids – you don't get chance to save up do you? But I shouldn't do anything hasty. I think you went a bit too far last time when you chopped his head off and hung it on your saddle-bag. He was only doing his job.

Have you been to the new leisure centre? The things they get up to! Rub each other with olive oil and then lick it all off. What a waste of lick. Tony wants to try it with ice-cream. How's your black eye? Make sure it's all clear before you go slicing your way up and down the new road. And don't drink and drive.

I'm trying to show my lot how to knit but it's like talking to a brick wall. How d'you get on with your lot these days? Tony says they pushed the IXth Legion into a bog again.

I'll have to go now – they're all stood outside with their knitting waiting for me to cast off for them. I dunno!

Luv to all,
Carrie Brigantum

PS How's your husband managing with only the one leg now? Not surprising he was a bit miffed is it? Do be careful.

Suddenly Otley was shaking me to my senses, my head cleared and a pub materialized as the Romans faded away.

'Are you all right?' he asked. 'You've been screaming and thrashing about on the back seat – I nearly ran off the road twice.'

'I've been having a nightmare,' I lied. 'I dreamt you'd run off with another woman – '

'I've got enough with you,' he said before I'd finished.

We arrived at what looked like an olde worlde inn on the outside with the same crash, bang, wallop on the inside as we had found at The Bluebell. We had a ploughman's lunch and prepared for a quick get away.

'You're a bit strange these days, you know. It's them bloody dandelions.'

'It's nice having two lives,' I said looking for an aspirin.

'No muckin' about, mind.'

'It's all academic, I'm not into muckin' about. We're doing this for posterity,' I reminded him. 'We shall be gone one day – don't want our grandchildren living on a rubbish tip and drinking poisoned water.'

'This music – it's like two cats copulating in a dustbin.'

A mini Madonna and her boyfriend jumped up and down, limbs jerking as if worked by an invisible puppeteer.

'They'll be brain-damaged by the time they get to our age,' Otley said as we got up to leave.

'We were just as bad – singing, dancing, roller-skating.'

'Yes, but we sang words – "Blue Moon", "Red Sails in the Sunset", "Walking in a Winter Wonderland". This is just chimpanzee noises.'

'I'll have to go and see what Mike's up to,' I said half to myself.

'I don't know if it's worth saving the world for them,' Otley said.

As we made a detour round the dancers I noticed three men with their heads together in a corner. If one wasn't that Viking I'm a Dutchman.

He whispered to his mate and glanced in my direction. I turned away quickly to look out of the window. Had he recognized me? He had the air of a man up to no good and I wouldn't like to tangle with him. When I looked back they were gone.

Seven

'I'm going to follow them,' Otley said. 'Drinking shorts this time o' day. Flash Harry.'

'What about Mrs Grindlewood-Gryke? She'll be waiting for us.'

'I'll ring her up while we're here – tell her you've got chicken pox or something.'

'Thank you very much, supposing she comes to see me?'

'You can put some spots on with your lipstick.'

We watched him going down the road, looking this way and that and making little dodging movements as if to outwit a hidden enemy, his yellow head shining like a buttercup in the sun.

'He must live round here,' Otley said.

'Unless he's going for a bus,' I replied, getting out my timetable. 'There's a Jumpa runs at ten to the hour only they've altered it now and it goes five minutes earlier. Then there's a Come and Ride on the hour but it's always late and you can't get it to stop anyway – they'd rather run over you. And there's the Circle one that goes all round the houses on a magical, mystery tour but you never know where that'll end up and – '

'Oh, shut up!'

Presently the other two conspirators emerged and climbed into a little, blue dumper-truck and went off in the other direction. We trailed them at a discreet distance as they turned off the main road into a country lane and then on to a rough cart track.

'I'm not going up there,' Otley decided. 'It only leads to the back of Crag Woods.'

'What are they going there for? Let's get out and walk up.'

'There's nothing up there, only the prehistoric fields,' Otley said. 'Must be archaeologists or something.'

'Perhaps they've got a metal detector.'

Curiosity got the better of us and we crept up the field in the shadow of the wall until we reached the open and could go no further without being spotted.

'There's an old British hillfort somewhere at this end of the wood,' I said. 'It's overgrown now but it would be nice to find it. I might pick up some vibes.'

'Shh!'

Suddenly there was a clatter as the lads began throwing large stones into the back of the dumper: pieces from stone circles and the foundations of round huts. Otley started forward, but I held him back. It would be dangerous to tangle with them.

'You follow them and see where they go. I'm going to look for the hillfort.'

'You'll get lost,' he said. 'Nobody ever goes in there, it's like the wood in Sleeping Beauty.'

'Lovely!'

'You're bonkers!'

I made my way into the wood as Otley sneaked back down the side of the wall to the car. I cast a backward glance at the two marauders, muscles bulging as they flung the great slabs of limestone about as if they were no more than a pound of apples. I shivered. I take my duty as guardian of our heritage very seriously but I would not be able to do it if I were pounded to a pulp.

If only I had brought my camera! The big one was dark with rosy cheeks and wore a checked shirt. His jeans were slung low on his hips revealing his bare behind when he bent over. The little one was ginger with an albino look about his eyes, he wore an off-white tee shirt with Fred Flintstone on the front, a hole in the back and jeans that made him look like a skinned rabbit. I think I would know them if I saw them again.

It was still and dark in the wood, full of secret places and here and there a dappled glade where flowers bloomed; little white tips of enchanter's nightshade bursting through the green; skitterings and twitterings of hidden life all around. Where are they all? Elinor says she saw a goblin here once when she was looking for Napoleon. She says you have to shut your eyes and recite that poem we used to say at school:

> *Up the airy mountain,*
> *Down the rushy glen,*
> *We daren't go a-hunting*
> *For fear of little men –*

Where am I and how did I get here? I'm sitting in a sort of crater with stones and gravel strewn all about. On top of a hill in a circle of trees and with the scent of lilies of the valley coming up from the woodland floor below. I picked up a shiny flint shaped like an arrowhead, then another and another. This must be *it*. The ancient British hillfort. I've found it. Wait till I tell them. Tony might be here. Oh, no! Where's my dandelion wine? Don't say I've forgotten it. It's here – hiding behind a tissue in my handbag. I gulped it down as fast as I could and leaned back into a clump of ferns with a smile on my face.

Now don't misunderstand me, I love Otley – he's a war hero like Errol Flynn – but he does get on my wick at times. This is just an academic exercise, one for the record, an Awayday into the past that British Rail has no ticket for.

I feel drowsy. There's a ladybird on my hand. Somebody said the other day that if we don't stop polluting the planet all the ladybirds will turn black and have red spots.

'*Cara mia!* Ima back, whereza ma leetle pizza pie?' It's Tony!

'Have you got the money?'

'*Mamma mia!* Izza gone.'

Oh dear! I shall have to find him a sporran to keep it in, we shall never save up at this rate. I rummaged about in the pile of junk that Nutty left behind – rusty knives, catapult, moth-eaten rabbit skins, horsewhip, cattleprod, manacles – until I came across something that looked like a squashed hedgehog.

'Notta wonna thoza prickly ones,' he complained.

I ignored his protests and fastened it round him anyway. He seems to have forgotten who I am.

'Cantta you knitta me one?' he pleaded with a dazzling smile and a wink of his roguish eye. I turned away so as not to be lost. Somebody has to keep a sense of proportion.

'I'm saving up to go to Rome, I thought you said you were coming.'

'*Si*, I go see Mamma.'

'Well, you've got two choices, either you go on as you are, losing all your money, or you put up with having an itchy thing so we can go to Rome.'

He seemed to be having trouble making up his mind so I picked up my cudgel and swung it around my head like I've seen Boudicca do.

'Who am I?' I said stamping my foot.

'*Cara mia* mine,' he began to sing.

'And who else?'

'Pearl of Isura.'

'And who else?'

'Kweena Brigantia.'

'Well then?'

'I 'ave an itchy thing.'

We were just finishing our gnocchi when Nutty came bursting in brandishing a sapling he had torn out by the roots in his fury.

'Where's that poncin' poltroon, scoffing my dinner and havin' it off with my missus?' he bellowed as he set about Tony thrashing him until the leaves fell as if in an autumn gale.

'You pig,' I screamed. 'I've got to clean them all up now.'

He made a move as if to grab hold of me but I hit him with the cooking pot and he went out like a light.

'I go,' Tony said as he ran off with twigs in his hair.

'And don't forget the ice-cream next time,' I called after him.

I'm fed up with men. They've got women all over the place. Nutty's got a bit of rumpy up in the hills, a Silurian they say, with black hair and green witch's eyes. She's welcome to him, I'm not jealous but he thinks he owns me and has a right to tell me what to do. Me, Queen Regnant of all the Brigantes, friend of the great Caesar and all his works. 'Get bloody stuffed!' Nutty says when I point this out to him. I'm going to pick some daisies and write a letter to Nero, he's different.

At the Villa Claro
AD 54

Hail Mighty Caesar!

I can't wait to see you in your new frock and thanks for the cast-offs, it's a change from my old tweeds. I do agree it's as well to set your stamp on the new reign right from the start; old uncle Caligula, God rest his soul, well he was a bit common wasn't he? It's all right going over the top as long as you do it with taste; and poor uncle Claudius dribbling all down his toga, you can hardly follow their example. A ballet dancing emperor is an innovation; though I'm not sure how you simulate the sexual activity standing on tippy-toes with one leg in the air, I expect that's a trade secret.

That recipe you sent me for sea urchins marinated in red wine and ginger is very useful. Of course we only had sand urchins and it turned out a bit gritty but it's good for brushing the horses down with, puts a lovely shine on them.

Your free gift is on its way and I think you'll find a sporran quite handy; all the fellers here wear them in front, know what I mean? but in your case you could sling it over your shoulder for a handbag.

Well I'll be off now I've got my accounts to do. Do you want to buy any sheepskins, porridge or dishcloths, battleaxes, scumbags or clothes-pegs? you've only got to say. Bye luv and mindowyergo.

Your friend and ally,
Carrie Brigantum

PS Nutty is laid out with a cooking pot on his head and I fear that when he wakes up I shall have to call the guard out again. Put it on the slate.

No I shouldn't try that with yoghurt she might not like it.

How nice and peaceful it is now the men have gone. I'll put this bunch of daisies outside the door in my hanging skull container and tidy the place up. It's a pity to waste these leaves. I'll make a dock pudding for dinner. I've got a splitting headache now.

'Quick march, quick march! Pick 'em up there you 'orrible little men.' There's no peace for the wicked, it's them again making straight for my flowerbeds.

'It's about time you learnt how to turn corners, you stupid oafs,' I shouted at them. Oh my head!

'Fourth Dalmatians – wait for it – halt!'

They came to a stop in the middle of my carnations and started picking them. Tony says it's to put in their wine and their salads. There's a soldier there putting one behind his ear. I dunno.

'Nah then,' the centurion said, 'in full kit, at the double, yomp!'

'We went yomping yesterday,' the men complained.

'I'm ready for a sit down.'

'Why can't we do a slow march for a change?'

'Because if you slow down here as like as not you'll be turned into a suet pudding, right?'

'Right, sir.'

'Fourth Dalmatians,' bawled the centurion, 'to avoid ending up as a spotted dick – at the double – march!'

Thank goodness they've gone, I'm going to have a lie down now.

I must have slept all night as there was a green glow of dawn in the sky when I heard voices calling for me.

'I'm here,' I called back. 'Through the lilies of the valley and over the rocks hidden in the ferns.'

'You come down here to us.'

'No, I want you to see it as well.'

Presently Otley and Nigel appeared at the crest of the hill and joined me in the crater. I gave Nigel the arrowheads to put with his other stuff, he was pleased. He said the Stone Age settlements round here would have been used by Ancient Britons to get away from the Romans. These old, limestone woods held many such secrets, it was just a matter of finding them under the centuries of growth.

Otley was wearing his army gear and squashed hat, his Swiss army knife hanging from his belt. He looked concerned. It's an act he puts on in front of others to make them think he's a caring human being.

'Are you all right?' he inquired, picking the goosegrass out of my hair and flicking the dust off the seat of my pants.

'I'm a bit stiff,' I said as I hobbled my way down the hill.

Nigel held my hand to help me down, giving me some hormone replacement therapy at the same time. Ladies of a certain age ought to be able to get a young man on the National Health. He brushed against me with his all-action jogging suit, and his hot-shot leisure boots sent an electric shock through my modest, made in Hong Kong sneakers.

'We'll get it scheduled as an ancient monument, clear the site of brambles and put a fence round it,' he said.

'Not the brambles,' I protested.

'As few as possible just to make a path,' Nigel went on. 'We'll call it Fort Claro and charge fifty pence to come and see it.'

'The local rep can do *King Lear* in it instead of in the old Baptist chapel,' I said eagerly.

'Yeah!' said Otley. 'Living history.'

The sun was up by the time we got down to the Jubilee Tower and Elinor called us in for tea and toast. She looked ravishing in an emerald-green satin kimono over coral silk pyjamas, and blue silk scarf tied Japanese bandit style round her forehead in a vain attempt to capture her flying tresses. Immediately Nigel was at her side. I hope they're not going to dance, she's got enough hormones as it is.

'The social services are going to dig out their old files,' she said.

'They're busy just now establishing a creative day centre for the elderly and infirm.' Was she looking at me?

We told her about our exciting discovery but all she said was, 'I wish we could find a Martello tower.'

'By the way,' I asked Otley, 'did you follow that dumper?'

'Yes, I did,' he said angrily. 'And they went up to Swire Sugden's and tipped it in his back garden. He's building a grotto.'

'Surprise, surprise!'

'Was he there?'

'Yes he was,' Otley said, clenching his fists. 'I heard him say: "Tip it here. The buggers stopped me from re-working that old quarry so I'll 'ave this lot instead." I'll murder him if I get hold of him.'

'We'll have a demo,' Elinor said. 'Put a picket on his house.'

'Inform the council and the Ancient Monuments Society,' Nigel said. 'Department of the Environment, County Archaeologist.'

'Tell the police,' I added. 'Friends of the Earth and Greenpeace.'

'Now look here,' my war hero said, thumping the table. 'There's about ten thousand bodies all with a finger in the pie. We'll be here till doomsday if we write to 'em all.'

'That's what they're for.'

'It only holds things up. By the time you've done making your inquiries through the official channels and hung about waiting for them to make up their minds it's too late.'

'Well, what do you suggest?' Nigel asked.

'Possession is nine points of the law,' Otley said, 'and I suggest going up there and bloody well getting them stones back.'

'How?'

'Hit-and-run raid.'

'When?'

'Dead o' night.'

'Who?'

'Us and the lads from the nail factory.'

'I want to come as well,' Elinor said.

'And me.'

'There'll be some rough stuff,' Otley said ominously. 'We don't want any women getting in the way.'

Eight

It was decided that Elinor and I would gain Sugden's attention while the lads made off with the stones. Tell him a story or something like Scheherazade, fan him, blow in his ears, anything. We would have to be in disguise, of course.

'Let's go down and look in the dead box,' Elinor said.

Nigel made his way to the dig and Otley to the nail factory, leaving me with the prospect of a delightful day. Dressing up, eating, deadheading the roses and a stroll by the river with Dorothy Wordsworth. I have only to open a page at random and catch a glimpse of 'Sate all the morning in the field' and 'Sheep resting' to feel at peace with the world.

Aunt Bedelia greeted me with arms akimbo and a face like a summer pudding. How did I expect her to get on with her dandelions when she thought I'd been stabbed with a poisoned umbrella from Bulgaria?

The morning sun filtered through the parlour palms as I took a relaxing bath. I much prefer a shower but Aunt Bedelia doesn't think you're clean unless you boil for half an hour like a suet dumpling. I shall have to look for a watering-can. The sun hitting the stained glass of the conservatory flooded the bathroom with colour – ruby, sapphire, emerald, amber and amethyst – transforming everyday objects into the brightest of jewels. Aladdin's cave could not be more enchanting.

'Hurry up, your egg's getting cold!' Bedelia called.

'What can we go as, then?' I asked later, as we helped Bedelia clear the breakfast things away.

'It's got to be something striking,' Elinor said. 'It's no good going as Doris Day or Mary Poppins, he wouldn't give them a second look.'

'Tiller girls?' said Aunt Bedelia.

Elinor chose to ignore that remark and we ran through a list of possible candidates: Fergie, Princess Di, Madonna, Lucrezia Borgia, Kylie Minogue or Imelda Marcos.

'Not somebody – some*thing*,' she said with her hand on her brains.
'Geisha girl?'
'That sort of thing.'
'Honky-tonk woman?'
'Closer.'
'Go-go dancer?'
'I know,' she squealed. 'We'll go as belly dancers.'
'Oo yes! Like the Fry's Turkish Delight one.'
'You'll be just right with your belly,' she added casting a glance at my sagging midriff.

We had fun making up our disguise – swirling skirts, sequinned boleros, yashmaks and all the beads we could lay our hands on. Most of the stuff was from the Amateur Operatic Society's production of *Kismet* left with Bedelia as she was in charge of the costumes.

I was to be in shocking pink and silver and Elinor in turquoise and gold. We practised gyrating in front of the long mirror, hips going round and round and in and out until a grating sound began to accompany my every move, and I feared I was in danger of displacing a disc.

'I think we've got it about right now,' I said as I collapsed onto an old divan, which gave out a loud 'boing' in protest.

'There's something missing,' said Elinor.

'It's the jewelled navels,' I said, pointing to my heaving belly button.

'That's it,' she said, diving into the chest and coming up with two red glass beads. 'We can stick these in with Superglue.'

'Supposing we can't get them out again?'

'Otley can run us over to the blacksmith's,' Elinor said. 'If he can get stones out of horses' hooves he can do that.'

We found some tropical make-up left over from Elinor's bucket shop trip to Majorca, and a box of false eyelashes entangling each other like a nest of tarantulas. What fun! Wait till I tell my husband.

Otley thought it was a great idea. Men seem to like that scenario: four wives and a harem of concubines producing endless numbers of offspring for their lord and master who, no doubt, is abroad causing mischief gun-running and putting up the price of petrol.

It is quite irresponsible on this over-populated planet to hold such anti-social opinions. The need is rather for polyandry, and I for one can't wait to have three husbands – an old one to do the washing-up, a middle-aged one for a game of Scrabble, and a young one for a bit of 'ow's yer father.

We were to meet the lads from the nail factory at the other side of the bridge, Otley said, at one o'clock in the morning. They'll be bringing a dumper from the scrapyard.

'They're a noisy lot, they'll hear you coming a mile off,' said Aunt Bedelia.

'We'll have to keep them quiet somehow,' Elinor agreed.

'Only till we get up there,' Otley said. 'It's no good trying to shift a load of stones quietly. It'll have to be smash 'n' grab and off with 'em, noise or no noise.'

'And we'll keep Swire Sugden out of your way,' I said. 'There'll just be him and Mrs Tiggy-winkle.'

'Don't overdo it then,' he cautioned. 'We don't want you on the front page of the *News of the World*.'

We ate our macaroni cheese and dandelion salad followed by a creamy, home-made rice pudding with a thick, nutmeggy skin.

'Can I have some more pudding, please, Auntie?' I asked holding out my plate.

'Why don't you grow up?' Otley scolded.

'Because I've been grown-up once and I didn't like it,' I told him. 'I'm going back down again now.'

I especially felt younger since holding hands with Nigel and my emotions were in a turmoil. Otley, Nigel, Nutty, Tony – and now belly dancing for Swire Sugden. I could laugh and cry and swear all at the same time.

'You're not yourself, old girl, since you came up here,' Otley said patting me like a pet peke. 'You'll be all right once we get back home.'

'I'm not going back to Low Riding, ever, this is my home.'

'What, Claro?'

'My roots are here, my soul is here, from the beginning of time.'

'Stuff and nonsense,' said Bedelia. 'Eat your pudding up.'

After we had tidied up and set the dandelions seething, Otley switched on the magic lantern to get the weather forecast. One said showers with sunny intervals, another said sunshine and showers and a third said some sun with outbursts of rain and temperatures below normal for the time of year.

'We know what the weather was like this morning,' Otley exploded. 'What's it going to be like tonight?'

'And now for tonight's chart,' the weatherman said, taking off the poached eggs.

'Oh, thank you very much!'

He could have saved his breath for the outlook was much the same except there were moon and stars with the outbursts of rain.

'Don't forget the snow on the hills,' Otley jeered.

'When I was a gel the summers were always warm and sunny,' Bedelia informed us for the umpteenth time. 'It's never been the same since they dropped the atom bomb.'

'Our weather's always been crazy, you've only got to read Cobbett's *Rural Rides* – he crossed over from Lancashire to Yorkshire in the middle of a snowstorm in August,' said Elinor.

'Yeah!' said Otley. 'I remember my old man fixing a swing up in the coal-'ole one summer 'cos it was too bad to go out to play.'

'And the Yorkshire Annals record that in January 1844 all the flowers were out, fields with green wheat showing and birds' nests with eggs in.'

'You read too much, you'll go blind one of these days,' Bedelia warned as she switched over to *Wish You Were Here*.

They settled themselves on the settee as if they were in the front row of the stalls and Otley made a place for me.

'Come and squash in here, love,' he invited.

If there's anything I can't stand it's sitting in a row to watch television. I prefer to sit sideways in an armchair with one leg over the back, the other on the arm and a cushion wedged between with my crossword puzzle book ready for when the boring bits come on. But all the squidgy chairs are entombed in the parlour with the tinkling glass.

'I'll go and have a lie down and then get my costume on.'

'Be with you in a minute,' Elinor called after me.

The rising moon veiled in a mist cast a pearly glow over the countryside in the manner of our little, portable camping lamp with its white plastic shade. Through the open window I could see the crows wheeling round the old oak tree, and the pale, darting wings of the ghost moths in their nightly mating dance.

The river wound in a silver ribbon round Claro as if we were gift-wrapped and waiting for Swire Sugden to collect. It's not fair, just because he's got more money than we have!

Smoke from the gypsy camp spiralled up from the trees in Grindlewood Park accompanied by a faint glow from the fire. No hiding place for them now the poll tax is coming, they'll be hounded from pillar to post – two hundred three-hundred-and-sixty-fifths of the poll tax here; seven three-hundred-and-sixty-fifths of the poll tax in Appleby every year when they gather at the horse fair for a week. Millions of town hall bureaucrats scribbling away trying to keep up with them.

'Oh, there's another eighty-eight three-hundred-and-sixty-fifths to come from somewhere, Norman. That'll be when they were up in old Ezra Higginbottom's field, and seventy days in Pontefract.'

'Are you ready yet?' Elinor inquired as she opened the door and advanced with a tube of Superglue.

Aunt Bedelia couln't stop laughing when we made our appearance.

'Tee hee hee!' she wheezed as she staggered about the kitchen dabbing at her eyes with the hem of her dandelion-bedabbled apron. 'You'll have all the dogs after you.'

'Well, I'd never have thought you could be such a come on,' Otley said. 'Good job we won't be down Claro when the pubs turn out.'

He was well-nigh unidentifiable himself, blacked up with soot and wearing a nylon stocking on his head with the leg hanging down his back like a liripipe. With his skin-tight, navy-blue Damarts for a combat suit, and webbing belt festooned with a torch, knife, hammer, washing-line, and a packet of sandwiches, he was ready for anything – robbing a bank, making a rabbit hutch or gutting a herring.

'Now listen,' he said. 'Here's the plan. We'll – '

'Take that stocking off then,' I said. 'You look ridiculous.' His mouth, distorted behind the tight mesh, gave the impression of two maggots struggling to get off the hook.

' – We'll meet the lads over the bridge,' he went on. 'I'll park the car at the front of Rio Grande while the lads load up at the back.'

'Whereabouts at the front?'

'Round the bend, under the trees.'

'Then what?'

'I'll be on patrol and when we're ready to go I'll give you a signal so one of you stay near the window.'

'What signal?'

'I'll flash the torch on and off three times, then I'll get in the car and hoot the hooter.'

'He'll hear you.'

'He's got to get his car out of the garage before he can come after us. We'll be away by then.'

It all sounded simple enough but supposing . . .

'What if he ties us up and drugs us?' I asked as Aunt Bedelia handed round cups of dandelion coffee and gingerbread men.

'And what if he wants an orgy?' Elinor protested. 'I'm not playing mummies and daddies with him.'

'Tell him a story,' Otley advised.

He looked at his divers-style watch with quartz analogue movement and centre sweep and began the countdown.

'Ten, nine, eight . . .'

'Get your coats on then,' Bedelia said as she handed Elinor a red moufflon jacket. 'And you can have this, May,' enveloping me in a scratchy, old duffle.

'. . . three, two, one, zero, we have lift off!'

'Have you got your vest on?' Aunt Bedelia called.

'Take no notice,' Elinor said.

Soon we were down at the bridge where dark shapes told us that the lads were waiting. Then the moon came from behind the clouds to reveal Judd, Jack, Gordon, Harry and Bob, wearing an assortment of army surplus and carrying picks and shovels.

'Where's the others?' Otley inquired.

It seemed that Freddie had a darts match on at The Bluebell, Mickey and Jimmy had picked up two birds at the disco, Ted's wife wouldn't let him come and Chas was baby-sitting for their Donna while she went to a ceilidh.

'We shall have to work quicker then,' Otley said.

'There's a JCB in the field up there,' Gordon said. 'He keeps it behind the sheds. We can use that.'

'Right, and we're taking the stuff back where it belongs and no messing about,' Otley said. 'Up to Crag Woods straight away.'

'Well, I don't want it, if it was gold bullion it'd be another matter,' Jack grumbled. 'I'm only 'ere because I 'ate 'is guts.'

'That's good enough for me,' Otley assured him.

'An' I'm only 'ere for the beer,' Bob shouted as he climbed into the driver's seat.

'Aye, aye, 'ow's yer father?'

'Up the 'Ammers!'

'Can anybody come?'

Elinor and I squashed into the front of the pick-up with Bob while the rest got in the back and settled themselves down to the clanging of metal. Our baubles and beads jangled merrily every time we hit a bump in the road, and I couldn't resist sneaking a look at my navel to see if my bead was still there. It winked back at me by the light of a street lamp and I gave a sigh of relief.

'Where are you ladies from then?' Bob inquired politely.

'Give you three guesses,' Elinor said, nudging me to be quiet.

'Beirut?'

'No.'

'Baghdad?'

'No.'

'Istanbul?'

'No.'

'I dunno then, where?'

'Up Claro.'

'Gerraway! There's nobody like that up there,' he guffawed.

Our disguise had passed the first test, its eleven-plus as it were, but would it be good enough to fool Swire Sugden? It could be said he had an A-level in skulduggery and we would be fortunate to outwit the master.

Nine

'Leave the gate open,' Otley whispered as we slid out of the car. 'And no hanky-panky – just kid him on a bit.'

We scrunched up the gravel drive as quickly as we could and then rang the doorbell. Elinor tore at her skirt and tousled her hair signalling for me to follow suit. We were, she decided, fleeing from the immigration officer who wanted to deport us back to Ankara.

'Suppose we say different things?'

'Don't you say anything,' she told me. 'I'll do all the talking.'

Presently the lights went on and Swire Sugden appeared with a shotgun in his hand. He wore a navy and red striped towelling robe over black and white spotted pyjamas, and his bristly chins shook in fury.

'Whaddya want at this time o' night?' he demanded.

'Help!' Elinor cried. 'They're after us.'

'Who?'

'Immigration.'

'It's nowt to do wi' me. Clear off! You've been up to summat!'

'It's all a dreadful mistake – ' she began.

'Been shoplifting in 'Arrods, I expect,' he interrupted.

'We're just simple belly dancers,' Elinor went on, 'working our way through college and – '

'Come in a minute,' he said.

We stumbled into the lounge and fell on to a large plush sofa, panting heavily. A standard lamp with a red shade made the dark corners glow and struck flames off the crystal chandelier, giving the room an aspect of Dante's inferno.

'Have a drink.'

Whisky gives me migraine so I only made a pass at drinking it, and when he wasn't looking I poured it into a pot of begonias. Elinor knocked hers back and held her glass out for another.

'My father will kill me if I go home,' she said. 'I came here to get married, but I went to medical school instead. He cut off my allowance so I have to go belly dancing in my spare time.'

'You poor thing!'

'My intended has my passport and he's in Venezuela in oil; he sent me a photo of the refinery and five thousand bolivars to go and join him, but some things are beyond price. When I'm qualified I intend to work alongside Mother Theresa in Calcutta.'

'Never mind that. When I build my leisure complex we shall want some belly dancers.'

Elinor looked a bit wild now and got up to dance. I thought I'd heard the sound of stones being hurled about and gave a strangled cry. For the first time Swire Sugden's glance fell on me.

'And what ill wind's brought you here?' he inquired.

I put on a dumb show, gesticulating, clutching my stomach and pointing to my mouth. Surely that was another stone being dumped. I stood up and wiggled my hips.

'Poor Fatima cannot speak,' Elinor explained. 'Her tongue was torn out for tittle-tattling to the eunuchs on sentry-go in the seraglio.'

'What a lot!' he said, pouring out another drink.

That sounded like the cue for a song and I made a mental note to give it to Mike when I went over to water the busy Lizzies.

> *I lost my heart on sentry-go,*
> *When the moon was low,*
> *In old seraglio,*
> *Boop-boop-a-doop.*

'If you've got some music we can give you a twirl,' Elinor said falling over a pouffe.

Sugden slipped a cassette into the stereo and settled back to enjoy the show while I helped Elinor to her feet and arranged myself into a seductive pose. She stuck out her right foot and her left hip ready for off.

'Wild thing!' the cassette belted out.

Once we had got over the shock we found the rhythm and adapted ourselves to it – a sort of slow swing from side to side like the pendulum of a grandfather clock, then a little bumps-a-daisy backwards and forwards, describe a circle with your behind and end up setting your jewelled navel a-quivering like a newly turned out jelly. I paced myself while Elinor took on every beat as if it had challenged her to a duel. Her blue eyes flashed reflecting the blue-green of her swirling skirt and her raven locks flew this way and that, for all the world like the flying mane of a black Fells pony.

'Go for it, you spicy bit o' shish kebab!'

Sugden made a grab at her and I moved over to the window, nothing moving outside but wasn't that a boulder crashing into the back of a truck? Elinor had her arms round him now and he was slobbering all over her. Well, I do believe she's enjoying it, the brazen hussy! I don't know what Napoleon would think.

'What's all that noise down there?' Mrs Tiggy-winkle called from somewhere up above.

'Go back to sleep, Millie. It's only a couple o' the lads dropped in for a jar.'

Elinor uncoupled herself from Sugden's embrace and as he went to switch off the music, he cast a glance in my direction.

'I'm sure I've seen that little fat one somewhere,' he said.

Of all the cheek! Granny always said I was cuddly when she patted my gingham frocks in place over my podgy tum; not like that bag of bones next door who never got any malt and cod-liver oil.

'Well, thanks for your help,' Elinor said, giving me the wink not to say anything. 'They'll have gone now so we'll be off.'

'You can stay here the night.'

'It is not permitted in our culture,' Elinor replied.

'They won't know.'

'There are spies everywhere,' she went on. 'We'd be flogged to death in the marketplace.'

'I'll give you anything you want.'

'You are very kind effendi to this daughter of a miserable dog.'

'We could do with some new talent round here.'

'It is written,' she said, lowering her eyes.

We'd never get away at this rate. Suppose he tried to keep us here? I wandered idly round the room looking for something to hit him with: black TV, video and hi-fi unit; revolving cocktail globe; nest of tables with a buddha cigarette lighter; corner whatnot with a picture of Doris

Day, a china duck and photograph albums made to look like books. Elinor and Sugden were holding hands now and he was whispering in her ear, the red glow from the lamp falling on his beetling eyebrows giving him the aspect of a maudlin Mephistopheles.

What were the lads doing? Why was it taking them so long? Where was Otley? If only I could give him a signal that time was not on our side. I could not keep quiet much longer. Then I spotted the alpenhorn on the wall by the corner bar, I've always wanted to have a go on one ever since I went up the Jungfrau with a yodeller in his little leather bum-freezers. I took it down and gave it an almighty blast. The lovers sprang apart and Sugden pointed an accusing finger in my direction.

'Yer can't blow them without a tongue,' he bellowed.

Elinor made a dash for the door just as Otley replied with three toots and Mrs Tiggy-winkle called down the stairs again.

'Is that them out the back with the JCBs?'

'What?' Sugden roared.

Elinor hesitated at the door and beckoned for me to get a move on.

'Run,' I screamed.

Sugden made a grab at me and I beloured him with the alpenhorn until I heard the car drive off. In the struggle my wig went askew and he snatched it off my head.

'It's that bloody lot from Claro again,' he shouted.

Mrs Tiggy-winkle appeared in a yellow candlewick dressing-gown with her hair screwed up in pipe-cleaners under a boudoir cap.

'I thought it was your lot doing the grotto,' she said.

'Doin' the grotto?'

'When I saw them with the stones.'

'Saw 'em with the stones? Why didn't you say?'

'You told me to go back to sleep.'

It was no use pretending now and I sank wearily on to the sofa clutching my stomach, my jewelled navel had a sting like a hornet by this time but the bead could not be prised loose. I remember the time Jimmy Scattergood told me behind the cowshed that you breathe through your belly-button and if you stick a piece of Sellotape over it you die.

'Have you got anything to get this out?' I moaned.

'Such as what?'

'White spirit, nail varnish remover, anything.'

'No.'

'Try that vodka,' Mrs Tiggy-winkle suggested.

'It's a sin to waste good liquor,' he scowled. 'Especially on that white trash.'

'I shall die,' I gasped.

'You don't want a dead body on your hands, do you?' she said, handing me a miniature Smirnoff. 'Keep a sense of proportion.'

With a great deal of manipulating and the aid of a potato-peeler we managed to winkle out the foreign body and I threw it into my handbag where it clinked against my dandelion wine. They'll be up in the old field now replacing the stones and I could have sneaked away up to the fort to see Tony. Wait a minute! I'll see if I can get into the jacuzzi again and have a session in there.

'Sorry about all this Mr Sugden,' I lied, 'but you've got no right taking those stones.'

'You lot got a petition up and stopped me working the old quarry, didn't you?' he reminded me. 'Bloody nosy parkers.'

'Well, we didn't want juggernauts going up and down all day shaking Claro to its foundations.'

'The whole bloody lot wants bulldozing,' he said viciously.

'He's only building a grotto for my birthday,' his sister explained as she handed me some tea. 'Because I didn't want a satellite dish.'

'Yes, but not with those stones. You're destroying our heritage.'

'Heritage did nowt for my old mother when she were in t' workhouse,' he said. 'Heritage is only for them as can afford it.'

'Leave something for posterity,' I pleaded. 'Soon this country will be one vast hypermarket with a fifty-mile-wide motorway running through it.'

'And which d'you think posterity would rather 'ave then – that or a pile of old stones?'

'Maggie says we need entrepreneurs,' said Mrs Tiggy-winkle.

I suddenly felt shy sitting there exposing my navel to a strange man and I got up to put on my coat, but where was it?

'You're not going yet,' he said menacingly, 'till we decide what to do with you.'

I knew he couldn't call the police and wondered what he had in mind, bastinado, thumbscrews or a fate worse than death? I shivered, they could feed me to the concrete mixer, incorporate me into that barbecue they were building and nobody would be any the wiser.

'I must go to the bathroom,' I said, jumping up and down. 'And while I'm there, d'you mind if I have a swizz in your jacuzzi?'

'Stay there,' Sugden snapped as he went round checking that the doors and windows were locked.

'If you're keeping her here – ' Mrs Tiggy-winkle began.

'I feel so dirty,' I butted in. 'This whole business is distasteful, a man's home is his castle.'

'It is,' he agreed. 'Unless t' council wants to knock it down, then yer out.'

I clutched at my midriff again and bent over double, Sugden picked up his shotgun and pointed it at me.

'Any monkey tricks and I'll blow yer brains out.'

'Oh dear, I've got a splitting headache,' I said, standing up again. 'Have you got any aspirins?'

'Come on,' Mrs Tiggy-winkle said, taking my arm. 'His bark's worse than his bite,' she reminded me.

'What's up wi' Buster then? I never heard him bark?' he called after us. 'Fine guard dog he is.'

'I heard him growling but I thought he was having nightmares,' she called back. 'He always does when he's had Cheeky Chops.'

'Codswallop!' Sugden exploded. 'It's your fault for lockin' him up in that shed wi' a whoopee cushion and a bendy toy.'

'I'll leave you to it then,' said Mrs Tiggy-winkle as she set the jacuzzi swizzling. 'Headache stuff's in the cabinet.'

Tony, my darling, where are you? I took a greedy gulp of my dandelion wine and placed a small piece of stone from the fort between the gold-plated taps. I poured some sea-salt into the water to give my navel a spa bath and stepped in. There's garlic in the air!

'*Cara mia* mine!'

'Tonee!'

'Wherzza ma fagioli?'

After we'd eaten we went for a paddle to look for freshwater pearls. He looked so handsome in his replacement feathers. Suddenly there was a bellow of rage and Nutty leapt out from behind a tree.

'I've bin watchin' yer, yer mincin' milksop,' he roared, swinging his club at my darling. 'Get back to where yer came from yer bleedin' puff!'

'Minda my 'at,' said Tony.

I left them to it. I've got a letter to write to my pal Boudicca. She hasn't got the hang of this new money yet and she's in trouble with the tax collector. I dunno!

At the Villa Claro
AD 54

Dear Buddy,
    Sorry to hear about your dislocated hip, do be careful riding that mad stallion to Colchester on your one good leg. About the money, try and learn it off by heart.
    2 Dupondiuses make 1 Sestertius (nasty black ones)
    4 Sestertiuses make 1 Denarius (wonky silver ones)
    25 Denariuses make 1 Aureus (yucky gold ones)
If you get one with two heads on rubbing noses that's Nero and his mummy but don't believe everything you hear about 'em. He seems like a nice boy.
    That old Druid's still hanging about; I do wish you'd come up here for a week with your chopper, Tony's got a smashing mate I could introduce you to – Mario, he's a doctor – there's not much he can't cure but you have to be careful, he puts vinegar on everything, know what I mean?
    Have you got the girls married off yet? Nero's looking for another missus, he's fed up with Octavia posing for coins all day long. When he wanted an orgy she told him 'Get lost you spotty-faced, short-arsed little creep', she's for the knackers yard.
    Well I'll be off now luv, gotta parcel the dishcloths up for Byzantium. D'ya wanna buy a reconditioned ballista for the kids adventure playground? I've got one going cheap – 4 of them horrible, little black coins with goblins on, 2 of them wonky ones of that ugly old git with spikes in his head, and that one when Nero forgot to put his teeth in but don't tell him I said so.

Luv and kisses,
Carrie

PS Not at full moon with a swizzle-stick, he'll go blind.

'Mamma mia! look what izza done to my 'at.'
    My poor darling staggered in with a dented helmet and a black eye and I proceeded to apply some tutti-frutti to it.
    'You will get into fights,' I scolded. 'What d'you expect?'
    'Izza no me fight, izza 'im.'
    'Never mind, have a lie down till I make you some – '
    'I no wanta that porridge, izza like sick.'

'Don't be silly, it'll stick your ribs together.'

''E stikka ma ribs,' he said, nodding in the direction of the hills. 'You no stikka.'

He's run off, where's he going to? 'Tonee, come back here!' The scene faded and I found myself hugging one of Swire Sugden's towelling gowns in purple and green stripes. I dressed quickly and put it on. Now I'm not going back in there for them to make mincemeat of me. I opened the bathroom window and squeezed myself through.

Ten

I was fleeing down the road before I realized I had left my iodine bottle on the side of the bath along with the fragment of rock. Too late to get them now and I could only hope that Sugden wouldn't try them and be turned into a prehistoric monster.

I arrived home breathless just as Otley was arranging his hat and buckling on his belt. I fell into his arms.

'We were coming to look for you,' he said.

'He has a gun,' I panted. 'They were going to put me in the cement mixer – brick me up in the barbecue and – '

'Sit down, love, and have a cuppa,' Aunt Bedelia said, abandoning her seething pots. 'I expect it was a plastic one out of the *Exchange & Mart*.'

A whiff of her old smelling salts and ten minutes in the squidgy chair put me right again. They had got the stones put back into place and all the lads were sworn to secrecy. One thing we didn't want, Otley emphasized, was the civil service writing it out in triplicate; and as for invoking the law, you might as well take up Mandarin Chinese.

'Listen to this lot,' Otley said, picking up his do-it-yourself law handbook. 'Possession involves two concepts, *corpus possessionis*, which means control over the thing itself, and *animus possidendi* which means intent to have control over the thing itself.'

'Would you believe it?' Aunt Bedelia mused. 'I didn't know you had to be dead first.'

'And *profit à prendre* is the right to take something from the land of another,' Otley went on. 'Unless it's water taken from somebody's river, in which case it's called an easement.'

'And is it good for rheumatism as well?'

'"And an easement,"' he continued, '"must be appurtenant to land, while a profit may exist in gross, which means that it may be enjoyed by its owner or owners unconnected with the enjoyment of land."'

'They want stringing up, disembowelling and boiling in oil,' Elinor exploded. She's a wild child.

It was, Otley claimed, quicker to hit them over the head with a frying-pan than get mixed up with that sort of thing, and if anybody asks you know nothing about it.

'There's enough gobbledegook with the driving licence, never mind that lot,' he said, flinging the book away in disgust.

What would Swire Sugden do next, we wondered. There was a rumour that he was putting the pressure on old Miss Jago, the herbalist, to sell out her dinky little shop, her box of delights, so that he could turn it into a massage parlour for the Japanese who would come rampaging through the Chunnel in 1993.

Miss Jago was ninety if she was a day. Her father before her had cured all Claro's ills when folks couldn't afford a doctor; a glass of sarsaparilla on a hot June day; comfrey for a broken bone; coltsfoot for a cough; hawthorn for a dicky ticker and a sympathetic rub of tiger balm for a gardener's aches and pains. In those days you only sent for a doctor to make sure somebody was dead and Jago's was one of Claro's ancient institutions. Miss Jago, a familiar figure with her hennaed hair, bright eyes and puffed cheeks sprouting whiskers like an elderly hamster, could be seen every Sunday on her way to the cemetery with her capsizing walk, as if fighting a galeforce wind.

'Over my dead body,' said Elinor.

'Hear, hear!' Otley responded. 'We'll keep an eye out.'

I wonder if it's any good writing to Princess Diana because they do all this back to nature stuff, grow organic vegetables and herbs, talk to the flowers and that.

Your Royal Highness Ma'am Rhyming with Spam,
  Dear Di,
  I know you but you don't know me; I'm May and I've just been talking to the snapdragons, they're a cantankerous lot and I've had to move dear, little Mrs Sinkins to sheltered accommodation as they give her the vapours. Those gorgeous hydrangeas with the blue flowery hats remind me of the Queen Mum with their gracious nods, and they love a good old knees-up when we put Chas 'n' Dave on singing 'Dahn ter Margate'.

The reason I'm writing is we've got a fragrant Olde Worlde Herbaliste in Claro of the type popular with judges when they've got the gravel. It's handy for those women's ailments when you want a witch – know what I mean?

Well, there's this Swire Sugden, an entrepreneur, who's after turning it into a knocking-shop. We were wondering if you could see your way to putting him in the Tower for a spell, upside-down in that oubliette if it's empty. If not could we put his name down and he can go in with the ravens while he's waiting?

By the way, I've noticed you slipping out of your shoes a time or two (the old plates o' meat get sweaty don't they?) well if you put silverweed in it helps, but don't try slices of cucumber you'll go skidding about all over the place.

Well, I have to go now luv. They're playing the national anthem and my husband insists I stand to attention. He's a war hero you know.

Yours sincerely,
May Craven, Ancient Briton
PS How are the little kiddiewinks? You could murder 'em sometimes couldn't you?

'How are we going to stop this man?' Elinor went on, her blue eyes snapping like jumping crackers.

'He seemed taken with you,' I reminded her. 'He hardly noticed me till I hit him with the alpenhorn. Perhaps you could lead him up the garden path a bit.'

'But not too far,' said Otley.

'Well,' she said hesitantly. 'I don't want to get crossed lines with Napoleon. It's important to keep on his wavelength.'

It was easy to picture the Little Corporal sitting on a cloud with his walkie-talkie, waiting for his earth-bound love to get back from Sainsbury's and directing the traffic in his spare time.

'He'll not be worrying about you,' Otley put in. 'Ten to one he'll be having it off with Lillie Langtry or somebody.'

It must be crowded up there with all the spirits, but Elinor says they're down here as well, all around us. Sometimes you can sense them, like the half-seen flit of a bat at dusk. It's a bit creepy, but nice to know that one day you can whizz about the universe at random without having to bother about a metro permit.

'Let's go and see Miss Jago then,' Elinor suggested.

'We'll go,' Otley said, nodding in my directon. 'You and Aunt Bedelia can pop up to Sugden's and kid him on a bit.'

'I'm doing my dandelions,' Bedelia protested. 'If you don't do them straight away they nod off just like children.'

'Elinor can see Sugden and Otley can go to Jago's,' I said as I started to clear the table.

'And what are you going to do then?' Otley inquired.

'I'm going to have a lie down in a minute.'

'I don't want to go up to Sugden's on my own,' Elinor said, with a sideways glance at Otley. 'I had enough last night wrestling with that big baboon.'

'We'll dip for it,' said Otley reliving a childhood memory.

'Eena meena mikka makka, arrh arrh dominakka, chicarikka ompong, ping pong piney, arakkara weskkanchoo, O-U-T spells OUT!' he concluded, prodding me in the stomach and explaining that it meant I had to go to Jago's while he and Elinor went to see Sugden.

'But she can't seduce him with you there, can she?'

'She can just make eyes and invite him to the ox-roasting.'

'And I'll tell him Miss Jago's got some good stuff for Saturday night droop,' Elinor added.

'Well watch it,' Aunt Bedelia warned her. 'Don't bite off more than you can chew!'

I had been looking forward to a lazy day with Dorothy Wordsworth and a call in at the villa to see Tony, so I popped the *Journals* into my handbag with a fresh supply of dandelion wine just in case. Slip into Elinor's blue cotton barn-dancing frock and sandals; I'll have to go home to water the busy Lizzies and fetch some more clothes; I wonder what Mike's up to; we've got to go and see Mrs Grindlewood-Gryke yet and bake some gingerbread men; hope Miss Jago's in. Figaro here! Figaro there! The shantung tea-gown hanging by the window caressed my cheek with a butterfly kiss as a sudden breeze caught at its arms, how nice it would be to take tea and receive admirers in it, but I fear it would be not so much a sin with Elinor Glyn on a tiger skin as a merry ding-dong on the old chaise longue.

'Are you ready?' Otley called impatiently. 'I want to be back in time for *River Journeys*. It's Michael Wood going up the Congo.'

They dropped me off at the bottom of Claro and chugged on over the bridge. Elinor waved gaily and whispered in Otley's ear. They're up to something – how does she know about Saturday night droop and she a virgin?

Miss Jago lived in what used to be the old apothecary, soot blackened stone and Georgian windows with their bow fronts like Tweedledum and Tweedledee each side of the dusty, black door. A bell clanged as I entered.

All the perfumes of Arabia filled the air from half-open mahogany drawers and blue and white Staffordshire jars. A glimpse of exotic names fast disappearing and leaving only their outlines: sandalwood, spikenard and sassafras; juniper, jessamine and jacaranda; attars of this and pot-pourris of that; hyssop, vervain and valerian and a huge jar seemingly full of cockroaches but which turned out to be carob beans. Now I remember, we used to get them in a lucky dip with a sherbet dab and a stick of liquorice with our Saturday pennies.

'Yes?' Miss Jago croaked across the counter.

'Have you got any aniseed balls?' I inquired absent-mindedly.

'Can't get 'em now. Anyway, I stopped selling sweets years ago,' she sniffed. 'Kids came in and pinched 'em on their way to school.'

'Do you still sell sticks of liquorice then?'

'Oh yes! They're medicinal.'

'I'll have one of those twirly ones like barley sugar.'

I turned as if to go and then fell against an oaken chest with my eyes closed, one hand holding on to the lid and the other clutching my stick of liquorice.

'Are you all right?' Miss Jago asked anxiously.

'I feel faint, do you mind if I sit down a bit?' I replied, may God forgive me for deceiving a poor, old woman.

Miss Jago steered me through the parlour and out into the garden, and I gained the fleeting impression of cats and cobwebs before I emerged into the light.

'Sit here and I'll make you some mint tea,' she said, pointing to a faded deck chair set among the hollyhocks. It collapsed as soon as I sat in it.

'Sorry, I forgot to prop it up,' she apologized coming back with the tea. 'It's as right as rain with a brick under it.'

The little, walled garden was a riot of blooms – pansies, sweet william, stocks, and Canterbury bells; clematis and honeysuckle entwined in a passionate embrace, with a rambling rose playing gooseberry. A dazzle of rose and violet, crimson, yellow and cream.

'It's lovely here, we shall miss you when you've gone,' I blurted out.

'Gone?' she queried, her whiskers twitching in agitation. 'If you've come from that new funeral emporium you're too late. Mine's paid for -- I've got a budget account with the Co-op.'

'No – ' I began.

'And I'm leaving it all to the cats' home,' she went on. 'They're going to look after Tiger Tim and Fluff, they have fresh fish every day and hard-boiled eggs and they like a bit of tinned salmon on a Sunday.'

'We heard you were selling out to Swire Sugden.'

'Oh him! Well, he's made me an offer. He says he'll get me a place in that new old folks' home at Scarborough.'

'We don't want you to go, though.'

'He can be nasty when he doesn't get his own way, you know. I don't want to get across him,' she said, scratching her red head.

'He's got problems.'

'What problems?'

'We've heard he suffers from middle-age droop, especially at weekends when he's had a few. That's why he's so aggressive, goes shooting guns off when he can't do it. There was this programme on Channel 4.'

'I can soon cure that.'

'He tells everybody he's got a bad leg but we know what he means,' I said giving her a wink.

'Well, bring him here for his bad leg then,' she said, winking back.

Miss Jago's father, Silas, had been an amateur archaeologist and the spare room was crammed with flints, nails, keys, brooches and pottery. Wasn't that a Roman altar in the corner gathering dust? A broken tombstone here showing a snatch of bare knee under a natty mini-skirt? And there was a rogues' gallery of coins set out in a glass case, emperors of all shapes and sizes, some with laurel wreaths and some wearing fanciful crowns like Miss Universe.

'He picked odd ones up when they were laying the drains,' Miss Jago explained. 'He sold a silver one of Caracalla and bought this shop. You'd want a hoard to buy it these days.'

'If we found one we could buy it.'

'Well, I'd sooner it stay as it is than go for a massage parlour, that's for sure,' she said. 'And I'm off on a world cruise never mind old folks' homes.'

What have I said? There isn't a herbalist among us. I've got a bucket of mint and a parsley pig at Low Riding – I wonder what Mike's up to – and we did try to grow organic cabbages but the caterpillars devoured them. I regret not having taken it up when I was younger but there was no time, what with dancing, cycling, swimming and roller-skating after we'd earned a crust of bread.

I was always interested and once experimented shaking yarrow, sowthistle, horsetail, fat hen and nettles up in a bottle of water, and was just about to drink the green, swampy result when Granny dashed it out of my hand and gave me some treacle and brimstone instead. Anyway, we'll cross that bridge when we come to it. The gypsies are good at that sort of thing and if we find one who can read, like Matthew Arnold's Scholar-Gipsy, we can rent it out. But we haven't bought it yet.

'Would you sell it to us then?' I pleaded as I followed Miss Jago back down the rickety stairs. I felt dizzy the vibes were so strong here and if I didn't get out into the fresh air I would expire and be forever entombed in a limbo-land of cobwebs, camphor and catacombs.

'If you've got the money, yes,' said a sceptical Miss Jago, 'but I don't want pushing out, you'll have to see my estate agent.'

'Who's that?'

'Pringle and Grott in Bradford.'

'Aunt Bedelia went to school with old Mr Grott and – '

'I know your Aunt Bedelia very well,' she broke in. 'She got her dandelion recipes from here and she used to bring her little brother in a sailor suit for tiger nuts.'

Miss Jago hoisted up her green, crimplene skirt and climbed on to a chair, showing an expanse of pink knickers. I grabbed hold of her in case she fell and a shower of yellowing scraps of paper rained down on my head. A spider hung on a silver thread, the cats waited below.

'They're all here,' she said, 'recipes for potions, balsams and aphrodisiacs – I'll try this one on him.'

The dust cleared to reveal stuffed owls and weasels in glass cases, a grinning blackamoor holding a tray, framed certificates and testimonials, a parlour palm growing out of an elephant's foot, a begonia in a chamber-pot, a flatiron that you had to spit on to see if it was hot enough, frills, furbelows, knick-knacks and whatnots. Oh, my head!

'Will you drop a line to Mr Grott then?' I inquired.

'I'll see,' said Miss Jago hitching up her drawers.

Eleven

We could sell our house in Low Riding, I mused, walking back along the riverside: I'm not leaving Claro, I've found my patch of paradise and if my husband doesn't want to stay here he can get stuffed. I've had enough of being married anyway – 'May, where's my blue socks? You've ruined my best shirt! Isn't there any treacle pudding?' – I can go and live in a caravan in Biffy Bennett's field if nobody wants me, but I'm sure there's a cache of silver somewhere round here if only we could find it.

I sat down at my favourite spot by the culvert and opened Dorothy Wordsworth's *Journals* with a sigh. She was off into the woods with Coleridge again. Some nasty-minded people might think they were going for a puff at the old hookah but they were only pursuing their muse. I took a sip of dandelion wine and read on while a dainty, orange-tipped butterfly flickered in and out of the cow parsley.

'Who's there?'

'Izza me!'

'Tonee!' I cried, putting away my knitting. 'You're just in time for a spot of crackling.'

'Ima knackered,' he said.

My poor darling had run all the way with a bag of money for me hung round his neck as I'd sewn all his pockets up. His lorica segmentata was in a state of collapse and I tied it up again with a dinky little bow.

'But why didn't you ride?' I asked as I frisked up his feathers.

'They tooka my 'oss.'

There was no time to lose, Nutty was after him so we buried the bag of silver in a copse behind the villa, then Tony hid under the bed and I went to wash the pots up in the river.

'Gotcha, yer toffee-nosed trollop!'

I screamed as Nutty popped up out of the water and grabbed hold of my plaits. He dragged me up the banking, flung me over the back of a horse and galloped off.

'Tonee!' I screamed when I caught a glimpse of his anxious face peering out from the latrines.

'Wait till I get hold o' that connivin' cockatrice!' Nutty roared. 'I'll macedoine 'is meatballs an' pulverize 'is pizza!'

'Help!'

'Nah then,' my husband said when he set me down. 'Are yer comin' up in the 'ills wi' me or are ye stoppin' dahn there wi' them bloody puffs?'

'I can't afford to turn good business away,' I explained. 'We're showing a profit this year and I've just got the books straight.'

'Are yer or aren't yer?'

'No.'

'You maffickin' muffin I'll – '

I picked up a rock and held it ready to dash his brains out if he came at me with his cudgel.

'Get away from me, you smelly old goat. I'm fed up of you coming home drunk every night and living in a hut that stinks like a horse's pizzle.'

'Don't you love me any more then?' he asked in disbelief.

'No, you stupid git,' I screeched. 'How many more times do you want telling?'

Ping! Something hit him on the head and knocked him out and I was rescued by a patrol of Balearic Slingers. A multi-cultural society has its advantages, and it is possible to kill people at long-range now.

When I got back to the river I finished the washing-up and then had a lie down at the villa before writing a letter to Nero.

'Izza bugga,' Tony said.

At the Villa Claro
AD 55

Hail Illustrious Caesar,

I'm pleased to say your soldiers came to my rescue again, but it was them with the funny bloomers; I would have preferred the IX Legion as befits my status, however, they are still stuck in Boudicca's bog.

It must be fun sleeping with all and sundry, old and young, male and female, bondman and free, grandmothers, grandfathers, horses and goats. No, I'm sure that isn't what's giving you spots.

That fertility god you sent me, Priapus or somebody, with the big thing; I didn't know where to look, we have to keep him in a dark corner with his back to us. Is that why all your other statues have got no eyes?

I'm sorry your soldiers are dizzy when they come home on leave, going round in circles all the time up here. We could do with a good, straight road, you've built Boudicca one haven't you, and what does she do? goes charging up and down all day long cutting everybody to ribbons. I've told her to be careful, she's got a pile of arms and legs and the head of a centurion who was bending down tying his bootlaces at the time.

Your mother is a bit of a nuisance isn't she? wanting to get on to all the coins when you'd rather have the goat-boy – I expect she's proud of her little cheeky chops so take no notice.

Well, I have to go now luv so cheery-bye and don't do anything I wouldn't do.

Your loyal friend,
Carrie Brigantum

PS No, we don't do it sideways, that's the Chinese, but Boudicca can do it on horseback facing the wrong way round, standing on one leg and with her eyes shut.

My darling Tony made the macaroni cheese while I was writing. This fast food is so convenient as you do not have to catch it first, pasta having no legs. I remember the time Nutty said he would make the supper as it was my birthday and off he went on horseback with his hunting spear. I didn't see him for six months, then he came back with a maggoty monarch of the glen slung across his saddle and a wee bit o' Caledonian crumpet to transform it into Scotch broth. He never could resist a pretty face and now we've got a skirl o' lads and lassies doing the Highland fling all over the place.

'*Cara mia,*' Tony said. 'You lika bambino?'

'Yes, yes, I lika,' I agreed.

'Inna minnit,' he said, taking off his hat.

'But not just now, I've got the accounts to do.'

'Money, money, money,' he said as he replaced his hat. 'I go.'

'*Arrivederci,* luv. Thanks for the macaroni cheese.'

Oh, dear! this high finance: ten of these mouldy old copper coins of the realm equals three pigs; one of these with Diana of the Ephesians swinging on the parallel bars balancing a jug on her head equals five horses. Here's one of Auntie Agrippina with curlers in. It makes my head ache but somebody's got to do it.

'Mrs Craven, wake up it's raining!'

Nigel and the lads from the nail factory had been out drilling and were just off home when they caught sight of Elinor's blue frock down among the greenery.

'Aye aye, 'ow's yer father?'

'Can anybody come?'

'Have a banana!'

I dusted myself down, picked up my book and set off up the field for Claro.

'Cheerio lads,' Nigel waved as he ran to join me. 'Same time tomorrow. We've got to practise that tortoise manoeuvre again.'

'We haven't all got dustbin lids yet,' Harry called.

'Thanks, I'd have got a soaking,' I said, trying to run along between the drops. One of the predicted showers had just started.

'I thought it was Elinor at first. She's a worry, isn't she, threatening to throw herself in the river if they don't mend that hole in the ozone layer soon.'

'It's all talk,' I said. 'She's a wild child.'

'Thank goodness it was only you,' he sighed.

Suddenly the rain stopped and the sun came out sparkling the world with silver. Folk memories came flooding into my brain as I shook the drops from my hair like a wet dog.

'It's here somewhere, I sense it,' I cried, pausing in a little hollow.

'What is?'

'The silver that we buried in my other life.'

Nigel looked around him in disbelief then mopped the raindrops from his head and face with a large, khaki handkerchief. His dark hair and moustache glistened with red and purple lights under the hot sun.

'Silver?'

'It was in a leather bag. We buried it round here behind the villa, but it was all wooded in those days. Now it looks different.'

I picked up a branch and began to poke about in the grass. Nigel made a move as if to help and then stopped.

'I don't honestly think there was a villa here, Mrs Craven, as much as I'd like to take it seriously.'

'There was, there was,' I said, prodding at a patch of bare earth.

'There were very few villas up here,' he went on. 'And they were built later in the Roman occupation.'

'This one was built early for me.'

'We have to be careful of hoaxes. Remember the Piltdown Man?'

'Well I'm not responsible for that, Nigel, be fair!' I protested.

'You know what I mean, we have to be scientific about these things,' he said as he turned to go. 'We can't allow ourselves to be held up to ridicule.'

I threw my branch down and followed on behind. If only I could find it! But I'm not going to get lumbago digging for it, I shall just have to wait until the WEA class get up as far as the hollow.

'Will the dig reach that far up?' I inquired anxiously.

'It depends on whether the funds run out.'

'What funds? They're doing it for free, aren't they?'

'Nothing's for nothing,' he said, giving me a knowing look.

What we did agree about was that Swire Sugden had to be stopped by hook or by crook from turning this village scene into a concrete jungle. There would be no room for us folks, us simple peasants with no money and no clout who just want to go on enjoying our own, little green patch.

'D'you know they're building a new school in what used to be that lovely park? They've chopped six chestnut trees down already,' Nigel said. 'In spite of us getting up a petition.'

'I know.'

'And somebody's bought that big house up Moorside and put a notice up saying it's a private road,' he continued indignantly.

'We've always gone up that way when we've walked over to Ellerby's.'

'Well, you've got to go round by Burgin's Intake now,' he said.

'Of all the cheek! How can they turn what has always been a public road into a private one without a by your leave?'

'And you know that green walk round the edge of the park where the wild roses grow?'

'Yes.'

'Well, they've made it into a dog run.'

'I'm surprised they don't give us rat poison and get rid of us once and for all,' I exploded angrily.

The steam rose from our clothes as we toiled up the hill and Nigel held out his hand. That feeling again – not like old comrades at a reunion as when Otley and I get together, more like the first day of that holiday in Ibiza when I sat with my pina colada and Juan gave me the eye. I was wearing my gob-stopper earrings and my Marks & Spencer sarong; he thought I was Dorothy Lamour. Tony, Juan, Nigel, my eternal triangle, my loves, my soulmates.

'Don't you feel anything?' I asked as the electricity ran up my arm.

'My boots are soggy,' he said, looking down at his trainers.

'Don't you feel that you've been here before?' I prompted.

'I was here yesterday.'

'Tony!' I cried trying to shock him into a confession but he looked puzzled and made no answer.

'Juan!'

He let go of my hand and left me to struggle on alone. Of course, love is not the same for men, is it? For them the past has gone and the future is not yet here – a clean shirt, a Sunday dinner, a booze-up with the lads, a bit of rumpy on a Saturday night and Bob's your uncle. They've got no soul.

'Where have you been all this time?' Otley wanted to know when I got in. 'We were back in time for Daffy Duck and we've been all over the place.'

'I fell asleep,' I explained. 'And I've got some good news. There's a hoard of silver buried down at the villa. If we can find it we're rich!'

'Who says?' inquired Otley.

'I know,' I told him. 'I put it there.'

'You've been regressing again,' he said sternly, as if accusing me of masturbating.

'I can't help it.'

We exchanged news over the dandelion quiche and oven chips, and all agreed it would be a sweet move to snatch Miss Jago's shop from under Swire Sugden's nose. All the Roman stuff could go into Nigel's exhibition and the tatty, stuffed birds to the cats' home, something for everybody.

'Just a minute, we haven't found that silver yet,' Otley said. 'Aren't we jumping the gun a bit?'

'We can sell the house then,' I said in desperation.

'Now I know you're bonkers!'

'It'll turn up somehow,' Elinor said. 'It won't come to that.'

She and Otley had quite enjoyed their visit to the Rio Grande. Sugden was furious at losing his grotto but calmed down when told that no objections would be raised after all to his getting stone from the old quarry. He wouldn't be able to come to the ox-roasting as he had to see the planning department about a multi-storey car-park he wanted to put up when the cottage hospital came down. But he hoped to be in time for the Roman orgy in the evening.

'He said he didn't recognize me with my clothes on,' Elinor laughed. 'And he was hoping to see more of us.'

They sang the praises of Miss Jago and told Sugden how she had cured Claro's ills – little Jimmy's impetigo, old Sidebottom's prostate, Miss Umpleby's problem when her doctor said the only cure for it was twins, and Mrs Maddock's gammy leg she put right with a pot of yoghurt.

'Gammy leg?' he had inquired. 'I might go and see her myself.'

The tide was beginning to turn. It's the law of averages, you can only have so much bad luck then it changes to good.

'Yippee, hurray, balloo ballay!' I cried jumping up and down.

'Don't be silly,' Otley scolded. 'Sit down and eat your pudding.'

Ooh! It was date and rhubarb pie like Granny used to make – a big slice of delicious crust, pieces of hot, pink rhubarb and fat, juicy dates spilling out in a gungey glop.

'Is there any custard, Aunt Bedelia?' I asked.

'It's not school dinners, May,' said Otley. 'I expect we shall be having *fromage frais* or something.'

Afterwards Elinor went back to the Jubilee Tower to get in some dancing practice with Nigel and Aunt Bedelia made some of her dandelion coffee, which is caffeine free and good for the liver. Then we settled down to watch the magic lantern, a documentary about sewage outfalls.

'I'm never going to the seaside again,' Otley declared.

Then we discovered that cows were the cause of the hole in the ozone layer, eating and blowing off methane gas all day long into the atmosphere.

'You wouldn't think they could blow that far,' Aunt Bedelia mused.

'If it could be harnessed we could run the car off it,' Otley said, putting his arm round my shoulders. I picked up my crossword puzzle.

'Sugden says he's going to see Mrs Grindlewood-Gryke,' he announced.

Twelve

There was so much to do and so little time to do it. We needed a miracle like in the Bible, a flash of lightning and you get everything you want. I put the coronation mug filled with marmalade on the breakfast table and sat down. Edward VII and Queen Alexandra preened themselves like a pair of pouter pigeons, a blob of marmalade lodged on her majestic bosom.

'Did you know that coal is two pounds a gigajoule?' inquired Otley as he perused his favourite tabloid.

'No.'

'Neither did I,' he said, riffling through the pages at random. 'And there's a coupon here for you to vote for whether you think Fergie's got better legs than Di.'

I picked up the local paper to see what Claro had been up to. Crumpets! Miss Jago's aphrodisiac must be hot stuff. It was working already. Swire Sugden had been arrested for flashing and he'd only had one shot of her secret formula.

'Look at this,' I said, holding up the paper in front of Otley.

SHAME OF LOCAL TYCOON

Mr Swire Sugden, 45, the well-known entrepreneur, was apprehended by PC Charlesworth, 29, who went to investigate a scream behind the nail factory on Wednesday night. There he found Miss Cynthia Furtwangle, 75, of Pollards End, Claro, in great distress.

'At first I thought it was the vicar,' recounted Miss Furtwangle. 'He wears a raincoat like that, but I realized my mistake when he flung it open and shouted "Any more for the Skylark?" Fortunately I had my smelling-salts handy.'

The constable, who was proceeding towards the police station, asked Mr Sugden to accompany him in order to help with inquiries.

'I was only measuring the nail factory yard for a car-park,' explained Mr Sugden, 'when a nail went through my foot making me jump.'

'Poor Miss Furtwangle,' said Aunt Bedelia. 'A God-fearing soul like her, and her father always had a flower in his buttonhole.'

We would have to see Miss Jago as a matter of urgency and tell her not to give Sugden so strong a dose, just enough to put him in a good mood. I'll go on my own. If Otley comes with me he might be tempted to try it for himself and we're all right as we are, all passion spent.

It was a beautiful morning so Elinor and I went to pick some dandelions, leaving Aunt Bedelia in what sounded like a nest of cobras as she tested the bottles of beer for hissing.

The first wild roses were out in the hedgerows as the last of the May blossom began to fall, a patch of fireweed blazed on a distant heath and a little breeze wafted the dandelion clocks hither and thither across the meadows. Elinor caught one and began to blow it.

'He loves me, he loves me not, he loves me . . .'

'Who does – Nigel?'

'Who d'you think?'

Oh dear! She's not on about Napoleon again, is she? I wouldn't mind but she hasn't met him yet. At least I have met my Tony. She's not on the right wavelength, she knows that, but she still goes on about him as if she sees him every day.

'Have you seen him then?' I asked conversationally.

'I'll be seeing him tonight,' she said.

'Napoleon?'

'Nigel, stupid.'

'I thought he was lodging at the tower to be near the dig.'

'Only when it's convenient – when he wants some dancing practice.'

Somehow, in picking our dandelions, we gravitated towards the river where we found the WEA class scratching away at the bare earth. One or two were young unemployed but most were elderly and I wondered what would become of the class if they all dropped down dead.

'I shall go back to Doncaster,' said Nigel.

So far this morning they had turned up an old lemonade bottle and a collection of throwaway razors in a plastic bag, but they were still scraping merrily away with their spoons. It was better than bingo, they said.

'I think I've found something, Mr Nidd,' Doris called out as she ran excitedly towards him holding out a metal object. 'It looks as if it could be a Roman tool of some sort.'

Nigel took it and rinsed off the dirt revealing a rectangular hole at one end. We all crowded round him, eager to see what it was.

'It's only the key off a sardine tin,' he said flinging it into the rubbish bin, which was full to overflowing, the score to date being Roman Artefacts 25, Twentieth-century Junk 3,005.

'Hard luck, Doris. It was a good try,' her husband laughed.

'If we don't get results soon I'm abandoning the class,' Nigel declared. 'It looks like we're wasting our time.'

'We shall want our money back then,' they chorused.

'It's only a matter of time,' I told him. 'It's all there – the silver, the villa, my ring. At least keep going until after the jubilee, then you can show the visitors round.'

'Give the vibes a chance, she's only just got tuned in,' Elinor pleaded.

She looked charming in her Laura Ashley frock with the sprigs of forget-me-nots and primroses and her hair tied up with blue ribbon – Marie Antoinette playing at milkmaids. I tipped my dandelions into her handwoven trug which was half empty. She was a slow picker. I remember the time we all went pea picking down to Wisbech and I worked like stink while she flirted and gossiped her time away. Then when I presented the farmer with a bulging sack she called out, 'She's not picked all them herself!' and he only paid me half the money.

'Are you going?' she asked in a hurt little voice.

'I said I'd go and see Miss Jago.'

'What for?'

'You know – that in the paper about Swire Sugden.'

'I'll get these dandelions back before they get Saturday night droop as well.'

I left her walking up the hill with Nigel. What a handsome couple they made, knee-deep in herbage, just like Charles and Di in their organic garden. I made my way along the river bank through the sweet cicely, happy memories of aniseed balls as I squashed the stems with my fingertips and breathed in the spicy aroma. Fat Friesians made sad, moony eyes at the water and flicking away the horseflies and bluebottles with their tasselled tails, turned their backs in a huff as I passed. I used to wonder where those big, buzzing flies came from until one day, when I was getting a picnic ready, a slippy, hard-boiled egg shot out of my hands and disappeared out of my life for ever; then much later a swarm of bluebottles flew out of an old Wellington boot, which we used for an umbrella stand.

The rusty, old bell juddered and clanged as I pushed open the door at Miss Jago's. I looked around at the multi-coloured pills and potions, powders and tisanes, and wondered if she had anything for disappointment. Oh, well! I'll have another twirly stick of liquorice.

'Shop!' I called.

'Miaow.'

'Miss Jago!'

'Mowow.'

I peeped into the kitchen and the two cats rubbed themselves on my ankles. Tiger Tim leapt into the sink and looked longingly at the tap so I put them a drink of water down. There was no sign of Miss Jago. I went into the parlour, the blackamoor grinned and held out his tray of goodies and a stuffed owl seemed to fix me with his goggle eyes. Perhaps she's popped round to the shop for a packet of gingernuts. Grandfather clock ticking away in the corner with a jolly moon and stars winking at me; pair of pot shoes full of pot pansies; a wooden picture of dead ducks; moth-eaten teddy-bear waiting for a head transplant: Prince Albert in a Scotch kilt, Victoria in a tea-cosy.

'Miss Jago!' I called up the stairs.

There was no answer so I went up to look in the bedrooms and I found her in the spare room among the artefacts, dead as the centurion on the tombstone. I felt quite faint and sat with my back to her leaning against the Roman altar, I took a swig of dandelion wine to steady myself. Tony, where are you? It's no good calling for Otley, he said he was going fishing. The world began to spin taking me with it.

I didn't have long to wait, my dream lover never lets me down.

'*Cara mia!*'

'Tonee!'

''Owzza ma leetle fagioli?'

'I've got a splitting headache,' I said. 'That Nutty was round here again smashing the place up – he says he'll skin me alive!'

'Izza bugga, inni?' Tony replied with a shrug of the shoulders.

I was hoping he'd give me some money for an Awayday but he's lost it again and we can't remember where we buried that bag of silver; I keep looking for it but it's hopeless with the pigs rooting everything up, and the trees chopped down.

'I thought you were paid on a Friday?' I asked casually.

'I am pay but I loss.'

'Well, why don't you look after your flamin' money? I stitch all your pockets up and hang a leather bag round your neck and you still lose it. Are you a man or a bloody mouse?' I exploded.

'I a bluddy mouse.'

I can't be mad with him for long. I thought the Italians were passionate but I've never known him lose his temper. Even when Nutty tipped a cauldron of Scotch broth over his head he just sat there picking all the pearl barley out of his hair. I couldn't wish for a better gentleman-of-the-bedchamber.

'Will you do the spaghetti, luv, while I write my letters?' I called.

At the Villa Claro
AD 55

Dear Buddy,

I'm so excited, Tony and I are to be married as soon as we can get rid of Nutty. I want you to be my chief bridesmaid if you can get up here with your bad leg, but leave your chopper at home. Mario's going to be the best man; I should have a word with him about your problem as he will have his instrument concealed about his person, know what I mean?

That tax collector, he's a pest isn't he? I don't let him in – just because I've got a door it doesn't mean I've got to open it every time somebody knocks. Glad you cut off his money-bags; when you come up here have a go at old Droopy-drawers, he'll be at the wedding with his begging bowl.

I hear the IX Legion's got pneumonia because every time they get out of that bog you push 'em back in again. It's not cricket Buddy, poor souls they're only doing their job; we've got the ones with the pointed hats and funny bloomers up here, they eat rice pudding, talk about laugh!

Well, dinner's ready so I'm off now luv. Cheery bye and don't do anything I wouldn't do.

Your old friend,
Carrie Brigantum

PS I do agree, you might as well let your daughter marry that lavatory attendant if he's the only one with legs down there.

Here's Mario with his little black bag. He's got all the latest in medical equipment in his portable field hospital: saws and shears, hammers and chisels, gouges, forceps, grappling irons and a cabbage to practise on. Then when he's finished he eats it with a spot of oil and vinegar. If they run out of bandages they use cabbage leaves, put them in their boots when they've got blisters and use them for target practice when they run out of barbarians.

'Have you got anything for spots?' I asked him one day.

'Cabbages,' he said.

Tramp, tramp, tramp, tramp – they're here again with their big plates o' meat.

'First Tungrians – wait for it – halt!' bawled the centurion. 'Nah then, what's the trouble wi' you lot?'

'Well, it's like this, sir,' complained an infantryman shuffling his feet. 'Since we left Belgium we've had no Brussels sprouts.'

'Yer'll 'ave cabbage and like it!' the centurion ordered.

'My mother always gave us Brussels sprouts.'

'Yer can't put Brussels sprouts in yer flamin' boots, can yer?'

'No, sir.'

'Right then, shut yer bloody trap before I ram a cabbage in it.'

'Yessir.'

'First Tungrians – wait for it, you 'orrible little men – forward march!' the centurion barked, and they went limping off.

Jupiter be praised, they've gone! I was afraid he might come in and commandeer my spaghetti bolognese. We were just sitting down when – *Boing!* – a spear went past my head and lodged in the timbers behind me.

'She's got two of 'em nah, the pusillanimous puffin, I'll – '

It's him again, I'm off to get my knitting. *Arrivederci Roma!*

'*Presto! Presto!*' Tony hissed at Mario as I slipped out the back door. 'Izza bugga 'usband – *finito!*'

Where am I? I'm stretched out on the floor between the tombstones with Miss Jago. I'm not dead as well, am I? Oh, it's all right, I can stand up. Miss Jago's red hair lay on her head at a rakish angle. It was a wig after all, and her poor little bald head atop her garish make-up made her look like a pace egg done up for Easter.

I ran downstairs and picked up the telephone, and very soon the police and a doctor arrived. I explained that I had only come to buy a stick of liquorice and had found her there.

'Was there any sign of a break-in?' the constable asked.

'No.'

'She was ninety years old,' the doctor broke in. 'She's had a good innings and it looks as if she went suddenly – natural causes.'

'You'd have thought she'd last for ever with all this alternative medicine,' the constable said, turning to his colleague.

They don't say that about doctors. We had one who drank himself to death, another who died of galloping consumption and a third who absconded across the Irish Sea after swindling old ladies to buy himself a sunset home for gentlewomen in the stockbroker belt. Fair's fair!

'Health food freaks are human,' I protested. 'If you prick us do we not bleed?'

They took my name and address and let me go.

I paused on the way out for a last look round the shop – hop pillows, lavender bags and tussie-mussies; liver pills, blood pills and powders; coconut oil, bay rum and Hungary water; ozone-friendly furniture polish; balsams and bath oil; valerian, hyssop and thyme. Another institution gone from Claro. The next time we see it it'll be a Chinese take-away, a betting shop or a dry-cleaners, the latter being of no use to us as Granny always told us never to buy anything that you couldn't bung in the old wash-tub and scrub the living daylights out of.

I took my twirly stick of liquorice out of the big, glass jar and left seventeen pence on the counter.

I made my way up the hill to Claro with a heavy heart, something beautiful had gone from our lives. It's not the same thing, going to a doctor. They give you a tin number the size of a dinner plate and you sit in rows trying not to look at each other waiting for your light to come on. Bells ringing, nurses running hither and thither, children screaming, clerks consulting their records; and it's not as though you were wanting a leg off, you just feel a bit under the weather, that's all.

There was none of that with Miss Jago. What would we do without her? I hardly dare tell the others, they might blame me as I was the last person to call at the shop. The whole of Claro will turn against me, and the police arrest me in a dawn raid. I shall be put in the dock with my stick of liquorice.

'I put it to you,' the prosecution will say, 'that you purchased this cylindrical sweetmeat merely as a cover for your nefarious deeds. That your real intent was to divest this poor old lady of her life savings, and that furthermore, when she surprised you at your evil work, you suffocated her with a herb pillow made by her own careworn hands.'

'Take her down,' the judge will say.

Oh, Miss Jago, why did you have to go and die!

Later that evening, when we were watching the globes whizzing about on *Newsnight*, it occurred to me that Sugden now had a problem and it would most likely take the form of increased activity and aggression.

Thirteen

'What's this?' inquired Aunt Bedelia the next morning as she placed a cardboard box with holes in it on the kitchen table.

'It's a gerbil,' Otley said, having wrestled off the top and peered inside.

'Where's it come from?' I asked, examining the bundle of ginger fur with its twitching whiskers. Oh dear! It's got one of those long, rat's tails and I prefer hamsters with their round, cuddly bums.

'I found it on the doorstep when I went to fetch the milk in.'

'Somebody must have ordered it.'

'Well, I didn't,' said Bedelia. 'I ordered some mini gerberas for the rockery out of the *Exchange & Mart*.'

'They must have sent it on to the pets and livestock section by mistake,' Otley said as he replaced the lid.

'Never mind, we'll keep it, poor little soul. It must be hungry,' Bedelia said. 'What do they eat?'

'We shall have to get a book from the library,' I said.

'And it'll want a gerbilarium,' Otley said. 'An old fish tank will do.'

'It's been sent for a purpose,' Bedelia said mysteriously.

That afternoon I called at the public library and exchanged Gogol's *Dead Souls* for a book on gerbils. The computer had broken down and there was a long queue so I wandered round a bit. They're getting like Tesco, keep shuffling the goodies about like a pack of cards – and sometimes they get it wrong. I see that *Anglo-Saxon Poetry* is still on the shelf marked 'Humour' next to Spike Milligan's *Goodbye Soldier*. This looks interesting, a book about the world's cheeses, I like cheese. It was a heavyweight so I slipped it into my shopping bag while I browsed through the shelves. What a box of delights! Letters and diaries, secrets of the famous and here's Parson Woodforde getting his pigs drunk. Suddenly I realized the computer was working and if I hurried home I would be in time to catch *Walking the Pennine Way* so I got my book checked out and made a dash for the barrier. I pushed and pushed but couldn't get out, something was wrong with the thing, it was stuck. Buzzers buzzed, lights flashed and I felt a heavy hand on my shoulder.

'Miss Talbot, we've caught a thief!' a voice rang out.

My shopping bag was snatched out of my hands and a large book extracted. Oh, my goodness! The one about the cheeses, I'd forgotten it.

I was ushered into Miss Talbot's office for some finger-wagging. I explained it was all a mistake but she said she'd heard that one before. She was a pleasant, plump little body with faded, yellow curls, big blue eyes and a sweet smile, but you can't always go by looks. Green glass beads rested on her ample blue bosom and swung from her delicate pink ears, she put her head to one side giving the impression of an inquisitive cockateel.

'Aren't you the one we caught last year dashing out with a rucksack on your back?' she asked.

'I'd just got back from walking and called in on my way home . . .'

'Oh yes!'

'Then I got stomach-ache and had to run home . . .'

'Mmm!'

'Before I could get my books – I felt sick.'

'And what is it this time?'

'I slipped this book about cheese into my bag while I looked at the others, it's too big to hold in your hands all the time, and I forgot about it.'

'If you knew the things people get up to,' she confided. 'They spill coffee, drop their fag ends, smear the pages with treacle and once we even found a used condom inside *The Pope's Visit to Britain*, I ask you.'

'It's disgusting,' I sympathized.

'And they pretend they've got flu,' she went on in full flood. 'They sneak behind the shelves coughing and sneezing while they tear maps and diagrams out for their extra-mural studies, draw moustaches on the Queen and spectacles on Fergie and Diana.'

I said I'd be careful in future and having satisfied her that the only other book I had about my person was the one on gerbils I was let go. I caught a glimpse of Swire Sugden standing dejected outside Miss Jago's locked-up shop and I could have sworn he shook his fist at Claro as he turned away. Now what was that stuff they put in the soldiers' tea during the war so they wouldn't keep going off like randy tom-cats?

Otley was waiting with an aquarium when I arrived with the book and we went through the pages quickly. Sand to burrow under, toilet-roll tubes, food bowl, gravity-feed water-bottle, stones and a gnawing block.

'He wants something to play with as well,' he said, riffling the pages. 'Cotton reels, mirrors, parrot ball, a wheel and a see-saw, a brass ball with a bell in it, tissue paper, ladder, twigs and a plastic ball to roll about in.'

'And they like old boots as well, it says here,' I pointed out.

'We'll have to call him Ginger,' Otley decided.

'I'm trying to think who he reminds me of,' Elinor said. 'I know that face from somewhere.'

'Not Napoleon,' Otley smirked.

'No, Napoleon had black hair.'

'And no whiskers,' said Aunt Bedelia. 'And he had a big nose.'

'I know who it is,' Elinor exclaimed. 'It's Miss Jago!'

As soon as she said it we could all see the resemblance, of course – the red hair, the inquisitive nose and the twitchy whiskers, the darting movements and the short, little arms when he stood upright.

'Elinor, you're not suggesting –' I began and then checked myself hardly able to give voice to my thoughts.

'Well, it's funny he arrived just after she'd gone.'

The Hindus say that if you come back as an animal it's because of something you've done wrong in a previous existence so I don't know what Miss Jago's been up to, but I'm ready to accept that Swire Sugden's Buster is Jack the Ripper and that Tiger Tim and Fluff are really Robin Hood and Maid Marian.

We dashed off to the pet shop in Bradford for fear Ginger would feel deprived without all his accessories. There's no call for one in Claro, most animals being farm dogs fed on raw meat and kept barking at the end of a stout chain; or sleek, fireside tabbies fed on tins of Kittywinks from the Co-op.

What a squeaking and a twittering, a rustling and a snuffling there was; feathers flying and hackles rising; wheels spinning madly and claws plucking a scratchy tune on the wire cages. Big Jim, the python, lay drooling at the scampering, white mice a mere flick of the fang away.

There was a notice on his cage saying: 'Special Offer, Half-price and Two Tickets to Fantom of the Oppra'.

'Shall we buy him?' Otley inquired.

'No!'

'I thought you wanted to see *Phantom of the Opera?*'

Well, I do, but I'm not going to risk getting myself strangled to see it. Besides, I saw the original at the local flea-pit when I was seven and it only cost me two jam jars to get in.

We packed our purchases into our biodegradable bag and the manager gave us a word of warning about the plastic exercise ball.

'Don't leave him in it for more than twenty minutes and don't put him in the sun, he'll dehydrate.'

'Oh, no, we won't,' I assured him.

At the bus station a group of harassed mums and dads trailing a gaggle of infants carrying buckets and spades were in conflict with a bus driver.

'I told you, we're not going to Skegness,' he scolded.

'Well, why have you got a blue bus with white waves all over it?'

'Computer broke down, it's not my fault,' the driver explained.

'You didn't say when we got on you weren't going to the seaside,' complained a fat granny licking an ice-cream cornet.

'You didn't say you wanted to go to Skegness,' he protested.

'It's common sense,' one of the daddies reasoned. 'A bus with waves on should go to the seaside.'

'And how about if you get a bus with nothing on?' the driver challenged. 'Does that mean it's going nowhere?'

The gaily dressed group re-formed and went in search of the toilets in a flourish of sun hats and water wings and with a clinking of buckets and cameras. Oh, my head!

Aunt Bedelia was waiting with a dandelion flan and oven chips and a dish of home-made lemon cheese to put on our semolina pudding.

'It's a pity you can't make this out of dandelions,' she said as she held up the bright, yellow curd. 'It's the same colour, isn't it?'

'Where's Elinor?' I asked, nodding at the empty place.

'She went to look in her reincarnation book to see if there was anything about people coming back as gerbils.'

Could it be the same as the Doctrine of Signatures in plant lore, I wondered. Lungwort has blotches and spots like a diseased lung and therefore was used to treat that condition. By the same token, if you look like a gerbil you come back as one. I think I'm likely to return as a packhorse complete with bulging saddlebags; Otley probably a puma with his green eyes and soft footfall; Elinor a Princess Stephanie bird of paradise; Aunt Bedelia, I can see her as a busy, little robin working like stink to keep a whacking, great cuckoo supplied with big, fat worms.

Before the evening was half gone I was already fed up with gerbils. Has Ginger had his nuts? Look, he's holding them in his little hands like a human. Have we given him enough sand, tissue paper, carrots? Will he eat potato peelings, turnip tops and congealed porridge? Look out! he's on the rampage in his exercise ball, crashing into chair-legs and ankles, it's all the same to gerbils; and you have to steer him away from the kitchen in case he dashes his brains out on the flatiron we use for a doorstop. I've got nothing against gerbils but they can be exhausting to watch and I'd rather have a quiet sit-down with a nice book.

When Otley and Aunt Bedelia settled down to watch Miss Marple I decided to have a stroll as far as the Roman camp to watch the sun go down over the hills. I picked up my handbag and my pink, bobble-knit cardigan and opened the door.

'Where are you off to?' Otley inquired without taking his eyes off the magic lantern.

'I'm going to see if I can pick up some more vibes.'

'And come back with a crock o' gold,' he sniggered.

'Silver,' I corrected.

Puffs of white clouds outlined in orange lay on the hilltops like discarded cottonwool buds daubed with lipstick. Grindlewood Park again a gingerbread house and the Rio Grande turned into a slab of cinder toffee. I sat down when I reached the level of the marching camp and fumbled for the dandelion wine nestling in the bottom of my handbag. Open sesame! I leaned back against a rowan tree and closed my eyes. That's him practising the coracle again, I can see his feathers going round in circles. Oh dear! he'll be dizzy as a drunken coot.

'Tonee – dinner's ready!'

'I sick, I no eat,' he called as he span round crazily caught in a whirlpool. I went to look for a big stick to rescue him with and clung on to an overhanging branch as I held it out.

'Jump in and swim for it, yer bleedin' puff,' a familiar voice came from behind the bushes, I dropped the stick and ran for my life with Nutty after me.

'Gotcha! yer boodlin' baggage,' he growled as he knelt on my back and twisted my arms behind me.

'Let me go, you putrid polecat!' I screamed. 'Help!'

'There's nobody 'ere they've all gone for a bleedin' bath,' he leered.

I'm done for now, he'll cut my head off and tie it on to his horse's tail by the plaits dragging it up hill and down dale on his way home to Malham, and I don't travel well.

'Let me go, I've got a headache,' I pleaded.

'Where's that money you buried?'

'I've lost it – pigs have eaten it.'

'Liar!'

He let go of my arms and pulled me upright by my plaits, his red hair, stiffened with lime, stood up in spikes like the bristles of a wild boar, his face fungus cascaded over his chest. I got hold of it and pulled, jerking him off his feet. It was me or him. I screamed and scratched, jumped on him and bashed him with a boulder; I pulled out a handful of whiskers and poked a stick in his eyes; he shook his head, made a grab at me and I caught him off balance with a kick in the conjugals that sent him hurtling down the hill.

'Carrie!' he called. 'Where did we go wrong?'

'And don't come pestering me again you grotty, old gralloch or I'll set the dogs on yer.' I don't like getting mad but I can if I want to.

I was very tired when I got back to the villa and found Tony there eating his pot noodles as if nothing had happened. His eyes were a bit crossed and he kept putting the noodles in his ears but otherwise he was none the worse for his ordeal. He said he'd been rescued by the Balearic Slingers who filled the coracle full of rocks and sank it.

'We maka bambino now,' he said when we finished the washing-up.

'I've got some letters to write,' I told him. 'You know what Nero's like if I don't answer straight away.'

'You write, I maka bambino.'

'Steady on – I'm not Chinese.'

At the Villa Claro
AD 55

Salute Almighty Caesar,
How clever of you to think of dancing in a Greek tragedy, but they want livening up don't they? I hear you're putting on a musical of Plato's Republic

next. Fancy your favourite musician doubling up as a gladiator, does he strike up a tune at the same time?

That sporran I sent you, you're supposed to wear it over your toga not under – no wonder you've got blisters on your whatsit, I'll put some more lanolin in the post. There's another consignment of dishcloths ready as well, cash on delivery, and send one of the praetorian guards with it under his helmet because the other nits can't keep their money for five minutes without losing it.

You'll have to wrap up well when you go to the Zuyder Zee to inspect the front line; you'll want a waterproof fig-leaf for starters, I can do you a chunky-knit, Aran one out of oiled, seaboot wool if you like, to match your British warm. Is the goat-boy going as well? Boudicca sends her luv and they're trying to get that centurion's head back on, but they've had to give him an extra pair of arms to prop it up with; it does sometimes come off again when he sneezes but luckily there's always been somebody there to catch it. Well, I'm off now so toodle-oo and good luck with the musical.

Your friend and ally,
Carrie Brigantum
Regina

PS No, I shouldn't murder Agrippina, Octavia, Poppaea, Acte and Britannicus all at once, it might look suspicious. Save some for later.

My darling Tony was asleep by the time I'd finished my letters and done the accounts, and the oil lamp spluttered out so I crept under the sheepskins and cuddled up to him. We shall never make a bambino at this rate but somebody's got to do the work.

'Come on, it's eleven o'clock,' said Otley as he shook me awake.

'Blast it! I've missed *Newsnight* and it's Donald MacCormick as well,' I exploded as I plucked the leaves out of my hair.

'Did you find that buried treasure, that's what I want to know?'

'No.'

The lights of Claro twinkled below us like the jewels of the madonna as we made our way home, the moon coming up to full hung in the sky like a Chinese lantern touching the world with silver. Otley put his arm round my shoulders in a comradely gesture.

'D'you remember that night on our honeymoon?' he inquired.

'I'm not going roller-skating again,' I cautioned. 'I had my leg in splints for weeks.'

'When you said you'd always love me,' he gave me a squeeze.

'I do, but in a different way; not less, just different.'

His manner changed and he pulled away sharply hurrying on ahead, then he said he was joining the Foreign Legion on the morrow but he'll not get past the pub. Besides, we need him for our fight with Swire Sugden. It must be all hands on deck and it's not going to be easy. He won't like it either in the French Foreign Legion, he grumbled at Skegness when the sand got in his shoes. I hope he was only joking.

Fourteen

The new cemetery was a cold, cheerless place set on the bleak hillside, neat and square with straight paths dividing it up as if it were a piece of graph paper. Miss Jago wanted a flying angel carrying a bunch of Good King Henry but she'll be lucky to get a brick with her name and age on; the council doesn't like flying angels.

The old, Victorian graveyard is much more homely, down by the river where the bird's-eye primroses grow and on nodding terms with the church, the alehouse and the fish shop. It's a wildlife sanctuary now and a nice place for a picnic, they do guided tours and parties of schoolchildren are taken for nature study. The last time we were there a tiny tot with a yellow notice pinned on his back saying 'Thomas, Wind in the Willows group' was causing a commotion jumping on and off a Holy Bible and throwing handsful of gravel into everybody's eggy sandwiches. Miss was very cross but she daren't smack him because his father would come up and give her a black eye.

It's the right place to be dead in but it's standing-room only now so we've got to go up on the cold hillside where the council can keep us in order and where we shall be frozen to death twice over. That is unless you want to be cast into the fiery furnace instead, but there's no happy medium and it's a job to know what to do.

'I can't leave my dandelions,' Aunt Bedelia told us as we left for the funeral. 'Miss Jago won't mind.'

'Don't forget to give Ginger a roll round,' Otley instructed.

'Where is he?' she inquired, peering into the fish tank.

'He's in his boot. Can't you see his tail coming out of the lace-hole?'

The whole of Claro turned out for the funeral and the little church was full to overflowing. The lads from the nail factory lurked self-consciously at the back behind a pillar as most of them were heathens.

I have a sneaking sympathy for that line of thought because I've tried so hard to be a Christian myself but without much success. I have prayed for a handsome, young cleric like Francis Kilvert to come along and convert me. I'd believe anything for love in a rectory and cucumber sandwiches on the lawn.

Distant cousins sat on the front row whispering to each other. They're going to get a surprise when they find she's left everything to the cats' home. Mrs Wainwright in a big, black hat from Pontefract, who hasn't seen Miss Jago in yonks since they fell out over her Harold doing the Black Bottom at Mrs Wainwright's wedding. Mr and Mrs Broadbent who keep a fish and chip shop and send an aroma of kippers wafting our way every time they stand up and sit down. Uncle Harry, who they thought was dead, proved to be alive and kicking and living in Heckmondwike. And then there was Dora, who said she was going to study scientific instruments in Geneva for her thesis but who ran off with a Zulu and is now the mother of a tribe somewhere in Swaziland.

'And as we thank God for the life of our sister Everelda Jago,' the vicar droned on. 'We commit her into thy hands.'

The coffin was trundled away like a supermarket trolley and we followed it out lingering by the church door in an embarrassed silence, not wanting to be the first to make a headlong rush for the nearest pub.

'The people who turned up!' I exclaimed over our half pints. 'Just shows what they thought of her, she was a good old stick.'

'Al Capone had a big funeral, that's nothing to go by,' Otley said. 'I remember old Mrs Banks, buried in a pauper's grave and nobody there and she were one of the kindest old girls you could wish to meet.'

'Her father found a lot of Roman coins,' I said as in a dream.

'Look, May, don't you think you should see a doctor? Between you and me, I'll be glad to get back home. I think you're going round the twist.'

'I'm not going home,' I mumbled into my beer.

'What about Mike?'

'He's not bothered about us, is he?' I complained. 'He's always telling us to go to Majorca.'

'You fuss over him too much, that's why.'

'Well, he's my baby, isn't he? and I haven't seen him for two weeks.'

'You've got Ginger now.'

'I don't like his tail.'

'Where did we go wrong, May?' Otley asked.

'We have to change in order to survive, it's one of the basic laws of nature – ' I began.

'Yes, but not out of all recognition,' he broke in.

'Don't you remember that moth on the telly that changed from white to brown to go with the tree trunk it was living on?'

Otley put his glass down and made for the door. He refuses to talk to me when I get scientific; I followed him out into the sunlight and he gave me a withering look.

'And that's exactly what you look like,' he snapped.

'What?'

'A dusty, dingy, brown moth.'

Well, I didn't want to go to a funeral in Elinor's dazzling glazed cotton frock with the red poppies and blue cornflowers all over it, so I had borrowed Aunt Bedelia's black skirt and blouse which I wore with a brown, boxy jacket. I thought I looked more like a liquorice allsort. There's no pleasing him. When I get dressed up fancy he thinks I'm on the game, and what does he think he looks like, all done up like the stationmaster at St Pancras?

We walked up the road to Claro holding hands from force of habit, leaving the Tweedledum and Tweedledee shop behind and passing the old men sitting round the oak tree. Upward currents of air kept the dandelion clocks airborne and turned the leaves of the trees inside out.

'It's going to rain,' I murmured.

'Will you wear that belly dancing outfit tonight?' he requested.

I can't imagine life without him but he does get on my wick at times.

Aunt Bedelia came running down the garden path to meet us, her fat cheeks stained with tears and dandelion juice.

'He's gone, he's gone!' she sobbed.

'Who's gone?'

'Ginger! He rolled off down the garden like a mad thing, the gate was open and he was out like a bouncing bomb.'

'Which way did he go?'

'I couldn't see when he got on to the grass, he disappeared.'

He could be anywhere and we decided to eat first before we looked for him. Another frantic afternoon, Figaro here! Figaro there! and no chance of sitting by the river with Dorothy Wordsworth, unless I slip her into my bum-bag and sneak off when they're not looking.

'What happened?' asked Otley as he inspected the empty gerbilarium in disbelief.

'Well, I had the door open because I was baking and you must have left the gate off the latch when you went to the funeral.'

'It wasn't me, it was May.'

'And I gave him his little nuts and his little fruit salad, bless him and put him in his little ball – never thought about the door – and off he went down the garden; Linford Christie couldn't have caught him I tell you.'

We got dressed up like Action Man again and Elinor joined us in the search but where do we start, I wondered.

'You two go that way,' I suggested, pointing in the direction of the bridge. 'And I'll make my way to the ford.'

'If you haven't found him by tea-time go home,' Otley called after me. 'If he's gone he's gone.'

'Roger and out,' I signalled.

I wandered around for a while and then found a spot by the river to have a rest; the moisture-bearing west wind had driven the bumble-bees from the purple heads of the thistles, and the oxeye daisies tucked their heads underneath their arms against the coming rain. I'll have a little read and then I'll go and see Tony. Now where was I, I asked myself as I riffled through the pages. Who's that coming through the undergrowth? For a minute I thought it was Coleridge been for a drag on the old hookah, but it's not – it's Tony, my dream-boat.

'*Cara mia!*'

'Tonee!'

'My leetle zabaglione!'

'Come and get your tutti-frutti before the dogs get at it.'

After dinner I did some knitting while Tony looked for his money, he said he had his moneybag round his neck coming through the woods and he must have caught it on a branch. I expect muggins'll have to go and get it; there's no peace for the wicked.

'I wash up,' Tony said. 'Bugga 'usband come.'

I stormed off in a temper leaving him with his feathers wilting in the steamy kitchen, I don't get chance to put my feet up.

'And when you've done that, you can parcel them bloody dishcloths up for Mesopotamia,' I screamed. 'You useless, bloody nincompoop.'

'I no nincompoop, I Italian,' he protested.

'Faggots!' I said.

I found his moneybag hanging on a beech tree and was just about to count the coins when I heard voices, so I climbed up into the tree and hid myself in the leaves. It was my husband with a big lump on his head.

'I'll get that connivin' cream puff if it's the last thing I do,' he said, brandishing his cudgel. 'And that cross-eyed conker that she lives with. I'll string him up by his bobolinks.'

I held my breath until they'd gone – he and the giant Caledonian swinging his claymore and lopping the heads off young saplings as if they were his worst enemy. A close shave in more ways than one.

I fell out of the tree when it was dark and slipped the money into my bosom. Tony was hiding under the bed when I got home and the dishcloths remained unparcelled.

'We maka bambino now,' he said.

I ignored him and picked up my new goose-feather pen.

At the Villa Claro
AD 55

Dear Buddy,

The wedding's off for now. I've fallen out with Tony and I thought I'd killed Nutty but I saw him today. Did you say you could get up here with your best chariot, the one with the big knives on? I'd like to learn how to drive it.

Be on your guard when the great Caesar comes over here, he won't like you calling him Miss Nero just because he wears a frock and lipstick of an evening, and he does like girls to be girls so keep your battleaxe out of sight; it's all a bit jolly hockey sticks and what he's really coming for is an orgy. He'll be bringing a pot of yoghurt.

No, I'm not coming down setting fire to Colchester with you Buddy it's too far, but good luck anyway. Do you carry your burning brand with you or do you light it when you get there?

Well, I'll have to be off now, Tony's waiting for his gnocchi and he can't do it himself.

Your luving friend,
Carrie Brigantum

PS *Never mind what Mario says, don't put vinegar on it it'll sting.*

I had no sooner finished writing when the chief Druid called with his begging bowl and this time I was ready for him.

'Clear off, yer snivelling, old ratbag!' I yelled, throwing a pot of flummery at him. 'And get some bloody work done for a change!'

''Ooza dat?' Tony inquired as he massaged my pressure points.

'It's our spiritual leader – idle sod,' I explained.

I feel nice and relaxed now. I think I will make a bambino tonight otherwise Nutty and his tribe of Scotch collops will inherit my throne.

Suddenly I was aware of the church clock striking five and a steady drizzle pattering through the trees on to my head. I packed away my wet things and hurried along the riverside towards the dig. Then, as I ran up the slope behind the villa, I caught my foot in a hole and fell. I felt something hard and when I looked it was poor little Ginger, defunct, an ex-gerbil. But what was that underneath him? I lifted out the ball and with it a mouldering, leather bag. It looked familiar somehow and I wrenched it open with trembling hands. It was full of coins!

I arrived home breathless just as the others were having their tea and watching *Blue Peter*. I held out my treasures with both hands.

'I've found them both!' I gasped.

Poor Ginger was given a decent burial under the roses.

'That's what they do at the crematorium,' said Aunt Bedelia. 'Mrs Stott went with a dibber to bury a lock of hair with her old man, and she dug one of his teeth up.'

'I thought they put them in caskets.'

'No, they don't, they just dig 'em in,' said Otley. 'It saves 'em buying bags of bonemeal from Woolworths.'

We emptied the bag of coins onto the table and although we couldn't identify them at this stage, I knew they were silver.

'We're rich!' I said, clapping my hands.

'Not yet,' said Otley. 'You have to go to court first.'

'What for? It's mine. I buried it and I found it.'

'Treasure trove,' he went on as he consulted his handbook. 'It's complicated and it all depends on the whim of some creep in a beetle suit; if buried with no intention of recovery as in a burial mound it belongs to the owner of the land.'

'We always said "finders, keepers" when we were kids,' Bedelia said.

'"If lost or intentionally abandoned it then belongs to the finder but it has to be proved first",' Otley read out.

'How the dickens can you prove what was in the mind of somebody dead these past two thousand years or so?' I said in alarm. 'I know, but they'll never believe me.'

'And if any gold, silver, plate, or bullion of unknown ownership is found concealed then it belongs to the Crown.'

'They get all the sturgeons as well. They're never satisfied,' Bedelia complained.

'What can we do?' I asked, gathering the coins back into the bag and clutching it to my breast. 'I'm not burying them again.'

'They'll be safe in the bank until after the jubilee,' said Otley. 'One thing at a time.'

'I thought that was Miss Jago, you know,' Elinor said, harking back to poor Ginger. 'He was the spitting image of her.'

'She'd only been telling me about her father saying there was silver somewhere about,' I agreed. 'And something about the drains – there's a culvert down there.'

'And she came back to find it for you.'

'Don't tell Nigel just yet,' Otley warned. 'He'll have to record it and then Doris'll tell everybody.'

We were all sworn to silence until we had dealt with Swire Sugden and settled the ownership of the meadows. If only we could find the Chatwin heir – oh dear! And I wonder what Mike's doing – he doesn't know he's the heir to a bag of Roman coins.

I was so happy that I snuggled up to Otley as we watched the red, blue and green dots and dashes swirling round and ending up as a number four on the magic box.

'I told you, didn't I, about the Romans,' I prompted. 'Now do you believe me?'

'No,' he said.

Oh, well! I'll go and have a bath. I still feel cold and clammy after this afternoon. The water not too hot, Mr Earnshaw dropped dead after he got out of a hot bath and his wife's not had one since. Just right, test it with your elbow and if you can't feel anything you can get in. Blood heat they call it, that's tepid if you're English and at boiling point if you're Italian.

Swish an oatmeal bag in it to make my skin like milk and roses. I don't possess such a thing as a lactating ass. You can almost float in these big iron baths and I must be careful not to fall asleep as I did once in the briny at Bognor Regis when I was picked up by a fishing smack well on the way to France. Mmm, that's lovely, now wash my hair in a camomile shampoo with a squeeze of lemon in the rinsing water and Bob's your uncle. I could write a book about baths, but I wouldn't know what to call it: *Baths You Have Loved? Baths Of The World Unite? Bathmen Of The Kalahari* . . . ?

Suddenly I saw a face at the window, peering at me between the rubber plant and the kangaroo vine. I screamed and ran out clutching a towel round me. Otley was engrossed in *World in Action* and just said sh!

'There's a prowler outside! Go and catch him,' I implored.

'It's only Mrs Grindlewood-Gryke's chauffeur with a bowl of soup for you,' he said wearily. 'She wants us to go down there tomorrow, if you've got rid of your spots.'

Fifteen

Grindlewood, built in the Palladian style, turned its nose up at the rest of us with its columns and porticoes and pilasters. We stepped into the cold marble hall and waited under a statue of George the Third masquerading as Alexander the Great.

'Poor old soul, he was as mad as a hatter,' Otley said.

Adam fireplaces and jasper urns, ancestors ten feet square and chandeliers about to drop on your head.

'I'm getting a migraine,' I said looking in my handbag.

Chinese dragons and Chelsea whatnots, massive tables groaning with silver plate. Big treasures and little treasures. Something for everyone. Open the box and take your pick.

'Greedy sods,' said Otley.

'Come in and have some tea,' a cut-glass voice invited.

'Oh, thanks!' said Otley. 'Nice place you got here.'

The Hon. Mrs Grindlewood-Gryke was a bossy lady, as you would expect. A cross between a vestal virgin and a bus conductress. Fair-haired, fresh-faced and hazel-eyed, she strode through life as if through a newly ploughed field. We followed the tweed skirt into a kitchen where its owner motioned us to sit, in the manner of someone training a dog.

'Are you better now, Mrs Craven?' she asked.

'Yes, thank you, your honour,' I bobbed.

'Good Lord! Have you been watching *Upstairs, Downstairs?*' she said.

We discussed our plans for the living museum and theme park and told her about the oak tree. She was anxious that Swire Sugden should not be allowed to spread himself around like a malignant tumour.

'This new money, these upstarts, they don't know their place – they think they can tell me what to do,' she went on.

'We don't want any more supermarkets and car-parks,' I added. '"They" can go on the bus.'

'If everybody plays their part we can keep him out,' Mrs Grindlewood-Gryke said. 'I'm prepared to fund whatever we put on.'

'Oh, thanks!'

'It's our bicentenary here at Grindlewood and we want to make it a year to remember,' she said, measuring the floor with her brogues.

'We'll be starting rehearsals tomorrow,' Otley announced.

'And we think we've found a Roman villa.'

'Good show!'

'We wanted to put you in the picture,' Otley said. 'There's a lot going on and we don't want any crossed lines.'

'I'll organize the ox-roasting,' she said. 'Eats are on me.'

'And we're trying to find the Chatwin boy – ' I began.

'He was stolen by the gypsies,' she interrupted.

'It's a wild-goose chase but you never know,' I said hopefully.

'And if you could meet Swire Sugden yourself he might listen to you being an honourable an' all that,' said Otley to my amazement, I never knew he was a royalist. Soon he'll be tugging his forelock.

'I'll do that,' she said, 'bit of MI5 stuff behind the scenes, eh?'

'While we dig away at the front,' I said.

The Hon. Mrs Grindlewood-Gryke, 'You can call me Mollie', had been a widow since 1979 when her husband was lost in a blizzard.

'In the Antarctic?' inquired Otley.

'In the Lake District,' she said. 'It was the year they made Dennis whatsisname minister for snow.'

There was only a daily who came in to dust and wash up, a cook and a gardener. This must be him just coming in through the side door.

'Excuse me, ma'am, but the dumper's gone.'

'Have you reported it?'

'Nay, I've got mildew – gotta see to that first.'

'It must be a headache running this place,' Otley said.

'Well, we do open to the public now, as you know, but oh! the bills, and the staff want paying,' she said as she showed us to the door.

'What a shame,' Otley muttered under his breath.

'Same with us,' I sympathized.

'But on a much smaller scale, isn't it?' came the cut-glass tone.

'Well, we've got smaller money.'

'And then there's the rates,' she complained.

'You'll be all right with the poll tax,' I reminded her.

'Then they want your blood and your kidneys as well,' said Otley.

'Keep in touch,' she called as the huge door rattled to a close.

When I want a change of scenery I'll ask her if she wants any help. I'll do it for nothing – just my food and a bed in the attic looking out over the chimney-pots.

'Now I've gotta round up some more lads for the Ancient Britons,' Otley said. 'We want a few good skirmishers.'

'Have you got your costume?'

'I've got that fur loincloth and a dustbin lid.'

'If it's nice I'll wear that silk gown,' I said.

'It's not *The Teahouse of the August Moon* you know!'

'I told you Nero sent me it so I'm going to wear it.'

'If you go round saying that they'll have you locked up in a padded cell.'

We walked down to the car-park, through the rhododendrons, round the lake and over the willow-pattern bridge. Bought a pot of Grindlewood goosegog jam at the gift shop and went back to the car.

'They put elderflowers in it,' I said looking at the label.

'Don't start screaming again,' he said.

We thought we'd run over to Low Riding and make sure Mike was all right. I had to water the plants and stock up the fridge as I don't want to be reported to the NSPCC.

'He's got the vote now – he's out of our jurisdiction,' Otley said eating a custard tart I'd just bought.

'Hello! I thought you were at Claro.'

Mike was wearing a jester's outfit with bells on, one leg red and the other leg yellow. A young man in an Acker Bilk ensemble lurked in the doorway and a girl in a red satin skirt and a chocolate soldier cap twirled a baton and stamped her feet. This must be Jilly.

'Where's the others?' I inquired.

'We practise in Hob Wood,' Mike said. 'Because of complaints about the noise. This is just a dry run then we're off to join them.'

'Have you emptied the bins and put the milk bottles out – ' I began.

'Yes, we have,' he butted in.

'Keep the windows locked at night and unplug the telly – '

'Mum, why don't you give yourself a treat and go to Benidorm for a fortnight? His folks have gone,' he said, nodding at Acker Bilk.

'We don't want you to be neglected,' I told him for the umptieth time. 'All the child psychologists say that mummy and daddy have to be there for children to grow up well balanced.'

'I'm a big boy now,' he said.

'And the government are emphasizing the importance of the family.'

'You know why, don't you?' he said mysteriously.

'Why?'

'Because they want everybody to have a Big Daddy with his leather belt keeping 'em in order – less for them to do,' he said.

'Whippin' 'em into line,' added Acker Bilk.

'They're all right. Let's go,' Otley decided.

'And Maggie's always on about Victorian values,' I persisted, 'the sanctity of the family group – '

'Mafia families as well?' asked Mike.

'Divorce – single parents – old folks in homes,' I went on.

'Families torn asunder,' warned Otley.

'Some families want tearing asunder,' said Jilly, slashing at the air with her baton.

'Ask the kids sleeping under the arches at Charing Cross about Victorian values. It's the same as in Dickens.'

Somehow I didn't think my message was getting across but Mike seemed all right. He'd washed his hair and piled all his plastic carrier bags into a corner instead of strewing them through the house like the clues of a treasure-hunt.

'We shall want you to play for us in the pageant.'

'When?'

'A week on Saturday, all being well.'

'What sort of stuff?'

'Well, if you could practise "Viva España" for us to march to that'll be nice,' I told them.

'And "Any Old Iron" for the Ancient Britons,' requested Otley.

'Is it a proper jazz band with tommy talkers like we used to run after when we were kids?' I asked him.

'Sort of.'

'Come on!' said Otley, opening the door and propelling me through. 'See you then, mate.'

'Bye, luv,' I called back, 'and stop poking your ears out with your biro you'll get mastoids.'

'Sometimes I wonder how he passed his O-levels,' Daddy said as we crawled over the cobbles and out of the village.

'Well, he did, didn't he?' I couldn't help feeling proud.

'What good is it doing him, capering about with bells on?'

'They can't get anywhere these days without exams,' I said, 'he'll be doing his degree now.'

'Jesus never had a degree,' said Otley.

We called for some fish and chips to take back for all of us, but I wasn't sure that I could eat them after seeing that documentary where they all had ulcers. Memories of a childhood paradise came crowding in. A bathe in a spanking-clean river, roly-poly down the grassy knolls, finish up your bottle of Spanish water and jostle at the chip shop on your way home. A glass of milk and an apple when you got in and a smack if you were late.

'D'you remember – ' I began when Otley came back to the car.

'Yes, I do,' he interrupted. 'When you pinched my bicycle outside the chip shop and ran into the back of a lorry with it and buckled the wheels.'

'You didn't worry about me all bandaged up, did you?'

'It was a new bike and served you right, anyway,' he said. 'You were as mad as a March hare.'

'Only when I wanted to be.'

'But you were a little cracker all the same,' he said holding my hand.

I hope he's not going to get too sentimental. You can love somebody without going all gooey. Then the next minute he's swearing. That's why I stopped going to the Olde Tyme Dancing with him. Bowing and scraping all night at the class, then effing and blinding all the way home.

'And don't forget to bow to your partner, Mr Craven,' our long-suffering instructor would call out.

'I'll give 'im a bleedin' thick earole in a minute,' Otley would mutter rolling up the sleeves of his frilly, dancing shirt.

Aunt Bedelia stayed to watch *Brookside* while we went over to the Jubilee Tower for the rest of the evening. You could get seasick at the top watching the clouds scudding across a full moon in a vast ocean of space. Elinor was wearing an Empire-line gown in the hope of seeing Napoleon.

We were in line with the Craven fault it seemed and in an electric storm the tower and all its domestic equipment spat and sizzled like a jumping cracker.

'I heard the battle of Waterloo once,' she said.

'How d'you know?' Otley inquired.

'Shouting, trumpets, cries of men and horses,' she explained.

'It could have been Marston Moor, it's nearer than Waterloo.'

'I'm not on that wavelength.'

'Give over.'

'Well, you can't pick anything up on your radio unless you're on the right wavelength, can you?'

'No, you can't,' I said, giving Otley a cross look.

'Well then,' she said.

'You know he had piles,' said Otley finally.

Before we went down to the kitchen Elinor patted all the Napoleana into place, violets and Redouté roses; a picture of him riding his horse, Marengo, and that one of him feeling for his wallet; matchstick models made by French prisoners of war and a tricolour flying at half-mast.

Nigel was in the kitchen looking at his diagrams and broken pots.

'Have you ever seen anything like this before?' he said, handing me a piece of a dish with feathers sticking to it. 'Surely they plucked the chickens first before they ate them.'

As I held it in my hand it all came back to me. It was the night Tony came over to tell me Nero wanted a British warm like his. I was just dishing up the ravioli and he hadn't even had time to take his helmet off when Nutty stormed in, drunk as a fiddler.

'Gotcha! yer prancin' pollywog,' he raged pushing Tony head first in the dish of pulsating pasta.

They had a right set to while I went to look for my knitting. Nutty ate everything in sight and went off to fetch his smelly Brits again.

'I'll show ye, ye mollicking mollymawk,' he shouted brandishing his fist at me. 'I'll swingle yer scalp for a sporran.'

What a mess there was to clean up, and I had to hit the cooking pot with my chopper to get Tony's head out. His helmet was a bit dented and it had lost its feathers but otherwise he was all right – just a bit dizzy that's all.

At the Villa Claro
AD 55

Dear Nero,

Salute! lofty Caesar! I hear you want a black British warm for prowling about the streets at night. What a good idea! Tony would like a new hat. He's learning to row a coracle but he keeps going round in circles, it must be tiresome for him when he's used to going in straight lines.

If you could send some more troops up here I'd be very grateful, but not the ones who eat sheep's eyes and have ten women each as they are a strain on the economy and we've run out of rice pudding. Thanks for the new road, I'm sorry Boudicca's churned it up. She didn't do it on purpose, it's her new chariot. And your Governor wasn't looking where he was going, it was very silly of him. As soon as we have found him another set of legs he'll be out and about again, do you think he'll mind walking on his hands for now?

Well I'm off now luv. Here's some calamine lotion for your spots. It's all them orgies, but you're only young once. Arrivederci!
Carrie Brigantum
Regina
PS The poison mushrooms are the pretty red ones with white spots. I do agree. It's pleasanter than chopping him up in little pieces.

I came to sitting on the sofa still holding the broken pot in my hand.

'It's the feathers off his hat,' I said.

I promised to have a look at the dig and point out where the tessellated pavement should be. It was looking good, Nigel thought.

'And by the way,' said Elinor as she handed round tea and biscuits, 'I found out that the Chatwin kid was traced to a gypsy camp at the Appleby Horse Fair but before the police could pick him up he'd disappeared again.'

'When was that?' asked Otley.

'In 1955 – he'd be about six years old then.'

The gypsies gathered at the horse fair came from all over the place so he could be anywhere after that. Although the case was still open the police had no hope of finding him after all this time.

'You know what?' said Otley.

'What?'

'It's the Appleby Horse Fair next week.'

'Let's go up there,' said Elinor. 'You never know.'

'And we can stay out all night,' I said hopefully.

Nigel couldn't leave his digging but wished us luck and we began to make our plans: go up on the Settle-Carlisle line for a day or two, split up to get round all the caravans quicker, then meet at dinner and tea to compare notes.

'We can only try,' Elinor said, giving Otley the best biscuits.

'They've not found Lord Lucan either,' he said.

Sixteen

As soon as we received the tree preservation order we rushed down to pin it on the tree. A guard was to be put on it and the vicar arranged to ring the church bells if it was attacked.

'And if they start digging,' Elinor said.

'Of course,' he agreed.

'We've got to keep our eyes open,' said Otley.

'And if they bring the chainsaw we'll make a ring round it,' I said.

'You've got to be prepared to die for what you believe in,' Elinor said passionately with a toss of her wayward locks.

'Well, er,' said the vicar, 'I'm not so sure about that but I'll certainly ring the church bells.'

'There's no need to play anything fancy,' Otley advised. 'Just a plain ding-dong'll do.'

We had barely finished congratulating ourselves and going round with the good news when Mrs Maddock's little boy from the post office ran to tell us it had been torn down.

'A chap got out of a big, black car and did it,' he panted.

'Not to worry,' said the tree officer when we phoned him. 'They'll tear everything down. It's the same with the notices about dogs fouling the pavement. We put them up one minute and the next minute they're gone.'

'What can we do?'

'Have you got any white paint?' he asked.

'We can get some.'

'Well, just paint TPO on it.'

'Won't it damage it?' I asked thinking of the noxious fumes.

'No,' he laughed. 'If they can stand dogs piddling on them they can stand a bit o' paint.'

We borrowed some paint from one of Otley's Ancient Britons, Gilbert Briggs, who was painting his windowsill, and the job was done.

'Thanks, mate,' said Otley giving him back his brush. 'Don't forget the manoeuvres after tea.'

Aunt Bedelia tut-tutted at all the goings on as we ate our spinach soup made with dandelion leaves and wild garlic.

'Won't make a bit of difference what you do,' she sniffed. 'They'd run over us with a steamroller if they felt like it.'

'We'll go down fighting anyway,' said Otley.

I keep forgetting he's a war hero. With his paunch and his varicose veins and his rumbling tum it's hard to equate him with John Wayne and Errol Flynn.

'Be careful now,' I cautioned. 'Don't do anything foolhardy.'

'Don't tell me what to do,' he snapped.

'I only said – '

'Nobody tells Otley Craven what to do – I'm my own man.'

I remember him saying that once before. He was celebrating a new job at Christmas and went out with the boys in his smart pin-stripes. Knowing what they were like for drink I tried to tell him but he wouldn't listen.

'Don't overdo it,' I warned him. 'Just have a little drink and then come back home.'

'Don't tell me what to do,' he said. 'Who d'you think you're married to – Little Lord Fauntleroy?'

Well, I waited up until three o'clock in the morning and he crawled in with footmarks all over his nice new suit where he'd fallen on the floor and let everybody trample over him, blood pouring down his shirt from a head wound, a balloon tied round his neck and a paper hat on.

I struggled to get him into bed and he started to do deep breathing exercises, which he knows I can't stand when I'm trying to get to sleep.

'It's stuffy in here,' he said.

I went and got the pressure-cooker to brain him with and was just about to bring it crashing down on his bonce when I heard Mike calling from the next room.

'Mummy, can I have a drink of water?'

Who would look after him when I was in gaol?

'This woman,' the judge would say, 'is so depraved, so much the slave of her own passions, that she had no hesitation in bludgeoning to death the father of her child on Christmas Eve.'

It would look bad. There would be no recommendation to mercy. I put the pressure-cooker back and went to bed on the sofa.

'Merry Christmas!' Otley said the next day when he surfaced. 'We had a smashing time last night.'

He still doesn't know how much more smashing it might have been.

'Sorry,' he said when he saw Bedelia's open mouth, 'it's my nerves.'

Sometimes I think we'd be better off if we did what the animals do. Have our little bit of fun then throw daddy out to fend for himself when the kiddiewinks come along. Have you seen how the king of the jungle behaves when the missus brings back a nice bit of venison? He's been sat there all day like a stuffed dummy, then he suddenly comes to life, grabs the dinner and runs off with it trailing between his legs, tripping and stumbling over it in his anxiety to have it all to himself. And birds are not much better. Daddy sits there flapping his wings and squawking while mummy builds a new house.

'Talking about steamrollers,' Otley said, 'it would be handy if we could get hold of one.'

'Look in the *Exchange & Mart*,' I said.

'Why do you want a steamroller?' Nigel asked, no doubt concerned about his dig.

'So that we can flatten that Swire Sugden and post him back through his letter-box,' Otley said, crushing his bread roll into a poultice.

'Now don't do anything silly,' Bedelia cautioned. 'It's against the law to squash people under steamrollers.'

'Just run him down with your car,' suggested Nigel. 'You'll get away with a fine and Bob's your uncle.'

'And if you can prove you need your car for work they won't take your licence away,' Elinor added.

Well, that wouldn't apply to Otley but it is the safest way to murder somebody. That and knitting needles.

After we had finished our toad-in-the-hole made with soya chunks and apple dappy, we cleared away and washed up while Bedelia did the ironing. The steam rose from the cavernous sink and the furniture loomed at us like shapes in a jungle night. Otley riffled through a pile of old sheet music releasing a musty smell of pipe tobacco and Evening in Paris.

'This'll be all right for the Ancient Britons as well,' he said brandishing 'The Stein Song', 'I'll give it to Mike when we go over.'

More songs with words, the sort that he likes best: 'Mexicali Rose', 'When it's Springtime in the Rockies', 'It Happened in Monterey'.

'You were a nice little girl then,' he said accusingly.

Passionate, throbbing tangos, 'La Paloma' and 'La Cumparsita' were more in Elinor's line and Nigel was eager to continue his dancing lessons.

'We'll tape them,' Elinor said, 'and take them to the church hall.'

Sid and Ethel Parkinson, retired dancers, were starting a class. It was only a pound a time including tea and biscuits; fifty pence for OAPs, UB40s, students and disabled, which was most of us in Claro.

More steam, more dust stirred up until we ran for the door gasping. The windows had not been opened for years and had forgotten how it went.

'It's time for the practice,' Nigel said, consulting his Timex. 'No need to get dressed up for it.'

'Oh!' said a disappointed Otley, putting down his dustbin lid.

I picked up Dorothy Wordsworth's *Journals* hoping for a quiet hour or two by the river while they were manoeuvring. As the Queen they wouldn't expect me to do much. Elinor wanted to be Cleopatra.

'She didn't live round here,' Nigel informed her.

'It doesn't matter, they won't know any different,' she said.

'Right then – Watling Street Guard fall in!' he ordered.

'Hey up!'

'Quick march!'

'Erewiggo, erewiggo, erewiggo!'

Jostling, thumping, grunting, slapping, guffawing, raspberrying as the lads from the nail factory got fell in. Jack, Judd, Freddie, Bob, Mickey, Jimmy, Ted, Gordon, Chas and Harry.

'I'll go in front as the standard bearer,' said Nigel as he placed himself at the head of his patrol. 'Of course, on the day I shall have an eagle on a stick.'

'Oi oi how's yer father!' Harry shouted.

'Watling Street Guard, forward – wait for it – march! Left, right, left, right!'

'They didn't say that, did they?' Otley objected as he waited under the trees with his bunch of Brits.

'Patrol – wait for it – halt,' called Nigel.

Some halted at the right time and others didn't, resulting in a bit of a rugger scrum.

'Aye aye, put some water in it next time!' Freddie advised Mickey who was lying flat on his face in a clump of nettles.

'Clumsy sod,' he said when he got up shaking his fist at Gordon with the big feet who was marching behind him.

'Of course they didn't say that,' said Nigel as if to an elderly sloth suffering from senile decay, 'but it's no good me saying, "Sinister, dexter, sinister, dexter," because they won't know what I'm talking about, will they? They'll trip themselves up trying to keep time to that, won't they?'

'I never thought,' replied Otley.

'You can carry verisimilitude too far, you know,' Nigel went on. 'It's no good if nobody knows what you're getting at.'

'Oh no! You're quite right, it isn't,' agreed Otley.

'Right then, let's go,' said Nigel. 'Watling Street Guard, forward – wait for it – march. Left, right, left, right.'

'Erewiggo, erewiggo, erewiggo,' they chanted as they set off.

'Up the 'Ammers!' they roared as they charged headlong and then half stumbled and half marched to the far end of the meadow.

'Come back here! What d'you think you are, football hooligans?'

'The Campbells are comin',' they sang as they charged back.

'Patrol – wait for it – dismiss,' ordered Nigel.

The Ancient Britons surged forward and began forming themselves into lines, Elinor in front as Boudicca in a pretend chariot and Otley as Venutius, the belligerent Brit, consort of our Brigantian Queen Cartimandua.

'The Celts didn't march,' Nigel said, dismissing them back into the bushes. 'They were brave fighters but undisciplined.'

'What have we got to do then?' inquired Otley.

'Just mill about and attack in a rabble when you feel like it.'

'Oh, that's easy!' came a chorus of approval.

'Where's Cartimandua?' I heard Nigel calling urgently.

'Never mind her,' said Otley. 'She was useless anyway.'

'Traitor!'

'Quisling Queen!'

'Burn her alive!'

'Bury her in quicklime!'

I crept along the riverside until I reached the culvert and hid myself among the banks of sweet cicely to read my book. The aroma evoked the sights and sounds of childhood – aniseed balls clicking against molars like billiard balls on the green baize cloth. A group of whirligig beetles span round and round on the surface of the water putting me in a daze.

That's Tony going round in his coracle again. He doesn't seem to be able to master the technique.

'*Mamma mia!* 'Ow you stoppa thissa machina stupido?'

'Ye'll stay there till yer radicles roll off and yer congles coagulate, ye pestilential pokeweed!'

Oh, no! It's not him again. I'll just ignore him.

'Tonee – dinner's ready.'

'I'm having it,' said Nutty, barging his way in to the dining-room.

'You won't like it, it's spaghetti,' I told him as I put the pot on the table and went to fetch the tomato sauce.

'I can go fishin' with it,' he said, stuffing it in his pockets, 'I've used all my maggots.'

'Just look what a mess you're making – I've got to clean that up.'

'Yer gettin' worse than them poncin' polecats, Carrie,' he complained. 'Yer never used to be like that till they came wi' their hot water and their olive oil – oil's fer boilin' people not for washin' in.'

'I'm afraid I must ask you to leave,' I said.

Tony came in then dripping wet and there was another punch-up. I left them to it and went up into my tree-house. I've got my accounts to do. There should be some money over this month. Every time Tony lost his army pay I picked it up. If they can build aqueducts you'd think they could engineer a wallet to keep their money in. They drop it all over the place.

At the Villa Claro
AD 55

Dear Buddy,
I did warn you about doing the Barbarian Chop. When you've taken the splints off your leg you can use them to strap your arm up. What a good idea to go round collecting all the spare parts! Sorry to hear you gave your husband the wrong leg though. Would you like to borrow Nutty for a few weeks? I'll donate one of his. They're at it again. I've got out of the way, I'm trying to do my accounts, I can't understand this new money can you? You did right chopping the Governor down and setting fire to the forum – but don't tell them

I said so. If you put his legs on backwards way he'll go home instead of coming up here.

Nero sends his luv. He's invited us over to his place for the circus and if we like it we can have one here. Seems like a nice boy. Don't know about you but I shall be glad to get away from my lot. Follow me round muttering and shaking their fists. It's a thankless task. I keep having hot flushes, know what I mean? but d'you think they care? they just follow me round saying 'Miss we've dropped a stitch'. That chief Druid was round here again. Nasty, old man, blood all over his nightie, been doing sacrifices I expect. Tony gets under the bed when he sees him coming. May Jupiter forgive me for saying this Buddy – but I do think his head would go nice on your mantelpiece.

It's all clear now so I'm off. Luv and kisses to all.
Carrie Brigantum

PS Sorry you got off on the wrong foot with the new commander. A scutum is a shield, didn't you know? I said to 'Hold his scutum at the top', not 'Boil his scrotum in a pot', silly goose! No wonder he was miffed.

'Watling Street Guard – wait for it – dismiss.'

Where am I? How did I get up here into this tree?

'Help, help! I can't get down,' I hollered.

Soon my rescuers arrived jostling, pushing, laughing, joking.

'Oi oi, does your mother know yer out?'

'Hey up, can anybody come?'

'Me Tarzan, you Jane!'

'Have a banana!'

The Ancient Britons had gone home tired of having to lurk in the bushes waiting to burst out in a rabble. I picked my book out of the sweet cicely still unread and made my way back to Claro.

Nigel caught up with me and I was glad to have company as it can get spooky in the half-light. An eerie, green glow in the sky behind the tower turned it into a ghostly galleon on a leaden sea; Claro itself, a crazy house, leaning this way and bulging that. It looked ready to collapse like a house of cards if Swire Sugden huffed and puffed hard enough.

'We've got down to the stone foundation,' Nigel said. 'It's against all the odds if it is a villa but I hope you're right.'

'It's only a small one,' I said, 'three rooms and a bathhouse, with a verandah facing south.'

'Really?'

'I'll draw you a plan. And I told you about the garden going down to the river, didn't I?'

'Yes.'

'Well, there's a jetty, they brought stuff up the river.'

I could see Elinor and Otley, and Aunt Bedelia standing with her arms akimbo silhouetted against the lighted windows. It looked as if they were waiting for somebody, could it be me? Oh dear!

Seventeen

Otley seemed to be very cross about something the next day but I didn't bother to ask what. I'm fed up of all this aggravation. I want to go and make daisy chains and eat rhubarb pie like we did in that magic, far-away land of childhood . . .

A penny to spend on Saturdays. Jelly babies, dolly mixtures, love hearts that said 'Kiss me quick', and if you saved up for two weeks you could buy a whipped cream walnut. Garden parties in the summer at Miss Annie's who went round muttering to herself and poking everybody with her parasol. But it was the scene of my first heartbreak. We held hands going to school every morning, Jimmy and I, and three times I stood on my head for him at Miss Annie's to prove my love. But Kathleen Mary Butterfield lured him away with a bounce of her fat orange curls, and I found them roly-polying down the hill together behind the shrubbery. It was a bittersweet time but he still held my hand going to school.

'Are you all right, May?' Aunt Bedelia inquired after breakfast.

'She's in her "Come into the garden, Maud" mood,' said Otley.

'Can we have rhubarb pie today?' I asked absentmindedly.

'I think all this is tipping you over the edge a bit,' said Bedelia with an armful of dandelions.

'She went doolally once before,' Otley told her.

'Haven't you got any tablets?' she wanted to know.

'No – I don't want any.'

'We do deep breathing exercises instead,' said Otley, throwing out his chest to expand his lungs, his paunch moving itself up a notch.

'The dancing'll do you good. It starts tonight, will you be going?'

'As long as there's no bowing an' scraping,' said Otley.

'Not in a paso doble there isn't,' I reminded him. 'They stab each other with their banderillas.'

'That sounds more like it.'

Bedelia never went out at night as she didn't want to get mugged.

'You don't know who's hiding in that snicket by the church – it could be the vicar or it could be Dracula, they look the same when it's dark.'

We were just wondering what to do next when Elinor came running in waving a letter.

'It's from Mr Scrape,' she shouted.

We could have another month he said, then they had no option but to sell to Swire Sugden. The boilerhouse bridge needed repairing before it pitched us all into the river. Estate cottages had to be modernized, and the school had to have all the lead and asbestos extracted so Portakabins would have to go up.

'Another month,' said Otley. 'That takes us into July.'

Elinor was looking forward to the dancing class with Nigel, and to the horse fair with Otley. How many men does she want? It was all her different incarnations apparently. One life is not enough for somebody with her hormones. I realized with a shock the same thing could be said of me now and I've got no hormones. Mustn't be too hard on her.

She did look fetching in her fuchsia velour jumpsuit that deepened her speedwell eyes to a pansy purple. And I noticed Otley was admiring himself in the mirror a lot these days, the predatory gleam back in his hazel eyes, sometimes gold sometimes green, according to where the light was coming from.

I'm still in my army trousers and my one-hundred-per-cent cotton shirt made in Bombay. I shall have to look in the dead box for something to wear tonight. A bodystocking and a black wig – like on *Come Dancing*. Otley won't recognize me.

We're trying to work up some passion for the pageant. We don't want to be cardboard cut-outs, we want the museum to be a real, living one. Bring history leaping from the pages of those boring, old textbooks – Battle of Hastings, 1066 – Magna Carta, 1215 – Great Fire of London, 1666. Big deal. And then when you're older, scutage, tallage, and how many old goats we've had for archbishops and popes.

Mrs Grindlewood-Gryke says we can do a Roman banquet so we got a book from the library about what sort of food they ate. You'd never believe it! Minced dormice, sautéed snails, calf's brain custard and pig's testicles in coriander sauce. But to be fair that was just the gourmets.

The legions lived on cabbage and polenta and wine that turned to vinegar with the shaking up it got. Anyway, we'll do what we can without going too far.

'You'll be needing some more wine,' Elinor said handing me another flagon. I took it and refilled the iodine bottle for my handbag.

'Did you lot say you were going up to Appleby?' asked Bedelia.

'On Monday, that'll be the sixth of June,' Otley said, 'and there'll be another two days of the horse fair left to go.'

'It'll give me a chance to get on with my baking an' that then for the WI stall,' she said with a nod of approval.

'Can you make a rhubarb pie again?' I asked.

Liquorice and rhubarb! The stuff of my West Riding childhood! The liquorice fields of Pontefract, exotic as a blaze of opium poppies, meant fresh, juicy roots to chew in springtime and little, round, black pancakes in the winter. And the road to Great Aunt Martha's lay between avenues of waving rhubarb, enchanting as the Golden Road to Samarkand to a small child eager to see the big, wide world.

'Snap out of it – you're grown up now,' said Otley, passing his hands in front of my eyes in the manner of a hypnotist. He turned and smirked at Elinor. Who does he think he is? Just because he's my husband.

'You know what?' he giggled, 'when she was a kid she used to think that cockerels laid pot eggs.'

'Shut up!' I screamed.

'That all black cows were bulls . . .'

'I'm warning you!'

'And you know that wavy, glass top on the weaving shed at Hubert Sampson's mill?' he pressed on regardless.

'Yes,' said Elinor.

'Well, she thought it was the seaside.' Snigger, snigger, snigger.

I flew at him ripping all the buttons off his shirt in one go, tore it off his back in two pieces, grabbed hold of his string vest and dragged him round the kitchen like a sack of potatoes.

'May – ' he started to say, but I crammed a cushion into his mouth before he could finish. He struggled to his feet gasping for breath.

'I'm only – ' he began. The door was open and with the strength of ten I hurtled him through it and into the herb garden where he came to rest in a clump of sage. With the fury that had accumulated over the years I pulled up some onions and flung them at him. Now he can get stuffed.

There was an embarrassed silence when I went back into the kitchen to tidy myself up. I had a drink of water as my throat was hurting, picked up Dorothy Wordsworth's *Journals* and sat down thankfully in an easy chair. I was feeling a bit dizzy now.

'May,' said Aunt Bedelia, 'I don't think you should let yourself get worked up like that. You'll burst a blood vessel if you're not careful.'

'Well,' I said, 'he gets on my wick at times.'

Eventually Otley came in from the garden rubbing his head.

'Are you all right?' they asked, like people do when somebody's been knocked down by a bus and lying stretched out in the road.

'I'm fine,' he said. 'Take no notice it's her age. It's not often she loses her temper, but when she does you can look out!'

Three pairs of eyes focused on me and I felt like the family pet, the Old English sheepdog that's lost its marbles and joined up with the wolf pack to go worrying innocent lambs.

'I don't know how you're going to go dancing tonight after that,' Bedelia said, making some dandelion coffee and handing round a tin of gingerbread men she had baked for the jubilee.

'I'll have a bath and then nip over home for my dancing shirt,' said Otley, looking at me. 'Are you coming?'

'I'll go and have a lie down, I've got headache,' I said. 'Make sure they've not left the oven on and the back door unlocked like they did last time.'

Nice, quiet bed, with a cool, cotton pillow for my throbbing brow and a playful breeze puffing at the open window, lifting its frilly skirt like a peeping Tom.

I was still wide awake an hour later so took a gulp of wine to help me sleep. The peonies on the wall faded and gave way to a thick, wooded hillside. Somebody crashing through the undergrowth. It's him on the white horse dropping his money all over the place, and those fellas with the funny bloomers following him.

'Balearic slingers – halt,' he shouted.

The men surged round him and jostled themselves to a standstill.

'If I've told you once I've told you a thousand times,' he said, 'your catapults are for stoning the Brits – not for shooting stickybuds at me, right?'

'Yessir,' they said.

'Right then, come and get these bloody things out of my hair.'

They milled around and tidied him up to his satisfaction and went on their way singing:

> *We are the Bally slingers,*
> *Watch your bum,*
> *Cos we've got*
> *Some stingers.*

At the Villa Claro
AD 56

Dear Nero,

Salutations O Mighty Apollo! glad your music tour went down well, playing the fiddle standing on your head while drinking a glass of water is very clever, none but a Nero could do it, but you really should not have set fire to the auditorium as an encore.

Looking forward to the circus, but could I ask you not to throw me to the lions until I've got my accounts in order? I don't know if Buddy will be coming, she doesn't want to be parted from her chariot.

Yes, it is a shame about the Governor. I can only apologize, we'll try and get his legs on the right way again when he comes back from Spain. Did you say you sent him to Germany? oh dear!

How are you getting on with the plebs? They can be a bit thick at the best of times; you know that amphora you sent me? well my lot only went and peed in it – I have to go now, Tony's coming for his Osso Buco. Luv to all and Arrivederci Roma!

Carrie Brigantum

PS What you asked me. It was with a dab of lanolin. Know what I mean? Oh! if you don't get Nutty soon I'll gouge his eyes out with a swizzle stick, cut off his conjugals, marinate him in oil and vinegar and barbecue him in the forum. And you know me – I don't like violence.

I felt the blood racing through my veins as I put my bodystocking on. Was I getting hormones again? A black lace top and red satin flounces, a sleek, black wig with a bun at the nape, a thick plastering of theatrical make-up and brass curtain rings in my ears. I'll slay them!

'Stone the crows! You're not going out like that, are you?' said Otley.

I tossed my head. If I'd had some castanets I'd have clicked them in his face. Had he forgotten this morning already? I'm in a stamping mood.

'What do you think you look like, then?' I said.

'How d'you mean?'

'In your brogues and cavalry twill topped with mauve broderie anglaise frills.'

'What's wrong with it?'

'You look like a schizophrenic transvestite.'

Just then Elinor appeared in kingfisher-blue sequins, tight and glistening like a mermaid's tail.

'How are you going to dance in that?' Aunt Bedelia asked.

'It's slit up each side,' she said showing an expanse of thigh.

'Don't go and get yourself raped,' Bedelia cautioned, 'and go in the car – you don't want all the dogs in Claro after you.'

Nigel had a bolero and cummerbund over a white, silk blouse and flared, velvet trousers. His moustache seemed to stand out more than usual. He must have put some Cherry Blossom boot polish on it.

When we made our entrance at the church hall everybody stared. Most of them were wearing their twin sets and pearls, cotton frocks, jeans and tops, Sid and Ethel Parkinson in evening dress from the fifties. They were doing a sort of Nordic cha cha cha with Dutch doll movements, hands and feet turned out at right angles and clockwork jerks of the head. Then they pawed the ground like a circus pony, held their arms above their heads and twirled round like a gyroscope, and finally did a bumps-a-daisy only from the front instead of the back.

'Now let's all do it. Everybody on the floor, please.'

Dom-peromp - stamp - derompompompedom, derom – stamp – perom – stamp went the music as we clattered round the loose floorboards. They all seemed to be watching us and waiting for something spectacular to take place. A young blade in the corner eyed us closely every time we went past. I thought I'd seen him before somewhere.

Now Sid and Ethel demonstrated a samba, doing scissor-cutting steps backwards and forwards, then with hands on hips somehow entwined, and heads looking behind them, they went round in a circle.

'I'm not doing that,' Otley said.

Then a rumba – seductive, swaying, sinuous rhythm. Hips going in the opposite direction to the feet, ending in Ethel standing on one leg like a stork, the other leg wrapped round Sid's waist and he bending over backwards with his head touching the floor.

'Now let's all try it,' he said.

We did all right until we got to the last bit and I got my foot caught in Otley's pocket when he tried to bend down, he fell and flung me over his head knocking my wig skew-whiff.

'Leave that bit out if you can't do it,' Ethel advised.

Last came the paso doble. Stamp – stamp – stamp – stamp – tarraa, rah – 'The other way, Vi' – stamp – stamp – thud – thump – 'Careful with your Doc Martens, Ted' – stamp – stamp – stamp. This was more like it. The march of the Watling Street Guard. *Olé!* Ethel knelt on one knee while Sid stuck his banderillas in her. Next he jumped in the air with his feet together and his knees bent, then he knelt on one knee while she leapt into the air. Now he pretended to be waving his cape at the bull and executed a neat veronica, then she kicked her leg up backwards and touched her heel with her fingers while he looked scornfully on with one hand behind his back palm facing outwards. Finally she knelt again with her head down and he stood on his toes with arms stretched out and up like a condor going for the kill.

By this time nobody was paying any attention, just stamping round any old how. The lights flickered on and off for the last dance.

'Quieten down, ladies and gentlemen, please!' implored Ethel.

'And take your partners for a tango,' Sid announced.

Elinor and Nigel were soon into their stride, two kinds of molten metal poured into the same mould. Any minute now they would be kissing. I felt quite embarrassed and excused myself to go to the cloakroom.

'Don't be long,' said Otley. 'We can catch the chip shop if we hurry.'

Out into the spooky snicket and down a few yards towards the churchyard. It was quicker than pushing through the front door and round to the side again. It was a ramshackle arrangement like most things in Claro. The inside door was chained, bolted and locked and had not been opened since old Mr Stott, the caretaker, had been buried with the key.

Picking my way over the cobbles, slimy and damp with centuries of hiding from the sun, I reached the musty room where I collected my raincoat from the attendant.

'They're going to try and get that other door open,' she told me.

I was just walking back past the big, black marble vault belonging to the Chatwin family when somebody dodged out from behind it and grabbed me from the back. I tried to scream but he put his hand over my mouth.

'I knew it was you lot from up Claro,' he said.

Eighteen

I was bundled into the back of a car with a scarf tied over my eyes. It smelled of petrol and TCP. Who would want to kidnap me? KGB, CIA, PLO, IRA, MI6? I wasn't doing anything, only Latin American dancing an' that. Perhaps it's that bloke who locked the gates in Gibraltar so they couldn't get into Spain. They get upset about anything these days. I daren't wear that nice fur coat that cousin Freda gave me in case I get bombed by the Animal Liberation Front. We use it for a bedside rug in cold weather.

'Get out!'

Where had I heard that voice before?

He pushed me towards the light and through a door then took the scarf off my eyes. I might have known. It was the Rio Grande. Swire Sugden and his three chins were waiting for me.

'I recognized her when her wig fell off,' my abductor said, holding it up with the scarf.

'You were spying when you came up here the other day, weren't you?' said Sugden looking through the contents of my handbag. Tissues, aspirins, notebook and pencil came tumbling out. He gave it another shaking. Sticking plasters, safety-pins, lipstick, comb, bus pass, piece of string, rubber bands, Vick inhaler, dried rose-hips that I picked last autumn and forgot to plant, and a cracked, yellowing snap of Otley and me roller-skating at Margate.

'You left a bottle o' poison last time, didn't you?' he said, holding up the iodine bottle, his grey eyes shining like a puddle in the road.

'That's not poison, that's Aunt Bedelia's dandelion wine.'

'We'll see what the police 'ave to say about it,' he said, putting it in his pocket.

'I've seen 'em putting the notices up and goin' round knocking on doors,' my assailant told him. Of course! It was the red-faced Viking talking to him, the same chap who had been in the pub. He must have been lurking in the church hall, though I couldn't see him properly in that dark corner. Had he been following us all this time?

'Mr Millington-Smythe informs us that you're trying to trace that Chatwin heir,' said Sugden, pouring out a drink and handing it to me. I expect it was drugged.

'No, thanks,' I said, handing it back, 'but I wouldn't say no to a cup of tea.'

'Millie!' he called, knocking back the drink himself.

Mrs Tiggy-winkle put her grey curls round the door to see what he wanted and tittered when she saw me captive again.

'How's your leg?' she asked. 'That Buster's a naughty boy at times, but he likes to watch *All Creatures Great and Small* on a Sunday, doesn't he, Swire?'

'Can we 'ave some tea and bacon-flavoured crisps?' he inquired.

I felt better now and decided to lie my way out of a tricky situation.

'It's nothing to do with me,' I said. 'It's my husband and his cousin who's behind it all. They're stark, raving mad.'

'I can vouch for that,' his henchman said, folding his arms and placing his legs astride like the Colossus of Rhodes. 'You should 'ave seen 'em tonight – all done up like poncin' poll-parrots. Talk about laugh!'

'I've got the idea,' said his boss, giving me the once-over.

I felt that he was beginning to soften towards me.

'Just tell them lunatics o' yours to lay off or I shall 'ave to bring in the heavy mob. I'm not 'aving my business ruined by a lot o' bleedin' idiots who couldn't run a chip shop.'

Chip shop! My chips will be cold by now. I bet Otley has scoffed them all, greedy pig. How can I get away from here? I put my cup down and got up out of my beplushed and bedizened chair.

'Well, I think I'll be going now,' I said, moving towards the door.

'Just a minute,' wobbled the blue chins as he came looming up to me like an ocean liner in a fog.

'Yes?'

'This bottle o' poison's goin' to the police station.' He pushed my handbag at me. 'You can 'ave all the other rubbish.'

'Thanks,' I said. 'I nearly forgot it.'

'And you're not goin' yet.'

He came nearer with his powerful shoulders bulging under his Mafia suit. I could sense his enormous strength. The sort that builds skyscrapers, bridges, motorways and chunnels. The sort that never takes no for an answer. How are we going to keep him away from our tree? If I get out of here alive I shall write to Mr Gorbachev. I'm sure he could use a man like Sugden.

Dear Gorby,
  You know that tunnel you want to dig under Siberia from Murmansk to Vladivostok? Well we've got just the man for the job. He's even standing by with his spade right now.
  He's a good all-rounder and when he's finished the tunnel he'd be pleased to join the Bolshoi ballet as a roustabout.
  Well, tovarishch, I've got to get my boiler suit on as I'm in line for this year's Mother of Industry washing machine. Dossvidanya! Oh Lord of the Kremlin and may your onions never shrivel.
      Maya Cravenova
      Britonski Ancientski
PS Maggie sends her love.

'What you staring at?' the SS man was saying into my face.

'Nothing,' I lied. 'I was just thinking how much like Rambo you looked – masterful like.'

'Aye,' he agreed. 'He showed them Viet Cong a thing or two, I could do with a few like 'im round 'ere.'

The patio door stood open and a flurry of vanilla-scented air blew in from the laburnums. The moon lay in the tree-tops like a squashed Gouda in a dish of broccoli. With tomato sauce I could eat it.

'I think I'll walk down, it's a lovely night,' I said.

'Jed'll run you down when he goes back,' the boss ordered. 'It'll be company for 'im.'

'My husband will murder me,' I said.

He lit a cheroot, opened the drawer of a walnut table, took out some plans and spread them out in front of me.

'Nah look 'ere,' he said. 'When they get that Chunnel going we'll be on the mainline to Glasgow, right from Paris. It's a good place to break the journey.'

'I know – I told him, but he's ignorant, he won't listen,' I said.

'I've got plans for hotels, a leisure centre, holiday chalets, supermarket, a car-park; jobs for everybody, revitalize the whole area.'

'Great, but they don't want that tree cutting down. Stupid, isn't it?'

'We could do with a night-club and a massage parlour an' all,' said the Viking, full of enthusiasm.

'An' that bridge 'as got concrete cancer.'

I followed the direction of Swire Sugden's nicotine-stained finger as it prodded at the blueprint.

'What, the boilerhouse bridge?' I said in disbelief. 'What do you mean?' Computer viruses, concrete cancer, whatever next?

'Chloride corrosion from the salt put on the roads in winter. It's rotting away all the concrete edifices,' he said through his cheroot.

'Well, would you believe it!'

'That bridge won't stand another flash flood, an' yer know what t'Wharfe's like when it rains, don't yer?'

'It fills up fast,' I agreed.

'Yer can be paddlin' one minute and swimmin' the next.'

'It's an ugly thing anyway, and it'll be no loss if it does get swept away,' I said boldly.

'Yes, but not when t'Mayor and Corporation's on it,' he laughed.

'Can't you just build a new bridge then?' I asked, getting up to go.

'No, it's all part of me plans, it's all or nothing,' he said.

'But nobody wants it do they?' I pleaded. 'Nobody except me that is,' I added hastily in case he decided to throw me in the dungeons.

'Yer don't think I'm goin' ter build a new bridge just for you lot in Claro to go and fetch yer dole money do yer?' he said crossly.

'Oh, no!'

'Idle bloody sods – they want to get some work to do. I didn't 'ave all this handed on a plate,' he said as we walked out into the backyard. 'I was dragged up down Monkey Park, went to school wi' me arse hanging out; I've worked for everything I've got.'

'Some people work hard all their lives and still have nothing,' I reminded him, thinking of the fifty pounds I've saved for the gas bill.

'I know but that feckless lot up at Claro had that grand, old house given an' they've let it fall to pieces round 'em.'

'They don't care,' I lied.

'Nah then,' he said finally, 'if yer can talk some sense into 'em there'll be summat in it fer yer, right?'

'Oo, thanks!'

'If not – this bottle o' poison goes to t'police.'

Mrs Tiggy-winkle came tripping out to wave us off and Buster's chains began to rattle inside his kennel.

'Down boy!' she said. 'You got her last time, wait for somebody else.'

I caught a glimpse of JCBs grazing in the adjoining field like a group of hybrid giraffes; and was that a dumper truck with its shell tipped up like a rutting tortoise? I'll tell Mrs Grindlewood-Gryke.

We flew down the moorland road like a bird, disturbing the sleeping ducks at the tarn. Through the quarry and the conifer woods and out into the main road where the yellow lights make you look like something in a Hammer horror. He pulled up at the bridge and got out to show me the concrete cancer. Black cracks and gaps yawned in the pillars. He gave me a sudden grin, purple mouth full of little, ivory bits like when you cut into a pomegranate and he was gone.

'And where d'you think you've been to this time of night?' Otley wanted to know when I got home.

'We were just going to ring the police,' Bedelia said.

'Thought you'd been murdered,' said Elinor, still in her fishtail.

'Time is irrelevant unless you want to catch a bus – ' I began.

'Don't be so flamin' cheeky,' said Otley, 'we've been all over the place looking for you.'

Needless to say they didn't believe my story. They think I'm on the game. Folks are always ready to believe the worst. Particularly husbands.

'Have you eaten my chips?' I asked him, feeling hungry all at once.

'Of course I have,' he said. 'No good keeping 'em for you when we thought you were dead.'

'Here you are, luv,' said Aunt Bedelia giving me a mug of cocoa and some bread and mousetrap cheese. 'Hope you don't have nightmares.'

'I swear it's true,' I told them yet again. 'May God strike me dead if I tell a lie.'

'And if he doesn't, I will,' said Otley.

'Now now, none of that!' said Bedelia.

In the films he'd sweep me into his arms and say, 'Thank God you're safe, darling!' and his uncle in the States would die and leave him a million dollars. Wonder how much Swire Sugden's got?

'He's not such a bad chap, you know,' I yawned. 'I've seen worse.'
'He's got no soul,' Elinor protested.
'All he's got, besides his big mouth, is money,' said Otley.
'We could do with both, couldn't we?' Bedelia said as she bustled us off to bed.

What a good idea! With his money and our soul we could think up a scheme to please everybody. I'll put it to him the next time he kidnaps me. Rebuild the Roman villa and use it for a hydro and health farm.

We went carefully up the rickety stairs, wall bulges out here, and roof dips down there, torn matting and straying hooky rugs. Round a dark corner with an irate husband behind you. Mind you're not found lying at the bottom of the steps with a broken neck like Amy Robsart. I expect Leicester told Queen Elizabeth she'd had one of her hot flushes.

We came to a stop outside my bedroom door and he made a lurching movement. Was he going to strangle me with his tie? No, he was still wearing it. I stumbled into the bedroom and he followed me in.

'You were a right come-on in that get-up,' he said, patting my wig. 'I fancied you all over again.'

'Did you?' I said astonished.

'I saw you lasht night an' . . .' he began to sing a romantic song from our courting days, but was cut off in mid warble as he tripped over my hiking boots and crashed into the wardrobe head first.

'You're drunk,' I said wafting the fumes away.

'Think I'll shleep here tonight, it's been a long time,' he hiccupped.

'I've got headache,' I said, kissing him goodnight. 'See you.'

'I saw – ' he struck up again with a mouth like a railway tunnel.

'Be quiet!' I said flinging a pillow at his gaping maw.

He flung it back, missed me and knocked a motto off the wall.

'"East, west, home's best,"' Otley read. 'Thatsh a bloody lie!'

Aunt Bedelia had the bedroom underneath and I didn't want her knocking on the ceiling with a broom handle so I decided for once to put up with his snoring and deep breathing exercises. I pushed him on to the bed and started to take his shoes off.

'You can sleep here, but be quiet now,' I hushed. He sprang up at once and made for the door as if he'd been propositioned by a dirty old man in a public convenience.

'No fear,' he said as he went out, 'I don't want AIDS.'

What is he talking about? I've been a virgin for the past ten years.

Never mind, I'll go and see Tony. A drink of wine, sit by the window looking at the moon and watch the shadows of the trees dancing on the wallpaper.

> *Red, white and blue,*
> *The Queen's got the flu,*
> *Caesar's in a dustbin,*
> *The dirty kangaroo!*

It's those urchins after the chap with the Beatle hairstyle again. I know the big, fat one at the front. Wait till his father gets home! There's that nice family sitting round the table on the wallchart, they're smiling at each other while mother does the washing up.

'Mummy, why are your hands so nice and soft?' the children will ask.
'Quick march – left, right!' It's the legions coming this way.
'Pick 'em up there, you 'orrible little men!' says the centurion.
They've gone straight through my rose garden and flattened it. I wish they'd learn how to march round corners for a change. Now here's a gang of Brits following them and picking their money up.
'Four sesterces make one denarius; how much is that in the old money?' they're grumbling. 'Is there enough for a pint o' stingo?'

Aquae Sulis
AD 56

Dear Buddy,

Tony and me have come down here again. It's the only place you can get a bit of hokey-pokey, sizzling by day and guzzling by night, talk about dolce vita! when you get your splints off come over for a week.

Has the Governor got back from Spain yet? Do try and get his legs right he's supposed to be in Germany. Did you say your husband's got one of his?

That nice, young centurion I sent over with the olive oil last week. I said he was a primus pilus not 'prime his piles', you should make an effort to learn the language now we're in the common market dearest Buddy.

Pleased to hear you can ride bareback standing on your bad leg. Nero wants you for the circus, he seems to have taken a fancy to you and was asking about the lanolin – say no more! Tony's back now so we're off for some gnocchi.
Your luving pal and fellow monarch,
Carrie Brigantum

PS About that Druid. If there's no room on your mantelpiece, could you not put him on a stick for a scarecrow? He's taking all my money. I try to be out when he comes begging but that stupid Nutty gives it all away. Who's going to look after him when he's old? not the Druids, muggins that's who. Just higher your chariot blades on a level with his neck and drive past when he's not looking? but don't tell anybody I said so.

'Come on, lazybones, it's nearly dinner-time,' Otley scolded when he brought me some tea up.

'I'm not hungry, I've just had some gnocchi,' I mumbled in a daze.

Oh dear! I wish I'd stayed at home to clean the oven after all. It's like having two husbands now I'm under pressure from Sugden as well. What will he do if I fall into his hands again? Where will it all end?

Nineteen

When the Lord made Sunday he meant it for a day of rest, a day of peace and quiet after the turmoil of the working week. He didn't expect us to come rolling out of the pubs drunk, and the Yorkshire pudding to get flung at the ceiling with the gravy running down the walls like the tears of a black madonna.

'Go and have a drink while the dinner's ready,' Aunt Bedelia said.

I was going to go and sit by the river with Dorothy Wordsworth. I haven't found out yet what they got up to in their opium den with Coleridge and de Quincey. Making out they'd gone to see the daffodils.

'Let's all go,' said Elinor, hooking Nigel and Otley with her arms.

Reluctantly I put down my book and followed them down the garden.

'An' don't have all the dogs barking,' warned Bedelia.

Otley was presentable in his cords and silk shirt; Nigel in his best jeans and sneakers padded along like a puma; Elinor, as usual, ravishing in a cream, cotton two-piece, with a raspberry top, mouth to match and sky-blue earrings and chiffon scarf. I trailed on behind, haggard and dishevelled in my army gear, still half asleep and cross at missing my day in the cow parsley.

'Come on!' Otley kept saying impatiently.

He's got no sympathy. I was dragged out of bed half asleep after being kidnapped the night before. All they did was sit watching Polish films on Channel 4 till I came in. He seems to be in a bad mood about something.

It was noisy in The Bluebell. Kylie Minogue dancing round the jukebox and Michael Jackson fighting to get out of his pushchair. We went round the corner out of the way only to find the lads from the nailery there.

'Hey up! Look who's 'ere!'

'Aye aye! Watch yer pockets!'
'Quick march!'
'Oompah oompah!'
'Stick it up yer joompah!'

Laughing, jeering, jostling, joking, shuffling, elbowing, singing, stamping. Oh, my head! I sat with a tomato juice in front of me for some time straining my ears to hear what Nigel was saying.

'I'll deal with you later,' Otley muttered at me.

What does he mean? I'll ignore him. I turned towards Nigel.

'How's the villa going?'

'Great,' he said. 'We're getting down to the real stuff – mosaics, some wall plaster, animal bones and there are signs of a hypocaust.'

'There's a temple, and an altar to the Goddess of the Wharfe. Tony had it made for me and – '

'She's mad!' Otley interrupted. 'What'll you have?'

Everybody was drinking too much and I felt like a Mother Superior at the bottle factory outing. The lads were nudging each other and pointing at me.

'Does yer mother know yer out!'

'Oi oi!'

'How's yer father!'

It was silly to draw attention to myself. If you can't lick 'em, join 'em. May as well go to bed in a drunken stupor after dinner, same as the rest of them. They'll think I'm anti-social if I don't.

'Take it easy,' Otley said, getting alarmed. 'Don't start asking for green chartreuse.'

'I must say,' said Elinor, sipping a gin and tonic, 'you seem to be getting some good vibes. You're right on the wavelength.'

'I could write a book but nobody would believe it,' I said.

'She went off her trolley in Margate after drinking that stuff,' Otley went on, 'singing, dancing, roller-skating – turning cartwheels on top of the cliffs. I just managed to catch her as she was going over the edge.'

'It makes me feel good,' I explained.

'Well, we don't want you feeling that good again,' he said.

'Come on,' said Nigel, 'I'll buy you one.'

'Oo, thanks!'

The potent blend of aromatic herbs and brandy slid down my throat like a liquid flame. Hot sun, bright flowers and green fields got into my blood. The stuff of life. Suddenly I wanted to sing and dance.

'Roll out the barrel,' I sang as I leapt into the middle of the floor. 'Altogether now!' I shouted as the lads got up to join in.

'Sit down, May,' said Otley.

'Trossachs!' I said, showing him a clean pair of heels.

Round and round the tables. What a lark! The jukebox ran itself out but we had a good, old knees-up. The stained-glass knights and their ladies looked down their noses at us rollicking serfs. Who cares if I've got boots on? Clomp, clomp, stamp, stamp, kick, ouch! clomp, clomp.

'May,' Otley began as he groped his way towards me.

'Leave 'er alone, she's enjoying 'erself,' the lads told him.

'All join up for a conga,' I called over the racket, and soon we had a long snake winding its way in and out of the tables and finally through the door. If the Common Market snake's like this I don't mind.

'May – come back here!' I could hear Otley's voice growing fainter.

'Never on a Sunday, la la la, tara ra, ti dumpty dumpty dummm,' we chanted as we conga'd our way round Claro. Doors opened and shut and curtains were lifted and dropped. Children and dogs joined in.

How blue the sky is! How fresh and green the grass! How musical the river and how charming the trees whispering sweet nothings as we pass! Legs rose and fell as we made our undulatory way like a giant centipede.

'Hey up!' shouted the lads.

'Erewiggo, erewiggo, erewiggo!'

'We won't go over the bridge, it's got cancer,' I said, pointing to the gungy concrete. Gales of laughter at the very idea. We turned back through the village again and up to Claro. Children and dogs were snatched by anxious owners. By the time we got to the pub stomachs were beginning to rumble.

'I could eat old Hagen's hoss wi' two pennorth o' chips,' said Bob as we went our merry ways.

It was a long pull up the hill, and I felt more like doing a roly-poly down it. As I passed the bottom of Crag Woods a figure emerged from the undergrowth. It was Tumbleweed. Poor soul! He wasn't going to sit in a bog to eat his Sunday dinner, was he?

'Hi there!' I called out.

'Oh, it's you!' he said. 'I wondered what all the racket was down there.'

'Have you had your dinner?'

'I've got my sandwiches,' he said, holding up a soggy parcel.

'Throw them away and come back with me.'

'I'll save them for later,' he said, stuffing them into a soggy pocket as he squelched up the road alongside me.

I stopped to pick a rose as we made our way down the garden. I'll give it to Otley, he will be pleased. Tumbleweed hesitated and turned as if to go back and I put my arm round his shoulders.

'Aunt Bedelia won't mind,' I assured him.

What a delicious aroma coming from the kitchen – roast beef and Yorkshire pudding. I don't eat meat myself but can appreciate the smell of a Sunday dinner. At Christmas I give Otley my turkey and he gives me his Brussels sprouts. I pushed open the door and bounded in.

'Only a rose – ' I began as I held out my offering to my husband and I was just about to start on the second line when a Yorkshire pudding with onion gravy flew past my head and stuck with a plop on the ceiling. I could have eaten that.

'Don't start bringing your fancy man here with you,' Otley said.

'I knew I shouldn't have come,' said Tumbleweed.

'He's not my fancy man – it's Tumbleweed,' I explained, leading him to a chair at the table.

'You admit you've got a fancy man, then?'

'No, I haven't.'

'Well, who's that you were having nookey with last night?'

'It was only a dream,' I told him. 'I was eating some gnocchi with this Italian – I didn't say nookey.'

'I've no objection to dream lovers,' Otley laughed.

'I'm sorry about that,' I apologized to the household as we ate our dinner in silence. Roast potatoes, carrots and greens mixed with dandelion leaves went with the meat; then bread and butter pudding – Prince Charles's favourite recipe cut out of a magazine. Bedelia was watching *EastEnders* so we cleared away and washed up ourselves. Got the pudding off the ceiling with a fish slice and mopped up the trail of onions running down the wall like sheep streaming down the mountain side. I didn't ask if Tumbleweed had enjoyed his dinner.

'Don't forget we're going to Appleby tomorrow,' Elinor said as we tidied up the kitchen. 'We'll have to be up early.'

'What a coincidence, I'm going up there too,' Tumbleweed told us. 'Might bump into you eh?'

'Come with us,' I invited.

'I think you'd better stay at home,' Otley cautioned.

'No fear, I'm looking forward to it.'

'Have you been before?' Tumbleweed inquired. 'It's a bit wild.'

'No, but I'm dying to see the gypsies.'

'I have met one or two on my travels,' he went on.

'You can show us round then,' I suggested.

'What made you want to go this time, then?'

'We're trying to trace the Chatwin boy,' said Elinor. 'It would solve all our problems if we can find him.'

'Stop 'em selling out to Swire Sugden,' Otley said.

'Best o' luck,' said Tumbleweed.

We arranged to meet him on the early train at Skipton the next day and off he went to his bog.

'If you've got your heads together over this I'll – '

'You'll what?' I said, squaring up to him with the fish slice in my hand like a machete.

'I don't know what I'll do,' he said recognizing the gleam in my eye.

'Don't you love me any more?' I asked, putting the fish slice down and quivering my bottom lip.

'Of course I do, but you get out of control at times, May. Have a bit of decorum as befits the mother of a college student,' Otley said, softening his tone. 'Imagine if Mike picked up the paper and read "Wife lops husband's head off with a fish slice on a Sunday afternoon" and found out it was us.'

'He'd never pass his exams,' I said with a sob.

'Drink this dandelion coffee and go and have a nice herb bath to clear your head,' said Aunt Bedelia. 'You never had any Yorkshire pudding to line your stomach after all that booze.'

All eyes turned to the ceiling and then fixed on Otley.

'I'm sorry,' he said. 'I didn't know it was May's.'

I ran a fragrant bath through muslin bags of mint and lavender and flung my clothes onto a chair eager to get in. I remembered a memorable dip in a mountain stream, astringent and awakening; but this was something else again, a luxurious wallow. If there's one thing better than an icy plunge it's a decadent soak in a scented bath. Peel me a grape!

Aquae Sulis
AD 57

Dear Nero,

Hail again Mighty Caesar! How I bless the day you came here with your hot baths. My proles are a bit wary of them, when they see the steam they think they're going for a mess of pottage. It's those nasty Druids, they'll eat anything.

You know when you've rubbed the olive oil on and licked it all off again? well what's that funny little stick for?

Tony's showing me how to play knuckle-bones, I don't know whose knuckles he's using, he gets them from Boudicca, if we come across the Governor's we'll send them back. Did you say he was in North Africa? if we can't do anything about his legs we'll give him a new head when he gets back. Have to go now, Tony's waiting in the steamer. Tarra!

*Your friend and ally,
Carrie Brigantum,
Regina.*

PS What a good idea to have funeral games! You want cheering up don't you? I'm sure the gladiators will enjoy a spot of tiddlywinks with Uncle Nero before they die – but mind you don't end up on the funeral pyre yourself going leap-frogging over the mourners like that. You're lucky it was only your toga got singed.

'Left, right, left, right.' It's the legions again making straight for my garden with their big feet.

'Watch where you're going you clumsy clots!' I shouted throwing a cabbage at them.

'Oh, thanks!' said the centurion. 'We'll have this for our dinner.'

'Neverra minda,' said Tony. 'We go and 'ava some fagioli – justa like mamma uzzda to make.'

We were just sitting down to our dinner when the chief Druid came in sight with his begging bowl and Tony got under the bed.

'Not today, thank you,' I told him for the umptieth time.

'It's for the starving multitudes,' he whined through his matted beard, holding out the crock of gold in his blood-stained fingers.

'You've got all my money and I've had no dinner meself for three days,' I said. 'Now be off, or I'll set the Romans on ye.'

'Them pusillanimous popinjays, they couldn't find their way to skinning a cat on their own,' he sneered. 'There's got to be eighty of 'em and another to tell 'em what to do.'

'They know how to have a bath,' I said looking at his grubby hands.

'Any sacrifices today?' he wheedled, looking around for any likely victims.

'Clear off, you dirty old man!' I shouted, throwing a stone at him.

'Wait till I tell your husband!' he shouted back.

''Eeza not here aza well izzy?' Tony inquired peeping out from under the bed.

'No, you can come out now, luv, and finish your fagioli,' I said.

Suddenly I was aware that my decadent bath had gone cold and the church bells were clanging the faithful to evensong. There are so many tunes they could play. Why do they just go ding-dong? The first time I heard 'Oranges and Lemons' was when we stayed with Cousin Alice in London. We went to a fancy-dress ball, Alice and Ted as Jack and Jill, Otley as Captain Bligh and myself as Dick Whittington. Coming home at dawn, exploring Dickens's alleyways and squares, I somehow got separated from the others and went rushing round frantically trying to find them. Pudding Lane, that's where the Great Fire started. In a ghost town, silent and deserted as the *Marie Celeste*, I gave myself a history lesson.

> *Up and down the City Road,*
> *In and out the Eagle,*
> *That's the way the money goes,*
> *Pop goes the weasel.*

I went, until I sank exhausted on some steps opposite a church. 'Oranges and Lemons' the bells began to ring as the worshippers arrived in their hats and gloves and Liberty scarves. Who did they think they were staring at? They'd get a thick earole in a minute. Of course, it's not every day they find Dick Whittington sitting on the steps outside. I'd forgotten. But I sat there and listened to the bells. Perhaps they would play 'Turn Again Whittington' if I waited long enough.

'Are you all right?' inquired an anxious Christian with a bag of peppermint creams.

'Yes, thanks,' I said, taking one, 'I'm waiting for my husband.'

'Is this him?' she asked pointing to a sober gentleman in a bowler hat and pin-stripes coming towards us.

'No,' I said. 'My husband's Captain Bligh, he's wearing a cocked hat and the bottom half of his pyjamas . . .' She fled before I could finish.

'Are you coming out of there?' Otley called. 'Other people want a bath, you know.'

I wrapped myself in a beach robe and spread my wet towels out on the winter hedge to dry. I opened the conservatory door to slip out to my bedroom the back way and noticed a pair of eyes peering at me from behind the rubber plant in the far corner, distorted by the old glass.

'Who's there?' I called from the bottom of the steps.

'It's only me,' said Otley, 'I was worried, I thought you'd fallen asleep and drowned yourself, been knocking but you never answered.'

'I'm fine, had a nice, long soak.'

'Thank goodness!' he said. 'Thought we might have to put Appleby off.'

Twenty

The next morning I borrowed some jeans and sandals from Elinor and wore one of Otley's tropical shirts with bananas and palm trees all over it. He bought it in the Swinging Sixties and had never worn it.

'Why don't you stay at home and help Aunt Bedelia with the dandelions?' he suggested.

'I want to go,' I said, putting on my cardigan.

'If you show me up I shall just go off and leave you,' he warned.

'All right,' I said.

We packed some cheese rolls and sardine sandwiches, spring onions and tomatoes, buttered scones and apples and pots of yoghurt. 'Don't forget your Thermos and plastic spoons,' said Bedelia.

'And we want some tissues,' Elinor added.

'Come on!' Otley said irritably. 'And stop fussing.'

A quick look in the mirror. A puff of powder, a dab of lipstick and a squirt of ozone-friendly aerosol to keep my hair subdued. I'm trying hard to look as if I've got decorum.

Otley wore his army-surplus gear and Elinor some natty breeks and a frilly blouse like Diana used to wear when she was Shy Di. We arrived at the station in time but where was Tumbleweed?

'Just made it,' this strange young man said as he flopped down beside us. Without the camouflage of pondweed and sphagnum moss he was unrecognizable.

Black curls and a peep of gold earring, moleskins and a velvet jacket, red kerchief knotted over a gleaming white shirt. You would think he was a gypsy until you looked closer at his blue eyes and the dusting of freckles over his apple-blossom cheeks.

The train pulled out of Skipton and soon we were in the Yorkshire Dales. Little grey towns and villages grazed among the hills like flocks of sheep. That's Pen-y-ghent, that's Ingleborough and this is Whernside coming up on the left, but first the viaduct at Ribblehead. I'll close my eyes till we've crawled over here. It's all done up in steel pins and scaffolding to hold it up, and I once saw a computer thing in a museum showing how it shudders when the trains go over. Now it's the Blea Moor tunnel. Oh dear! Shut my eyes again. Other viaducts and other tunnels. It's as bad as the Big Dipper at Blackpool.

'You're missing the views,' Otley scolded as people ran from one side of the carriage to the other in order to catch everything.

'I can see them from here,' I explained. 'It's when I look down I don't like it.'

Wild Boar Fell, the River Rawthey and the velvet-topped Howgills in the distance. Now we're in the Vale of Eden and the line runs west of the river until it crosses the loop at Great Ormside and into Appleby by its eastern banks.

'Right,' said Otley as soon as we got off the train, 'let's go and find this bloke.'

'Let's look round first,' I protested. 'There's plenty of time.'

Through the 'new' town of Victorian terraces that came with the railway and over the river into the old town. That's if you can get over the bridge. Crowds coming and going and jammed on the bridge itself. Leaning over the parapet to watch the young bloods in the river sprucing up their horses for the fair. Bare chested and wet trousered, the job done, they swank before their audience then gallop off to Fair Hill. The crowd begins to melt away and a bubbling froth is tossed along the river, dancing and swirling and disappearing from sight round the bend. I hope that's ozone-friendly washing-up liquid they're using.

Gig racing, horse racing, buying and selling of Fell ponies, Dales ponies, piebalds and skewbalds and painted gypsy ponies, mongrels and workhorses of all shapes and sizes. The clip-clop and slapping of hands echoes round the hills and valleys with the shouting, singing, laughing and quarrelling and slamming of car doors.

'Well, I don't know where to start in this lot,' Elinor said.

'There's always a gypsy king and queen somewhere,' I said, 'if we can find them.'

'This isn't fairyland, you know,' chided Otley. 'It's just a field full o' vagabonds trying to scratch a living.'

'Excuse me,' I said to an elderly gentleman coming towards us, 'can you direct us to the Gypsy Queen's caravan?'

'I know nothing about them hedgerow heathens,' he snapped as he went on his way, 'an' if you take my advice you'll watch your pockets.'

Otley was looking the other way as if he didn't know me when I tried again with a pleasant, motherly woman with a shopping basket full of goodies. She wore a cotton frock with little daisies and forget-me-knots sprinkled all over, and a fluffy, pink, angora cardigan. I expect she was on her way with a box of liquorice allsorts and a pineapple upside-down cake for her grandchildren.

'Excuse me,' I asked, 'do you by any chance know where the Gypsy Queen lives?'

'No, I don't and I don't want to,' she said crossly, 'I'll be glad when they've gone. They pee all over your garden though the Council provides toilets for them.'

'You're making a right fool of yourself, aren't you?' Otley said.

'Well, you go and find her then,' I told him. 'I'm going to have a look round.'

'I'm hungry – let's have something to eat,' he said, delving into the sandwiches.

We jostled our way through the multitudes until we found a patch of grass to sit down on. It was a warm, sunny day and my feet were starting to ache. A paddle would be nice later on. Didn't Tumbleweed say he'd been to the fair before? And was it Appleby? It was a long time ago and he was very small, he said, he could barely recall it. I wonder if that's where he met the gypsies.

'I had a book from the library,' Elinor said. 'About all the gypsy tribes – the Lees, the Smiths, the Boswells. If we ask for them by name they'll think we know them from somewhere.'

'Like when you write to the Inland Revenue,' said Otley. 'If you know their names they're not quite as nasty.'

'Can we have a paddle and go on the swings as well?' I asked.

'No swings here,' Elinor said. 'It's not that sort of fair.'

'We've got work to do first, playtime afterwards,' said Otley, jumping to his feet.

'We'll take the caravans nearest the town if you and Tumbleweed look for the strays further afield,' Elinor suggested as she sorted us out into mixed doubles.

'Hope Gypsy Rose Lee's out there somewhere,' Otley grinned at me. How am I expected to keep my decorum? I turned to my partner, Tumbleweed.

'This scene, does it jog your memory at all?' I asked.

'Vaguely, but it was all so long ago,' he said.

'Be at the station at quarter to seven. It's the last train,' Otley said as we went our separate ways.

'Can't we stay out all night?' I pleaded. 'Such a lovely day.'

'No, we can't, we've only got a cheap day return, haven't we?' he said.

Trust him to do that when we've got such a magnificent choice. Round Robins, Early Birds, North-West Rovers, North-East Rovers – you could have a week's holiday and never get off. He's got no imagination.

We put our litter back into our rucksacks as all the bins were full to overflowing, and Elinor and Otley set off in the direction of Fair Hill where all the caravans were resting. Some were traditional gypsy vardos but more were luxurious modern homes pulled by Range Rovers and Mercedes. Not all have to go round selling clothes-pegs for a crust of bread.

'Good luck, then,' I called after them.

'Mindowyergo,' Otley called back.

'I'm all right,' I shouted.

'Sure he doesn't mind?' inquired Tumbleweed.

'Just because you're married doesn't mean you've got to be Siamese twins,' I said loftily. 'We like to keep our individuality.'

'I agree, I agree,' he said, 'but not everybody thinks that way.'

We wandered round the old town of Appleby, taking in the Moot Hall, the Almshouses and castle with its birds and wildlife. Then, when I was feeling fit to drop, Tumbleweed said he'd show me Flakebridge Wood, which lay beneath a range of foothills under the Pennine Edge.

'Oo, that'll be nice,' I lied, I didn't want him to think I was a sissy.

We turned north-east out of Appleby and stopped on an old Roman road.

'This is the Roman road between Carlisle and Catterick,' he said.

I thought I felt funny. Who's that going tramp, tramp, tramp? It's them with their big feet again. Better get out of the way.

'Pick 'em up, you 'orrible little men!' the centurion's shouting.

'Permission to speak, sir?' requested a bold one limping up.

'Well?'

'We've all got gangrene from marching through that rose garden.'

'You've got two alternatives,' the officer bellowed at them, 'either you stay up here and get gangrene – or you go down south and have your legs sliced off.'

'We'll have gangrene, sir,' they said in unison.

'Right then, forward march! Left, right, left, right.'

They all went limping past with their scutums sagging in disarray, and all the dogs and urchins in the neighbourhood chasing after them.

> *Julius Caesar is no good,*
> *Chop him up for firewood,*
> *When he's dead, boil his head,*
> *Make him into gingerbread.*

'Gerrardavit – yer'll be old yerselves one day!' one of the veterans wheezed throwing a stick at them. 'Little buggers.'

At the Imperial Palace, Roma
AD 57

Dear Buddy,

Nero sends his luv and wants to put you in for the chariot racing next time. You'd slay them you would!

We had an orgy last night and I've got a bit of a headache today, I'm going to have a lie down in a minute.

We went steaming first to work up an appetite. There was this girl in a bath of asses milk, yuk! and it had all turned to cheese, so they put her on the table with a dish of figs for afters. They all lie on their bellies to eat, it saves them falling down.

Nero's gone native. He thinks he's Apollo and goes ravishing all over the place, all the girls are after him, his wife's not very pleased. They're not speaking now but he's very good to her, she has her favourite mushroom omelettes at every meal.

He's arranging a Greek tour presenting himself as the world's only singing, dancing, somersaulting potentate. This boy is talented. He's asked me to go along as wardrobe mistress, I said I'd think about it but I can't stand the heat. Longing for a breath of fresh air round the old philibeg, know what I mean?

Got to go now and have a lie down before the next orgy. Luv and kisses to all. Oh! Nero says will you send some more lanolin.

Your old friend,
Carrie Brigantum.

PS Will call and see you on the way back if you've got no battles lined up. I've knitted you a battleaxe warmer so you don't get frostbite when you go massacring in the winter time.

'Where am I?' I was lying in the middle of a green lane clutching a bunch of dandelions, my fingers gummy with the pungent milk oozing out of the squashed stems.

'I thought you were dead,' said Tumbleweed. 'You dropped like a felled ox.'

'I'm all right, just felt dizzy, that's all,' I said as I got to my feet and collected my belongings.

'Do you want to go back?' he asked anxiously.

'Pushing and shoving among that lot, no fear,' I said as we struck out for the woods.

A myriad becks tumbled down from the hills into the valleys and dales below, cutting a gorge here or following the old meltwater channels there. Time for a wash and a paddle and another sandwich.

'That's the old bobbin mill down there.' Tumbleweed pointed along the edge of the wood. 'Made of birchwood they were – this wood's mostly oak and birch giving way to conifers as we come out, with a view of the foothills.'

I listened carefully as I want to learn all the green I can in case Maggie comes our way. People are dead ignorant. If you ask them what taraxacum officinale is they think it's a new mini-cab service.

'You can see the line of the Pennine Fault running in a south-easterly direction,' he went on. 'Well, that's High Cup Nick, Murton Pike and Roman Fell.'

Roman Fell, he said, and on a geological fault. No wonder I got dizzy! The countryside had put on its summer dress, so many shades of green and everything fresh and clean. Wasn't it a paradise?

'That's what you think,' said Tumbleweed.

'How d'you mean?'

'Those Cumbrian fells to the west,' he pointed.

'Oo, aren't they lovely?'

'No good to man or beast since Chernobyl. They're still radioactive,' he explained. 'Still can't eat their mutton.'

'I've stopped eating meat myself,' I told him.

'They poison the apples as well,' he said. 'Didn't you know?'

'Everything's poisoned,' I agreed.

'That's why there's all this football hooliganism.'

'Before the war it was only Argentina that had football hooligans,' I said, 'poor people like that who had nothing to eat.'

We came out of Flakebridge Wood, down the road and into Dufton Gill Wood, following the beck that flowed over chocolate-brown sandstone.

'That's the Pennine Way,' said Tumbleweed, pointing up into the hills. 'Are you fit?'

'My feet are killing me; I'll be making my way back,' I said, sitting down suddenly. That's the trouble with men – they're either all or nothing. Men! I'd forgotten I had a husband. He'll be waiting at the station and we can't make it now. It's half-past six already. Oh dear! He'll be very cross. I remember when Mike was a baby and I went home with my shopping and left him at the check-out in Sainsbury's. I never heard the last of it.

It was early evening when we wandered round to Fair Hill to see what was going on. What a racket! Shouting, arguing, laughing, stereos and ghetto-blasters, horses, dogs and children. I bought some lucky white heather and a silver horseshoe from a little girl in jeans and a grubby tee shirt. She looked at Tumbleweed and then ran off.

'Come on,' he said. It was as if he wanted to see but not be seen.

The sky darkened and the moon came out, going from full into its last quarter, and bright as a chunk of Wensleydale cheese. Somewhere a camp fire was lit and we were drawn towards it instinctively. We stood back in the shadows hypnotized by the flames and a family group circled round them. The shape of a vardo loomed in the twilight and the whinny of a horse came from the trees.

'Mammy, Mammy, it's the Romany Rei!'

We were grabbed suddenly and hustled into the dancing light.

'What you doin' round 'ere, mush?' a wild-looking man in a torn shirt and ragged jeans wanted to know.

'We thought you were going to sing,' I lied, 'when we saw you sitting round the fire.'

'They's dukkered,' an old crone cackled.

'You come stealin' our mokes and we'll roast yer on the fire like an otchiwitchi,' the wild man threatened.

'We don't want your horses,' said Tumbleweed. 'It brought back memories – the fire an' all. I lived with you travellin' folk when I was a young 'un.'

'Then yer should know the old tongue.'

'If I've not forgotten.'

'Who's the rawni?' the old crone asked.

'She's my friend.'

'Country hantle? or one o' they didicoi besoms more like.'

'She's from Low Riding.'

'Kushti, kushti,' she muttered as she lit a clay pipe from the fire.

'Ask him the password,' a young woman said, with coral and amber beads jangling round her neck and hair like the plaited mane of a black, Arab stallion, 'the riddle-me-ree one only a Romany knows.'

'Rosie,' the wild man called and the little girl I bought the heather from came out of the caravan, 'riddle me the Gorgios.'

'What am I?' she asked looking at Tumbleweed, and then began to recite in a sing-song voice, 'with a stick in me hand and a stone in me throat, I walk through the land in me shiny, red coat.'

'You're a cherry, of course,' said Tumbleweed.

They all seemed to be pleased except the child, who was banished to bed disappointed, and we sat until the sky blackened, talking and sharing their hedgerow broth. It was a magic night until the spell was broken.

'Throw the slop-bucket on the fire,' said the old girl. 'It's bedtime.'

Suddenly there was an air of menace. The goodwill died with the fire and black shapes loomed up out of the dark. I began to feel drowsy and wondered about the hedgerow broth. Had they poisoned us? I stumbled away from the caravans and sat down by the hedge to wait for Tumbleweed. But where was he?

Twenty-One

I opened my eyes to the sun riding high over Fair Hill. A rough horse-blanket rubbed against my chin and a lacy canopy of cow parsley shaded my eyes from the bright light. I sat up and looked around. The vardo was gone. Had last night been a dream? No, there was Tumbleweed asleep under an old army greatcoat, a ladybird ambling about on his twitching nose. Good gracious! Have I been asleep under a hedge with a strange man not my husband? I don't know what Aunt Bedelia will say.

'Wakey wakey!' I called in a panic.

'I'm a cherry, I'm a cherry,' he declared in his half-sleep.

'Wake up, they're all going!'

I pulled the coat off him and flung it onto the hawthorn bushes where it rested upside down, spilling the contents of the torn pockets.

'Wait a minute,' said Tumbleweed, 'I recognize that coat. It's old Jackdaw's – a thousand years old if it's a day.'

'Is that a note pinned to it?' I asked him, pointing to a grubby bit of brown paper.

'"Old Jackdaw lies under the sod,"' he read out. '"He left this for the little Romany Rei I reckon you be he so take it bor an plant no gorja curses on his grave."'

'I'm not touching it, it stinks,' I said, looking at the mouldering debris in the hedge bottom.

Tumbleweed poked about with a stick and then picked up a small bundle wrapped in a piece of black plastic bin-liner.

'The saints preserve us!' he said as he struggled to open it. 'It's like trying to break into the Kremlin strongbox.'

'Or a packet of ginger biscuits,' I added.

We tried tooth and nail and finally impaled it on a thorn tree, tugging at it until the branch flew off and hurtled us into a ditch.

'It's only a handkerchief,' Tumbleweed said, holding it up.

It was made of fine lawn and had an embroidered monogram in one corner. It looked like 'CSM' with some kind of tiny flowers round it. Then there was a tobacco tin with a little boy's treasures – marbles, a long-dead spider, gaudy stamps from Helvetia and Madagascar and a piece of blue glass with a letter to Santa Claus wrapped round it: 'Dear Santa, Will you bring mi dadi back for crismas and a cowboi set.'

The signature looked like Spiggy Meu but it could have been Spiggy Lee. Tumbleweed put them in his pocket and we picked our rucksacks up to make our way to the station.

'The thieving old devil,' he said. 'He told me he'd posted that letter and sent my Christmas card home.'

'It is you, isn't it?'

'Who?'

'Lord Chatwin of Spignel Meu.'

'Good grief! Do I have to wear one of them velvet caps with knobs on?'

'And we've got Swire Sugden where we want him now,' I said. 'Wait till he finds out.'

'Not so fast,' he cautioned.

'How d'you mean?'

'We've got to prove it first, haven't we?' he continued. 'They're not going to take my word for it.'

Baldrics! There's always something and if you have to go to law they'll take you for every penny you've got. People have spent years trying to clear their names after some trifling misdemeanour or insult and ended up having to sell the roof over their heads. And when you've done you can't stop folks thinking what they want to think.

'Well, I've got no money, have you?' I asked him.

'No,' he said, 'and if I had I wouldn't spend it on that.'

We caught the half-past one train and settled down to enjoy the run. High, bleak moors and rushing becks. Lush, green valleys and wooded dells. Then round, rolling drumlins circling wide water-meadows and we were home.

'Did you say you sent a Christmas card?' I called as Tumbleweed rushed off to his bog watch.

'Yes,' he said, slowing down somewhat.

'Well, it wasn't there, was it?'

'I didn't see it.'

'It must have been posted then.'

'Yes, but – ' he began.

'Could be with your family papers if we can find them,' I went on. 'Wouldn't that be proof?'

'It's worth a try,' he agreed, 'and if we can appeal to Sugden's better nature we can work out a compromise.'

'He hasn't got a better nature,' I said despondently.

'We'll appeal to his worst then,' he laughed as he went on his way.

Oh dear! That's Aunt Bedelia with her arms akimbo again. Elinor leaning over the crazy gate and Otley with his field glasses. It's a long pull up this hill, I'm not going to run up and drop down dead.

'Where d'you think you've been to?' Otley demanded when I got in.

'I've been to Appleby,' I said, 'to the gypsy horse fair.'

'We know that, stupid, but where have you been all night?'

'At the horse fair.'

'With that fancy man?'

'I've been with Tumbleweed.'

'What doing?' he said, blowing himself up like those funny birds.

'Don't shout, I've got a migraine,' I said. 'You know I don't travel well.'

I fell down thankfully in the squidgy chair and drank some tea while he hovered round waiting to pounce again. Bedelia gave me some aspirins and a cloth soaked in cold water and vinegar for my forehead. I leaned back and closed my eyes.

'And what – ' Otley began.

'Leave her alone a minute,' Bedelia counselled. 'Let her get her breath back first.'

'She's had all night to get her breath back,' he complained.

Now it's suddenly quiet and Bedelia's gone in the kitchen to get the dinner ready. Elinor's looking through the records for another tango to practise with Nigel. They're both pale and passionate these days and she hasn't mentioned Napoleon for a long time. Lights flashing on and off in my head. I promised Swire Sugden we'd call it off. Find the Christmas card. Rehearse the pageant. Make some gingerbread men. Tell Otley. Where's Tony? What's Mike up to? I've got to water the busy Lizzies. Clean the oven with Mr Muscle. Don't leave it on again, you'll set the house on fire! The bridge has fallen in with the Mayor and Corporation on it. Forgot to tell them it had cancer! Help! Murder!

'May, are you all right?' Otley said, lifting the vinegary cloth from my eyes. 'You're screaming the place down.'

'It's that bridge, it's got cancer,' I explained.

'Oh yes!' he said as if he didn't believe me, 'and what were you doing all last night?'

'Tell you about it at dinner-time, it's a long story,' I said.

The late afternoon sun fell on the table as we ate our individual quiches and dandelion salad. A dish of apples stewed with dates, a cold, sago pudding if you were desperate and wanted your ribs sticking together. Plum cake and cheese and a mug of strong, black tea in case you were still falling apart. Elinor fetched a pot of Greek yoghurt out of the fridge as she was weight watching. I'm on the verge of it myself but can't decide whether to get fat and have a merry, unlined face, or be thin with a face like a fossilized Capuchin.

'What's Greek yoghurt made of then?' Bedelia wanted to know.

'I'm not sure,' said Elinor dipping her spoon in.

'It doesn't look any different to me.'

'It is different.'

'In what way?'

Elinor thought for a minute or two and then made her decision.

'It's slimier.'

'So is sago pudding and you never eat that, do you?' Bedelia tutted as she cleared it away.

'I'll push her face in it if she doesn't shut up,' Elinor threatened. 'She gets on my wick.'

They were very pleased when I told them the outcome of my night on the tiles and Otley sat next to me on the sofa with his arm round my shoulders. It was like a second honeymoon. Any time now he's going to ask me to go roller-skating.

'All is forgiven,' he said like Jesus.

'This is a nice record,' Elinor said, blowing the dust off an old seventy-eight. 'Anyone for a tango?'

Otley leapt to his feet eager to practise some passion as the strains of 'La Paloma' came throbbing out of the music box.

'Praaaaam, perampam – dip – pamperampam, peram, perampam – dip.'

Elinor twisted and swayed and twirled, her blue eyes blazing, the wick having been set afire by Aunt Bedelia. Full of hatred and Greek yoghurt she pushed and pulled at Otley sending him this way and that. Dressed in an embroidered, peasant blouse from Oxfam and a frilly skirt, she stabbed at the Turkey carpet with her stiletto heels sending up little whorls of dust and leaving pockmarks in her wake.

Otley's cavalry twill and brogues were doing their best to keep up and he was breaking out in a sweat. His green eyes were taking on a bluish tinge and hers were going green with so much exchanging of deep looks. They stamped round the sofa and did that tricky bit of acrobatics that Sid and Ethel showed us the other night.

'Look out!' I yelled as Elinor's heel just missed my left eye.

I was trying hard to listen to the music and not look at them so I picked the local paper up and opened it. Oh, they've started doing guided walks round the cemetery, and there's going to be an open day at the sewage works. That'll be interesting. They've even installed closed-circuit television and computers so that you can see it coming round corners. Biff, bang, wallop and then heavy breathing from somewhere not too far away. I don't like to stare at them.

'Watch out!' I warned as Otley's knee caught the back of my ear. I'm going to be knocked out for not staring as well.

'I'm used to Nigel now,' Elinor explained to me, 'but it's nice to have a change.'

'That's all right,' I lied.

'You want to learn to tango properly, May,' Otley advised. 'Livens up the old hormones – better than monkey glands it is.'

The record ran itself out and they flopped down gasping and panting like an obscene phone call. Otley on the sofa next to me and Elinor on the floor leaning against him.

'Have you seen Napoleon lately?' I asked conversationally.

'I don't think he's on this wavelength,' she said, 'I had thought of having a holiday in one of the Martello towers if I don't see him soon.'

'Is that where he hangs out, then?'

'Shall we go, May?' Otley inquired.

'No, I don't particularly want to see Napoleon myself,' I said. 'It's not my scene – them cocked hats and support tights leave me cold.'

'It'll be a change,' he persisted.

'I don't want a holiday, I like it here,' I said. 'My place is here with Tony – I mean Mike.'

'Who's Tony?'

'He's my Roman friend.'

'I think it's time you got away – you're stark raving bonkers.'

'We found the silver, didn't we? Just like I said we would.'

'We want May for the villa,' Elinor interrupted. 'She knows all about it. Wait till after the jubilee and then we'll go.'

'All right,' he agreed.

All right, Elinor. Yes, sir, no, sir, three bags full, sir. Oliver North's got nothing on Otley; he's going to salute any minute now. He thinks I'm jealous when I get annoyed at his bad manners. There was the time we were getting off a crowded coach on a day trip to Brighton and he pushed me back into my seat.

'Just a minute,' he said. 'Let the lady go first.'

I was fuming. When he went in the Dolphinarium I got the bus up to Devil's Dyke and had my sandwiches up there.

Then when we went on the train to Italy and all the way through France and Switzerland he chatted up one of the Marias, and when I tipped his minestrone soup over his head on Milan station he said: 'You'll have to excuse my wife, she's just an ignorant peasant.'

'Eet izza no wotta you theenk eet izza,' said the Maria.

Well, I didn't think it was anything but rudeness and I can't stand bad manners so I got the next train back and left him there.

'You know I love you,' he said when he got home after a month in Rimini and San Marino. 'I've been looking everywhere for you.'

Aunt Bedelia had charge of the television so we had to watch all the soaps in Christendom. Talk about Pandora's Box. I've got enough troubles of my own without watching other people's. I felt my eyes closing and picked up the paper to hide behind.

'You look worn out,' said Bedelia as she bustled into the kitchen. 'Have this hot toddy before you go to bed.'

I took the hot, spicy drink and it went down like a stream of molten lava. Soon the world was upside down and the walls caved in to admit the rider on the white horse.

'It's him again,' I cried.

'We'd better get her into bed,' Otley urged, 'before she goes sleepwalking down to the river and falls in.'

'Make a note of everything you see,' Elinor ordered. 'We want ideas for the pageant.'

'Scribble, scribble, scribble,' I mumbled. Like they said to Gibbon when he was writing *The Decline and Fall of the Roman Empire*. I wonder if he was drunk as well.

Who's that crashing through the undergrowth? It's the ginger one in the tartan longjohns and his mate with the coconut matting on his chest. They're looking for the womankind who have all gone off with the Romans.

'Mollickin' in them scented baths all day long. I want my dinner,' said the ginger one.

'Niminy-piminy, pasta-plonkers,' roared the blond giant, 'I'll curdle yer collops till they drop off.'

'Comin' here stealin' our slave labour,' bellowed the other shaking his fist at the sky.

'Show 'em a bar o' soap and they're anybody's,' said his mate.

'Won't even look at 'er new battleaxe,' grumbled Ginger as they went on their way looking for money.

At the Villa Claro
AD 58

Dear Nero,

Salute O Lord of the Dance. What a lyre! I am quite under the spell of your instrument, and how I enjoyed that sideways dancing! but do be careful you don't fall in the sea, Italy is not very wide. I look forward to your state visit to Brigantia. Please bring your own elephants and bed-linen.

Your fan club went wild when you did your Apollo act didn't they? I should give it a miss when you come up north, it's a bit chilly for that sort of thing, though I could knit you a winter fig leaf. Sorry you've had to send a new Governor after all. Haven't you got him back yet? did you say he was last heard of on the Silk Road and he should have been in Caledonia? oh dear! and Boudicca's got his legs ready. She's had to pull the IXth Legion out of a bog again. One of these days they'll just vanish from the face of the earth and never be seen again. Do have a word with them. What a waste it would be, all those roads and nobody to tramp on them!

Well I have to go now or I shall be roped in for the sacrifice and I don't like getting my hands dirty. The sooner you get that old Druid the better. I can show you where he hangs out – on the Isle of Mona – but don't let on I told you.

Luv to Octavia, Poppaea, Acte and not forgetting the goat-boy. Know what I mean?

Your friend and ally,
Carrie Brigantum,
Regina.

PS I forgot. Will you bring your own lions and Christians as well?

'May!' Otley called at the crack of dawn, 'Mrs Grindlewood-Gryke wants us to give her a hand.'

Oh clogs! I thought as I turned over.

Twenty-Two

My heart sank into my boots like Granny's lumpy porridge as we made our way to Grindlewood for a day's dusting and polishing. Mrs Bracken's varicose veins were playing her up and the doctor had told her to rest for a week.

'They've got no consideration,' Mrs Grindlewood-Gryke stormed as she met us with a supply of dusters and aerosols and impregnated cloths.

'Don't mind me asking, your honour,' I bobbed, 'but are they ozone friendly?'

'You'll have to excuse my wife, she's gone green like Maggie,' Otley explained. 'She sees holes everywhere.'

'Of course they're ozone friendly, never use anything else,' she assured me, 'and we've got wood-burning stoves.'

That's all very well if you've got a forest to keep it going like she has, I thought, but what if you live in a towerblock?

'I'll go and get you some wood,' Otley volunteered as he disappeared from view, leaving me with a duster in my hand and a country seat waiting to be polished.

'Come on then!' said Mrs Grindlewood-Gryke, tucking her skirt into her bloomers. 'Charge of the Light Brigade!'

I followed her spindly legs issuing from the bunched-up clothing up and down and along, in and out and under; squirting, rubbing, shining; kneeling, crawling, climbing; gasping, panting, grunting.

'I can do in a day what she does in a week,' she said, shaking her duster out of the window on to the roses below.

'If she's got bad legs – ' I began.

'It's idlitis she's got. Keep your circulation going and you don't get bad legs,' she broke in. 'She gives a quick squirt so I can smell it, then finds a nice, easy chair till she hears me coming.'

'She must be getting past it,' I panted. 'You want somebody younger.'
'They won't do it – they all want to be air hostesses these days.'
'I know,' I agreed as I shone a table she had just aerosolled.
'But she makes nice chocolate cake and she's handy when the cook's on holiday,' she admitted as she examined her face in the shine.

She wasn't lonely here on her own, she told me. There was always too much to do and although she hated it when she came as a young bride, she had grown to love it and would defend it with her life. There were house parties but a place like this needed a master to deal with things, like prowlers and gypsies camping in the woods.

'Gypsies?'

'They turn up every summer after Appleby Horse Fair – place is like a pigsty when they've gone.'

'But where can they go to?' I asked. 'Everybody moves them on.'

'They've claimed squatters' rights anyway. Been there since the house was built, generation after generation – never get rid of them.'

'Councils are supposed to provide sites for them but they don't,' I protested, feeling a sudden sympathy for an oppressed minority. 'If it was dogs driven from pillar to post there'd be an uproar.'

'I suppose you're right,' she conceded. 'But watch out if you go into those woods and don't take any valuables with you.'

'I haven't got any.'

I pretended not to notice her look of astonishment and got on with my shining. All the ancestors flicked over with a bunch of pink feathers on a stick. What fun! Was that my husband I caught a glimpse of through the open casement taking his ease on a sun lounger with a little pile of twigs by his side? That will keep the wood-burning stove going for ten seconds at least.

By the time we had cosseted one floor Mrs Grindlewood-Gryke's legs were criss-crossed by lines resembling a noughts and crosses grid, and my jeans, saturated with a witch's brew of chemicals, were gathering dust and fluff like a thieving magpie.

'Of course, we haven't time to give it more than a catlick,' she came to realize as we staggered up the grand flight of stairs to the first floor. I gave the pompous statuary a flick of the pink feathers as I went past. What a lot of pontificating panjandrums! For two pins I'd send them all crashing to the bottom. If there's anything more ridiculous than a periwigged Pooh-Bah in his frills and furbelows I've yet to see it.

'That's *the* Sir Mauger Grindlewood – East India Company,' she said as we came across another old buffer in stone with a bad smell under his nose. I expect he was like all the rest indoors, couldn't find his way out of a paper bag.

'Abigail, my posset's gone cold, can you warm it up for me?'
'Caroline, I can't undo my weskit buttons.'
'Emma, pull my boots off, there's a good gel.'

And what's all that on the ceiling? The Garden of Eden, The Creation, The Birth of Venus. You name it and they've got it. Big, fat Grindlewoods cavorting in their birthday suits, masquerading as gods and goddesses and Adams and Eves. Didn't they do well?

'This was Miss Delphine's room.'

A light, airy bower this, in spring green and primrose yellow with flower paintings and miniatures of rosy children on the walls. How did Miss Delphine get on with that lot outside? Confined to her room, no doubt, for refusing to marry the old humbug picked out for her. Ran away with the blacksmith who beat her with his bellows if his dinner wasn't ready on time, and now she lies buried underneath the spreading chestnut tree. Perhaps she would have been better off with the old humbug after all.

'Can you stay overnight?' Mrs Grindlewood-Gryke wanted to know. 'We can do a bit more tomorrow, and Mr Sugden's coming to lunch.'

I had planned a day by the river with Dorothy Wordsworth but was curious to find out what Sugden was up to.

'Of course.'

At last I'm coming out! My first venture into high society. Wait a minute, they do things different from us peasants, don't they? Must remember to spoon up my soup away from me and not slurp it all down my chin. Then again, they peel their apples with fancy, little knives instead of savaging them with their gnashers. I don't know what they thought about Nell Gwyn spitting orange pips all over the place. There must have been a veritable orchard flourishing in her wake, which could account for the sudden urge to build an orangery among the nobbery.

'Perhaps you could help Cook to wash up,' she suggested, bringing me down to earth with a bang.

'Yes, Mrs Grindlewood-Gryke, I will,' I said as if it was the one thing in the world I wanted to do.

'Oh, do stop bobbing up and down like a yo-yo,' she said. 'I said you could call me Mollie.'

'All right then – Mollie.'

'Did you say you'd found Chatwin?' she inquired as we caressed a rosewood cabinet. 'Arthur Negus went mad over this.'

'It's Tumbleweed.'

'I should recognize him when I see him – we were playmates.'

'Playmates?'

She had not thought it worth mentioning before as he was not likely to be found. She had gone paddling in the beck with him while his nanny and her Uncle Edgar took off giggling into the woods. Uncle Edgar even dammed a little pool so they could have a dip with their picnics.

'And he's got a birthmark!'

'Whereabouts?'

'I'll give you three guesses.'

'Are you sure?'

'I remember pointing at it one day and he said, "Well you haven't got one at all, yours is broken." It all comes back to me now.'

'There must be some other way of identifying him,' I said. 'We'll have to forget about that.'

'There's the photographs – and a card with no postmark. It was just pushed through the letterbox.'

I followed her to the Georgian wing where the rooms were more human size. A glimpse of rough woodland carpeted with bluebells and wild garlic could be seen beyond a daisy-sprinkled lawn; a wisp of smoke spiralled up from the trees; voices carried on the still air.

'That'll be the gypsies,' Mollie said, nodding her head towards it.

'What a lovely room!' I said, admiring its lightness and open aspect.

'See that ceiling, there's thirty thousand pounds worth of dry rot waiting to be done.'

'Oh dear!'

'It's like painting the Forth Bridge.'

'Bills must be a headache,' I sympathized, 'but worth it in the end.'

'I sometimes wonder – no one to hand it on to. Needs a man about, a son and heir before it's too late.'

'How old are you then?' I asked, forgetting my lowly status.

'I'm thirty-nine so there's still time – but only just.'

'Same as Tumbleweed.'

Suddenly she came alive and her hazel eyes lit up as she took out a large album from a walnut bureau.

'That's right,' she said, 'same as Tumbleweed.'

Starched family groups posed self-consciously in front of parlour palms and porticoes. Mollie was the only child of Thomas Arthur Gryke, manufacturer from Eaglesclough on the way to Huddersfield and don't let anybody forget it! He had the best for himself and he wanted the best for his Mollie. He got her the Hon. Charles Grindlewood, unfortunately.

'Poor Daddy, it was all such a bore,' she said, turning the pages over hurriedly.

'Surely not,' I protested. 'All those house parties, clothes, and a finishing school in Switzerland – '

'I grew up in the Swinging Sixties,' she broke in: 'Beatlemania, flower children, magic mushrooms. Daddy threatened to assassinate Bob Dylan unless I married Grindlewood. I was frantic; he was my hero.'

'They drive you mad,' I said, thinking of the time I was about to murder my husband with the pressure-cooker, 'did he do exercises in bed?'

'He did, and with somebody else most of the time. In the end I stopped sharing his bed altogether. I regret that because there would have been the children after he'd gone.'

After he'd gone! Otley's good at going. He's supposed to be helping. Still guarding his little pile of sticks no doubt, or even jumping over the broom with a Romany. You can't trust anybody, least of all husbands. A waterfall of yellowing snaps fell out onto the floor and Mollie picked one up.

'That's him!' she said, pointing to a dark-haired child with a scowling face about to be struck by a huge hand coming from the top right-hand corner. 'He wanted to go on the dodgems and Nanny wouldn't let him.'

It did look like Tumbleweed. Then there was the card. A shiny view: 'Deer Moly, Yestiday I went on the dojums with Jakdo I lik it heer. Yore frend Spiggy Lee.'

'If I can borrow these to show him – ' I said, picking them up.

'By all means and I'm looking forward to meeting him again.'

Mollie put the album back and we made our way downstairs with our collection of chemicals. Tired and hungry I gave the head Pooh-Bah a rap with the wrong end of the feather duster as I passed.

'What's that?' inquired Mollie, pausing on the stairs.

'I caught it in the banisters as I turned the corner,' I lied.

If only I had a crinoline to sweep down the grand staircase in! I have always longed to be a great lady but it's not easy when you spend your time queuing for slug-pellets and flea-powder. You tend to slink away in corners. And, oh, those fearsome pictures on the containers! I know what a flea and a slug look like, I don't want to be frightened to death every time I pick up the packet. If I want a video nasty I'll buy one. All they need to do is put a 'before' and 'after' circle, one with dots and one with nothing, like they do with lavatory cleaners.

I was almost too tired to eat in the old, flagged kitchen hung with gleaming copper pans and jelly moulds, but the macaroni cheese was as good as Aunt Bedelia's. Here's a crusty roll – mustn't show my ignorance and cut it with a knife, have to tear it to pieces as if it was my worst enemy. That reminds me – where's Otley got to?

'It's very obliging of Mr Craven to help out,' observed Mrs Grindlewood-Gryke over the coffee and slab cake.

'Think nothing of it,' I replied grandly. I don't know where he is, I'll smash his head in when we get home, taking care to use the rolling-pin, then I can tell the judge I was just rolling out the sausage plait when he took me unawares.

We chatted for a while about the trials and tribulations of being a stately home owner, and there are plenty of headaches I will admit, but I get headaches and nothing else – prices going up, wages going up, everybody wanting their ten per cent, she said. No use trying to explain that all some people get is ten per cent of little or nothing.

'Of course, I blame the Common Market,' she went on. 'Not like the Empire when we got everything cheap.'

'It'll be different when we join the snake,' I said.

'Oh frabjous day!' she giggled.

'And you're on to a winner with the poll tax, paying the same as us.'

'You keep saying that,' she chided as we cleared the table, 'I hope we're not going to have another Peasants' Revolt.'

'So do I,' I said, but I'm not bothered one way or the other.

Lovely bed with cool, white sheets and a voluminous gown beribboned like Queen Victoria's drawers. If I cross my hands over my breast I can think I'm dead and in paradise, but it's true what they say, you can get too tired to sleep. Thank goodness I've brought my dandelion wine. I'll go and see Tony now. That looks like Julius Caesar again.

> *Addy, addy, onkey,*
> *Caesar is a donkey,*
> *Mother is a scrubbing brush,*
> *Father is a monkey,*
> *O – U – T spells out.*

They won't leave him alone. One of these days he'll crucify them. Tramp, shuffle, the sound of marching feet – it's the legions. I hope they've learned how to turn corners, they're making straight for me.

'Lingones – wait for it, wait for it – halt!' bawled the centurion.

'Permission to speak, sir.'

'Granted.'

'It's the grub, sir – we're fed up of Yorkshire puddin'.'

'You'll 'ave Yorkshire puddin' an' like it. When in Albion do as Albion does.'

'You can sole yer boots with it,' said one protester.

'Or else it's all squidgy inside like sick,' said another.

'Nah listen 'ere – any more o' this an' you'll all go back to Gaul an' eat bloody frogs' legs – all right?'

'Right you are, sir,' they chorused.

'Right then! Lingones quick – wait for it, you 'orrible lot – march!'

'Left, left, I had a good job an' I left,' they chanted as they went.

Jupiter be praised! They've missed my rose garden and marched into the river.

At the Villa Claro
AD 58

Dear Buddy,

It was luvly to see you again. So sorry about your hubby's mishap though, it must be awkward having no arms and legs at all now, I did shout for you to stop but the wind was blowing the other way. When he stood in the middle of the road waving his arms it was only because he was hungry and wanted his dinner, now you'll have to trundle him about in a wheelbarrow like a dead sheep, you'll have no time for skirmishing. Do be careful.

Nutty raised an army of smelly Brits while I was away (present company excepted) and I fear a civil war. Hopefully the legions will fight it while I get on with my knitting. Nero has ordered ten thousand hides as they get through a lot of shoe leather with all that clomping. Can you help out? he's paying in gold and you can melt it down and make a new battleaxe that will never go rusty. He's rolling in it, he's even going to build a house with it. We could do with some of it over here so try and be a bit more friendly, dear Buddy, just think what it would buy! New houses with bigger holes in the middle to let more smoke out! Next time he sends you greetings do give him the right salute instead of the two-fingered one.

Tony's waiting for his Pot Noodles so I'd better be off. Luv and kisses to all in Iceniland.

Your fellow monarch,
Carrie Brigantum

PS Nutty's got a good pair of legs if they're any use to you, why don't you slice your way over here to see them? don't think he'd miss them as he's legless most of the time anyway. Know what I mean? don't tell him I said so.

Twenty-Three

It wasn't until I woke up at three o'clock that I remembered my husband. Where is he and what is he doing? Not that I care as I love my dandelion friend, Tony, more than I love Otley. But he's not going to get away with it wherever he is.

I dressed and crept along the endless corridors until I found the staircase and slid silently down the banisters under the disapproving eye of Sir Mauger Grindlewood. I'd just like to know what he got up to when he took his wig off, that's all!

All the doors were locked and bolted so I climbed out through the kitchen window and dropped into a bed of lavender. I crushed some of the flowers and rubbed them on my forehead as I'm told it has an invigorating effect on cabbages and thought it might do the same for me. Gardens are enchanting at night but you can only see the one little bit near you. It was irksome being trapped in my body as I wanted to be on the roof, in the rose bower, by the lake, in the woods, on the hills and in the valley simultaneously. It must save you a lot of time being a spirit and seeing everything at once. God doesn't know how lucky he is.

I followed the sound of voices coming from the bluebell wood, there was the acrid smell of wood-smoke and an orange glow lit my way through the wild garlic. Somebody was singing. It sounded like Otley.

'"O play to me gypsy,"' he warbled.

Had he gone mad? He'd never had a good word to say for them before, a bunch o' thieving magpies, he always said, living off the fat of the land while he had to pay taxes to keep 'em. What's he up to now?

If he only knew how stupid he looked! And who's that snuggling up to him? It looks like the beaded beauty Tumbleweed and I met at Appleby. Yes, there's the old woman and the wild man hacking at a haunch of venison. Suddenly a dog flung itself at me snarling and growling and they all stopped what they were doing to look in my direction.

'It's only me,' I said, flinching away from the dog.

'It's her with the Romany Rei,' the girl exclaimed.

'What are you doing here? You're supposed to be in bed,' Otley said.

'You know her?' inquired the wild one.

'This is my wife, May,' Otley replied with a hint of disappointment in his voice.

'Your wife?'

'Yes.'

'You never told us you were married,' complained the object of his serenade.

'You never asked.'

The carcase of a stag lay nearby in the process of being dismembered. It had to be done in the night, they explained, when there was nobody about and we could take some home with us providing we kept our mouths shut.

'I won't tell.'

'What were yer snoopin' about for then?'

'I didn't know where my husband had got to, that's all.'

'He was 'ere making up to an honest travellin' lass.'

'Now look here,' said Otley, 'you asked me to have a bite with you and that venison does smell good.'

'We didn't want yer singin' an' makin' moony eyes an' all that,' said the old girl, spitting into the fire.

'Nah,' the wild man broke in, 'any more o' that an' she'll put the eye on yer.'

'It must be nice living here,' I said, changing the subject, 'but how d'you go on for shopping?'

'Shoppin'?' he guffawed. 'We gets what we want and puts it in the freezer – got no use for shoppin' us.'

It seemed that what they wanted most was facilities. A site with lavatories, launderette and rubbish collection.

'You don't pay rates though,' Otley said.

'If they give us facilities we'll pay for 'em.'

'Fair enough, they'll get you for Poll Tax I expect.'

'Next time we see Mr Scrape we'll tell him,' I promised, with a rush of blood to the head.

'That silly old bugger,' Zylpha, the beauty, said, jangling her coral and amber beads and flashing her eyes at Otley.

'Comes round wavin' his byelaws at us,' her Cousin Jake took up the story. 'He 'ad us up once for "swimmin' without the benefit of suitable drawers" he called it.'

'Festering dungweed,' Grandma observed.

'An' then he prosecutes us for cuttin' animals up in a public place,' Jake went on. 'He says it comes under the Fireworks and Public Entertainments byelaw; an' there wasn't a soul for miles around.'

When we had finished laughing we sat round the embers drinking tea until the first green light of dawn showed in the eastern sky. Otley then decided he had better take the venison back to Claro before the community constable went on his early morning rounds.

'Don't forget we've got to see Cyril Gibbs at the council offices this afternoon,' he called out as I made my way back towards Grindlewood.

'If I can't make it, take Elinor.'

Maybe they'll elope to Gretna Green if they can't find a vacant Martello tower, then it will leave me with more time for my Roman friend and dear Boudicca not to mention Dorothy Wordsworth's *Journals* of which I have perused the first paragraph six times yet cannot seem to recall it to mind.

The kitchen window was still open and I climbed in after crushing another handful of lavender with the intention of taking it to bed with me for an invigorating sleep, if such a thing is possible.

The next morning Mollie and I resumed the polishing and dusting after eating our muesli and boiled eggs. I would rather have been down at the villa making figgy hedgehogs for Tony but a promise is a promise.

'Now if you'll give Cook a hand I'd be very grateful,' Mollie said as we fell exhausted against the banisters at the bottom of the stairs.

Mrs Cartwright was getting on in years, shapeless as a stuffed pillow, hands and arms scarred with the shiny tissue of a myriad burns, and eyes seemingly closed against a lifetime of hissing steam.

'Here you are, love, have a sit down and a cuppa. They think they own you body and soul,' she said, nodding towards where she last saw Mrs Grindlewood-Gryke.

'She seems all right,' I replied, 'environmentally aware an' that.'

'They're all right if they're getting the work out o' you but get sick an' it's another kettle o' fish.'

She grumbled on in this vein as she prepared the food and I ran about as the scullion. It is at times like this that I regret not doing a scientific O-level and becoming a brain surgeon so that no one would ask me to wash up or scrub floors. But then I don't like blood so I wouldn't want to be either a cook or a surgeon. There's not much to choose between them really; they both cut meat up but one eats it and the other pickles it.

'She wants me to make a thousand currant buns, five hundred sausage rolls and fifty chocolate sponge sandwiches, if you please, in time for the jubilee,' Mrs Cartwright exploded as she juggled with dishes and tins and bowls and ladles. 'Then if there's time she wants a "Guess the Weight" cake making as well – I've got to make it look as if it weighs five pounds when it really weighs ten.'

'Makes you want to spit,' I sympathized.

'I'm not trying to work all that out for a start,' she went on. 'I shall do it by the dollop like I always do.'

'How d'you mean?'

'Just putting in what you think, like in the old days. My old gran didn't bother with recipes and if anybody asked her for one she'd say "Oh, I don't bother wi' them things. I cook by t'dollop" – and it were always nice.'

I caught a glimpse of the outside world through a gap in the piled-up tins and dishes. The sun shone and the birds sang. Why aren't I out there enjoying it? I'm fed up, I don't make much dirt so why have I got to spend my life cleaning up other people's? I don't belong here. If it wasn't for Mike I'd be off but I'm afraid he might start snorting coke if I turn my back. It would be in the *News of the World*. What would the neighbours think? 'Teenager On Crack While Mother Gallivants With Dorothy Wordsworth'. I am going to have to write a letter of explanation to the Prime Minister.

Dear Maggie,

I feel I owe you an apology for abandoning your esteemed Victorian values. I cannot think what came over me as I was brought up chapel like you but unfortunately my father was a miner and not a grocer.

I happened to have with me the journal of Dorothy Wordsworth on my trip to the Dales as I had forgotten to return it to the public library, and you have my word that I dropped it the instant I was made aware that they were harbouring a drug addict. There is no connection between it and my son's fall from grace as I'm sure you will understand. It wasn't your fault that Mark got lost in the Sahara was it? You can tell them till you're blue in the face and they still do what they want.

It's the same with men as well isn't it? I know you'll understand when I say my husband's a one for the usquebaugh, I was about to correct him with the pressure-cooker once but I remembered my Victorian values just in time. I am not for one moment suggesting that you could do such a thing yourself because I think you would do it with more style and use a magnum of champagne.

I hope you will not think too harshly of me. My son will be out in six months and Mrs Gillick will be taking us under her wing in the absence of your good self.

Your obedient servant,
May Craven,
Ancient Briton.

PS I am so grateful for the £48 a week you let me have. It is riches beyond my wildest dreams and well worth fighting the Second World War for. I hear that the Ancient Teutons get twice that but it can't be true because they lost. Give my luv to Ronnie and Gorby.

'Do you like rhubarb?' asked Mrs Cartwright, depositing a number of baking tins in the sink.

'Oo, yes.'

'Good job you do,' she went on, 'because I cook it once a week to give the tins a good clean out.'

Swire Sugden had arrived and was taking an aperitif with Mrs Grindlewood-Gryke in the drawing-room. I hate all this la-di-da stuff but I wanted to hear what he said so I volunteered to serve their lunch and planned to loiter in the dining-room on the slightest pretext.

'Give 'em this carrot soup first,' instructed Mrs Cartwright.

A lot of nonsense followed about etiquette and right sides and wrong sides. Mustn't speak unless I'm spoken to. Who does she think she is? The Queen or somebody? Swire Sugden seemed very impressed with Mollie but then he hadn't seen her with her skirt tucked in her bloomers showing her skinny legs.

I hovered over the sideboard pretending to be looking for cutlery and strained my ears to catch the conversation.

'It's a very tempting offer,' Mrs Grindlewood-Gryke was saying as she expertly took up her soup without slurping it.

'All you have to do is drop your opposition to my development plans and I'll take you in as a partner,' Sugden urged as he mopped the orange-coloured dribbles off his chin.

'I could certainly use the extra money,' she continued. 'There's so much dry rot in this place . . .'

'Put your own house in order first, that's what I say.'

'But we don't want to see the meadow go.'

'What's more important, this magnificent building or a bit of grass?'

'It's not just a patch of grass, it's a principle at stake, thin end of the wedge.'

'You can't eat principles.'

'Unfortunately not.'

'And principles won't cure dry rot.'

While they were thinking this one out I served them with a summer casserole which Swire Sugden demolished and Mrs Grindlewood-Gryke toyed with absentmindedly. I made for the sideboard again to hover.

'I shall need to think about it, of course,' replied the honourable lady, 'Things are too far advanced – the jubilee celebration. To change direction now would let all those people down.'

'They're still living in the Stone Age.'

'This urban blight is spreading like the plague. There'll soon be no green left.'

'They block any kind of progress.'

'Some things are worth more than money.'

Neither was listening to the other talk and I thought it would be a good moment to fetch the rhubarb tart.

'Haven't they finished yet?' Mrs Cartwright demanded irritably.

'They're talking.'

'They've got no consideration for anybody else. They don't think I want a sit down. That's how Mrs Bracken got her bad leg, standing about while they chit-chat.'

'It's business.'

'What business?'

'He's trying to get her into partnership with him to go ahead with his holiday village.'

'They can do what they like for me – blow the place up for all I care

– I'll be off to my mobile home in Lytham St Annes before long.'

'Have you got relations there?'

'No, I want to be near my Premium Bonds. Ernie lives there.'

As I was hovering near the sideboard again, straightening the china, there was a sudden commotion outside and the gardener burst in with Mrs Cartwright hot on his heels.

'I couldn't stop him, madam . . .'

'Don't call me that, Elsie, I'm not a brothel-keeper.'

'He's on about the gypsies.'

'Watch where you put your muddy boots, Ramsons,' Mollie scolded.

'They've had one of the stags again. I found the umbles chucked away in the bushes. Stinks like a nest o' polecats down there,' he said.

'I'll deal with that riff-raff,' Swire Sugden bellowed, abandoning his rhubarb tart in favour of a punch-up. The gardener, Mrs Grindlewood-Gryke and I pursued him down the garden and into the bluebell wood.

'Well! That's all the thanks you get for slaving over a hot stove,' Mrs Cartwright shouted after us.

We found the gypsies about their business: Zylpha washing clothes in the beck, old Katie mending a torn jacket, Jake dismantling two old bicycles and trying to make one good one out of the spare parts, and Rosie, the little riddle-me-ree girl, splashing naked in the water. Oh dear! Bathing without the benefit of suitable drawers again!

'Come on, where is it?' Sugden demanded.

'Where's what?' asked Jake.

'The stag, that's what.'

'What stag?'

'You know what stag.'

I felt a migraine coming on as the old girl began to wail and Zylpha screamed a torrent of abuse. It was something of a pantomime, any minute now they would be saying: 'Oh no, I didn't!' and 'Oh yes, you did!' I was afraid it might come out that we'd got a cut as well.

'It was dead,' I blurted out. 'I found it on the barbed wire. It had got its neck entangled struggling to free itself.'

'Yeah,' said Jake.

'It belonged to me all the same,' Mrs Grindlewood-Gryke pointed out with the authority of a monarch claiming a sturgeon.

'I'll have you run in, you varmints,' Sugden threatened. 'It's time you scum were cleared out. Get back to Egypt where you came from!'

'We come from Rotherham.'

'Well, bloody well get back to Rotherham then!'

By this time I was thoroughly disgusted with these fat cats taking food from the mouths of the sansculottes. 'Let them eat cake!' the ghost of Marie Antoinette was calling. And whatever happened to *noblesse oblige*? In the old days they would be feeding the poor at the castle gate. Poor little Rosie stood dripping wet and shivering. My blood boiled.

'I told you, it's my fault and you can run me in if you like,' I said, turning to go, 'now if you'll excuse me, I've got a bus to catch.'

Twenty-Four

When the bus arrived it had 'Yorkshire Coastliner' emblazoned in foot-high letters on the sides with blue and white wavy lines depicting the sea. It disgorged a crowd of bewildered passengers carrying buckets and spades and shrimping nets who pushed their way back on again.

'This isn't Bridlington,' a harassed mum with a screaming child complained. 'Shut up, Diana, or I'll give you a backhander.'

'You didn't say you wanted to go to Bridlington,' said the driver.

'It says Yorkshire Coastliner on it, doesn't it?'

'That doesn't mean it's going there.'

'Well, where does it go to?'

'We turn round at Grindlewood Park and go back to the depot.'

'We've paid for our tickets.'

'What about getting a refund?'

A forest of hands clutching a variety of tickets waved about his head like the tentacles of a sea anemone and he began patiently to explain where they had gone wrong. Metro Saverstrip – only for journeys in West Yorkshire; Metro DayRover – you can get as far as Manchester with this if you're elderly or disabled and are permitted to take a dog or other authorized companion. Remember to rub the right date off with a copper coin of the realm or you can't go anywhere. Schoolcard holders can go on the bus if accompanied by no more than four adults – if they want to go by train they must have an Adult DayRover; a Family DayRover is for two adults and three child permit holders or one adult and four child permit holders with dog.

'We haven't got a dog,' someone protested.

'And where can we go with this?' inquired an anxious young couple.

'That's the Dalestour, Sundays only into North Yorkshire,' the driver said as he passed hurriedly on to the next customer.

'I thought this was for North Yorkshire,' complained an old lady. 'I'm going to see my sister in Kettlewell.'

'That's North Yorkshire, luv. It's a Dales Explorer, go as you please and get on and off when you want any day you like,' he assured her.

'Thank goodness for that!' she exclaimed settling into her seat.

'Only you're on the wrong bus,' he continued, 'you want the 800 Dalesbus – you'll have to pick it up at Ilkley.'

By the time he had sorted everybody out and told them how to get to Bridlington it was too late for me to use my free pass and I had to pay half fare. Still good value so I paid without protesting.

'It's these idiots,' he confided. 'They get on a bus and they don't know where they're going to.'

I closed my eyes for the rest of the journey as it had been a busy two days and I didn't feel like going to the council offices either. It would be too late anyway so I decided to take a stroll by the river and see how Nigel was getting on with the excavations.

Everything was cool and green and peaceful and the plashing of the water soothing after the noise and petrol fumes of the bus ride. Nigel was on his knees brushing the soil away from what looked like a green glass bottle.

'Have you found my ring yet?' I inquired. 'Cartimandua's ring, it's in the rose garden – I told you.'

'Oh, that ring! No personal objects yet, just keys, nails, basic pottery, a bit of Samian ware and some tesserae.'

'How much time have you got left for digging?'

'Very little. The money's just about run out. If we don't find something soon that's it!'

'It was a lovely villa and masses of white roses growing wild. That's why the Romans called this country Albion.'

He gave a wry grin and went on with his brushing.

'Tony told me,' I added.

'There can't be a villa here,' Nigel explained. 'It's more likely to be part of the marching camp, latrines or a workshop.'

I helped the girls to wash some of the sherds and then wandered down to my favourite spot by the river. Fishing into my green Marks & Spencer carrier bag I found some biscuits and an apple, some old sandwiches, which I threw into the water for the fish – and oh yes, there was still some dandelion wine left. I could do with forty winks right now and

Otley would never miss me. He would assume that I had been detained scrubbing the floors of the kitchens at Grindlewood Park. He seems to think that's all I'm good for, though I've told him I'm the Queen.

'Tramp, tramp, tramp the boys are marching.'

They're here again with their big feet. I like them, they've brought us central heating an' that, but we don't want all these roads cutting into the green belt; and you can't sneak up on anybody now when they can hear you coming a mile off. Oh, it's the elite this time, the IXth Legion lot in their natty mini-skirts and jangling horse brasses. They look a bit soggy from all the bogs they've fallen into.

'Ninth Legion into testudo formation – wait for it – march!'

'Not bloody tortoises again, *mamma mia!*' came a voice from the back.

'Can't we do lions or something for a change?'

'Or elephants?'

'Or crocodiles?'

'Tortoises is soul destroying.'

'You know why we 'ave to do tortoises,' the centurion bawled. 'It's so that if somebody drops a bloody great boulder on yer nut it'll bounce off again.'

'Well, you said we could go on a picnic today.'

'I didn't know you were goin' to go and walk into another bloody bog last night and get all the sandwiches wet, did I?'

'No, sir.'

'We've rescued them, sir.'

'We don't want squidgy sandwiches, do we now?'

'No, sir.'

'Right then, get fell in and form another bloody tortoise!'

They went squelching on their way dropping their money and I was able to get enough for some new feathers for Tony's hat to replace those he lost when Nutty put his head in the scruncher.

At the Villa Claro
AD 59

Dear Nero,

O mighty Caesar! I am distraught to learn of the demise of your mother and shut my ears to the ugly rumour that you had her put to death so that you could take up ballet-dancing.

Never mind what they say, luv, if you want to dress up as a woman that's your business. I expect you get fed up of wearing that boring old toga with the purple stripe round it.

Thank you for the silk, glad you were able to wrest it from the Governor before he set off to Lepcis Magna with it. We look forward to his arrival in Britannia again and Boudicca is saving some good legs for him; in fact they belong to a soldier of the IXth Legion who didn't hear her shout 'Get outta the way you stupid git' when she was trying her chariot out on the new road. It's not because he's Italian, she's not a racist, she slices our legs off as well if we're not careful. Her husband has just got a head and a torso now but their devotion is very touching, she takes him everywhere in her saddle-bag.

By all means do your British tour in the winter if you wish. I can incorporate a fig-leaf into your chunky-knit bodystocking but don't forget the cooling lotion as it'll be a bit itchy.

*Your devoted friend,
Carrie Brigantum*

PS I don't think you should marry that young man in the back row of the chorus, it's too soon after going to bed with your horse dressed up as a Praetorian Guard. People might not understand, you know how peculiar they can be.

Here's Tony coming for his gustatio, how handsome he is in his reconstructed hat. He appears dazed and is going round in circles.

'Have you been poisoned?' I inquire.

'I 'ave notta gotta the 'ang ovva da cocarel.'

He is quite determined to master the art of the coracle, though as Comptroller of the Queen's Household he need not concern himself with such trivialities.

'Never mind, luv, come and get your marinated mushrooms.'

We were just sitting down when Nutty burst in with his smelly Brits and they stuck their fingers in the cooking pot.

'What d'you call this poncin' pap then?' he raged, 'I can't eat this muck.'

'It's not for you,' I replied frostily. 'I thought you were at Malham.'

'Izza for me,' Tony explained.

'Then bloody well have it!' Nutty bellowed pushing Tony head first into the cauldron. I fled up to the tree-house for my knitting but a branch gave way as I grabbed it and I was pitched into the river. It was not long before Tony joined me in an attempt to free himself of the sizzling mushrooms.

'Ha ha!' Nutty laughed, 'that'll teach yer to come sneakin' round 'ere, ye mincin' mouldywarp.'

'Go and have a bath, you putrid polecat,' I screamed.

'I don't know what's got into you, Carrie,' he said, shaking his fist in the air.

'Buzz off!'

Poor dear Tony stood there with mushrooms in his ears examining his hat for damage. It's just not good enough, it's every time he gets some new feathers and as an officer of the Roman Imperial Army he must not be without feathers.

'Never mind, luv, we can kill another chicken tomorrow.'

'I no wanta chicken, I wanta peacock.'

'We haven't got any peacocks.'

'You izza queen, you find 'im.'

I floated on my back looking up at the puffs of white cloud dotted about the blue sky. I was beginning to get fed up with men and their tantrums but I do need a strong arm about, I'm no good with a battleaxe like Boudicca. Not that Tony is either but he's handy at sticking daggers in your back and that's better than nothing.

'May, what are you doing in there?' Otley's voice came from the trees on the river bank and suddenly he was in the water hauling me out.

He and Elinor had been to the council offices and I had still not come home when they got back. Aunt Bedelia was worried sick.

'I came to see what the Romans were doing,' I explained.

'You're mad,' he said. 'How is it I can't see them when I drink that wine, then?'

'It's like Elinor says, you're not on the right wavelength.'

'You might have drowned swimming when you're drunk,' he scolded.

'I'm not drunk and anyway you don't care.'

'Of course I care, there'd be nobody to sew my buttons on if you were dead.'

We gathered my scattered things together and made our way up to Claro leaving dribbles of wet in our wake. The Watling Street Guard were practising in the field and Otley looked on enviously. He would have liked to join them as he was tired of being a lurking Briton but his sense of loyalty would not allow him to defect to the other side.

'Aye aye, does yer mother know yer out?'

'Can anybody come?'

'Hey up, how's yer father?'

'Don't do anything I wouldn't do!'

Off they went raspberrying, guffawing and swearing in between snatches of song, just like the IXth Legion but drier.

'Any luck at the council offices?' I asked when they'd gone.

'Tell you about it after dinner,' Otley said with a smug smile.

Aunt Bedelia waited anxiously by the garden gate half hidden in the riot of dog roses and bindweed. The evening sun glowed from the west as brassy as a dinner-gong, throwing long purple shadows across the untidy lawn and into the bushes.

'We were worried stiff,' she chided as she bustled us into the kitchen. 'Had to go and leave my dandelions to look for you, now they've all gone to sleep.'

'Don't cry, I was coming back again – ' I began to explain.

'Well, I wasn't to know that, was I?'

A quick bath and a change into one of Elinor's cotton caftans, a blue ribbon to tie up my hair and a dab of powder on my freckles rendered me presentable enough to be fed. Pandora's Box was switched on and all the world's ills rushed out at us as we ate our cheese and dandelion flan and chips.

'Where's Elinor?' I asked as I spooned a gob of whipped cream over my gooseberry pie.

It seemed she was up at the Jubilee Tower practising the tango with Nigel and they would be down shortly with the papers.

'The papers?'

'We did a Watergate,' Otley explained, 'only in our case it was a Boilermakers Union Housegate, the old union headquarters. Cyril Gibbs says the council dumped a lot of stuff there that they hadn't room for in the new building.'

'What have they got in there?' Bedelia inquired. 'Don't know what it's like inside but it's as black as the ace of spades outside.'

'Old drawers and boxes full of dusty papers going back years, anything Jeremiah Scrape wanted to keep hold of, and he's got the key.'

'What's he keep all that stuff for?'

'In case it comes in handy, you know, like you save bits of string and wrapping paper.'

They had got in through a cellar window at the back and made their way up to a small office on the third landing where, according to Cyril, the sole employee had been there man and boy until he became fossilized and had to be removed feet first from his station. He had been dead a week before they realized he wasn't breathing.

We were just watching *4 What It's Worth* about all those people who go on holiday to the sunny Mediterranean, having booked a sea view, and come back with gastroenteritis from living over the dustbins and now want their money back, when Elinor came running up the garden path closely followed by Nigel.

'We've got them, we've got them!' she called excitedly as she burst into the room waving a large manila envelope.

'Shh!' Otley said, 'I want to see whether they get their money back.'

'Hello there!' Nigel greeted Otley. 'How's the Ancient Britons going, done any lurking lately?'

'To be honest no, lurking's boring and if it's all the same to you, Nigel old boy, lurking's out.'

'You're not dropping out altogether, are you? Give it a go.'

'We're going to march like you.'

'You can't. It would be historically inaccurate.'

'I don't give a toss, I'm not sitting in them wet bushes all day.'

'I know,' said Nigel, 'if you don't want to lurk you can amass.'

'We're not amassing either, we're marching.'

While Otley and Nigel squared up to each other Elinor emptied the contents of the envelope onto the table: family snaps, letters, postcards belonging to the Chatwins, the coat of arms well in evidence and having the same circlet of tiny flowers as the monogram on Tumbleweed's handkerchief.

'That's spignel meu, a little mountain flower something like cow parsley,' Elinor pointed out. 'It's an interesting story.'

During the Wars of the Roses Roger Chatwin fled to the hills with the infant son of Lord Clifford of Skipton Castle to save the child from certain death at the hands of the Yorkists. They lived with the shepherds and survived chiefly on mutton cooked with wild herbs, spignel meu they found to be a good substitute for rosemary and the child loved to eat the aniseed-flavoured seedheads. On the accession of Henry Tudor, the Shepherd Lord, as the young Clifford was known, was given back his lands and his faithful retainer knighted at his request; 'I am but a simple man, Your Majesty, and I know not how I should be styled,' the good servant protested. At which Lord Clifford whispered into the King's ear and both gave a hearty laugh. 'I dub thee Sir Roger Chatwin of Spignel Meu,' the King declared.

'Ah, isn't that lovely,' said Aunt Bedelia.

'I'm not milling about, I'm not lurking and I'm not amassing,' Otley said vehemently as Nigel pleaded with him yet again.

'All right, then have it your own way,' Nigel said resignedly, 'but we shall need to have different music.'

'I told you, "Viva España" for the Romans and "Any Old Iron" for the Brits.'

'There's something else in here,' Elinor said, dipping into the envelope and extracting a Christmas card.

'That's it, the trump card!' I said excitedly. 'We're winning!'

Twenty-Five

The next day we followed my ball of string into the woods to show Tumbleweed our treasure. It was so beautiful it broke your heart thinking what would happen to it if the developers got their way. Foxgloves and campion in their pink frills, stitchwort with its little white stars and golden marsh marigold hiding in damp hollows, a dappled canopy in cool shades of green letting in dabs of blue sky, the fresh smell of damp earth warmed by the sun.

'It'll be like Spaghetti Junction if that Sugden gets a foot in.' Otley muttered. He blew his nose and gave his behind a scratch as we picked our way through the lush undergrowth. I've gone off him since I met Tony but we do share a love of mother earth and I want to see this thing through. After that I'm making no more promises.

We found Tumbleweed guarding the bog asphodel and writing up his records surrounded by various specimens of damp foliage.

'We've got the papers and things!' I said waving the envelope, 'and your Christmas card's here as well.'

'How did you get hold of them?' he asked in disbelief.

'We did a Watergate.'

'You mean I did,' Otley corrected me.

He identified the photographs and was anxious to see the ones at Grindlewood Park. Yes, that was the card he had given to old Jackdaw to post but he really didn't want all this aggravation, he was happy the way he was.

'You owe it to the community.'

'Be a concrete jungle in no time.'

'They don't care about bog asphodels.'

'They'll have this wood chopped down for *Beano*s as soon as you can say market forces.'

'You're right,' he replied, clenching his fists. 'I'm a peaceable man but I'll murder 'em if they come up here with their bulldozers.'

'That's what we said, isn't it, Otley?'

'Have you seen Jeremiah Scrape yet?' Tumbleweed inquired, eager to get things moving now that he had made up his mind.

He would be at the next meeting in the church hall along with Swire Sugden, and were they in for a surprise! The irate villagers would have the paperwork to back them up this time. The trust for sale terms drawn up gave the trustees the right to manage the land and an obligation to sell it if it no longer produced a satisfactory income, with the proceeds of the sale going to the beneficiary, the consent of the beneficiary being necessary before the sale could take place. It was all in legal gobbledegook and took a bit of working out but Lord Chatwin had added some words of his own at the end: 'If my beloved Spiggy is found everything goes to him and his heirs.' You don't need a lawyer to explain that.

'Don't forget to be at the meeting tomorrow then,' we prompted as we trod carefully on the clumps of dry grass as if they were stepping-stones.

Otley put his arm round my shoulders as we made our way to Claro and began to whisper sweet nothings.

'You're not a bad old gel, you know.'

I tried not to cringe when he chewed my left ear making a noise like a pig in a trough. I hope I never go deaf and have to wear a hearing-aid; it will sound like the Atlantic rollers crashing up over the rocks at Land's End.

'How d'you feel about a second honeymoon?'

Now he's got his arm round where my waist used to be. It is embarrassing when you've got a spare tyre that keeps protruding between the bottom of your bra and the top of your roll-ons as if you were a snakecharmer with your pet python coiled round your midriff.

'We can go roller-skating again and Olde Tyme Dancing.'

At this I cowered away from him. Roller-skating yes, Olde Tyme Dancing no. Foul-mouthed peasant! I didn't know where to put my face when he told Cecil Ackroyd to eff off that night in the Temperance Hall.

'Here's a nice little dell. Let's have a sit down,' Otley suggested taking off his camouflage jacket and spreading it out on the grass.

'There's something I want to see on television,' I lied.

'What's that?'

'Er, um – ' I began.

'That's just an excuse. I don't know what I married you for, you've always been frigid – even when Uncle Joe sent that powdered rhino horn from Saudi Arabia.'

He snatched his jacket and put it on again.

'He got it mixed up with Aunt Isabella's ashes, that's why I wouldn't take it. I dug it into the roses instead.'

'You don't care a damn about anybody but yourself.'

'I do, I love you. I just don't want you to touch me, that's all!' I screamed at him as I ran off through the woods.

'I don't know what's got into you, May,' he shouted, shaking his fist in the air as he set off in pursuit.

'Buzz off!' I hollered, I shall leave him as soon as we've got this business sorted out. I'm not going back to Low Riding, I don't care how filthy the oven is.

We avoided each other all evening until it was time for the Open University programmes. Then Aunt Bedelia made some cocoa and managed to draw us into conversation. It was a programme about evaluations and the learned gentleman posed the question: 'Would you rather live for five years with two legs or twenty-five years with one leg?' It was something we had not thought about hitherto; it just shows how ignorant we are.

'How many legs would you like, Otley?' Aunt Bedelia inquired.

'I'd like to live a hundred years with the ones I've got now,' he said.

'What about you, May?'

'I'd like to live twenty-five years with ten legs or two hundred and fifty years with one leg.'

'I'd settle for a few years with four legs like a cheetah and be able to go at forty miles an hour,' Otley declared.

'And wouldn't it be fun having three legs and being able to go round in a circle like the Isle of Man flag?'

'It's interesting, isn't it?' said Aunt Bedelia, 'I wouldn't mind doing a degree in legs myself because mine are giving me gyp these days.'

It is feared in some quarters that television destroys family life but with us it's the opposite way round. We held hands all the way through *Live Aid*, having not spoken to each other for a week, and then rushed off to the Post Office as soon as we could with our three pounds. Once, I was waiting at the bus stop one Sunday with my bags packed ready to go to Sheffield when Otley came running up: 'Don't you want to see *Fragile Earth*? They're chopping down the rain forests.'

'Bastards,' I said, hurrying back home. It is without television that our family life would be destroyed.

We all squeezed into the church hall the following afternoon for a final showdown with Swire Sugden, the lads from the nail factory in a belligerent mood as they had just downed tools in protest against their foreman using bad language.

'Who the bloody 'ell does he think he is, bleedin' 'Itler?'

Mrs Grindlewood-Gryke and Elinor took their places on the platform with Jeremiah Scrape and Swire Sugden, who appeared to be in a hurry and frequently consulted his watch.

Apologies for absence, minutes of the previous meeting, agenda, jokes and folksy parables bored one and all for the first half-hour.

'Get on with it!'

'I've got a bus to catch!'

'We don't want to be 'ere all night!'

Swire Sugden spoke first, natty in his Mafia-type suit and blue chins vibrating with barely suppressed anger. He wanted to bring us into the twenty-first century. Claro had been a backwater for long enough. Conservation was all right but when did it lapse into deterioration? One day we would all be washed away when the bridge fell in.

'That bridge has got concrete cancer,' he warned, 'and if something isn't done soon there's going to be a disaster.'

There was much hilarity at this and requests to mend the bridge.

'No, it's part of the package. All or nothing,' he replied. 'The bridge is the council's responsibility. I'll repair it as a favour if my plans go through.'

'We don't want a holiday camp here.'

'It'll be Scandinavian chalets, very high class, with saunas and smorgasbord in the buffet.'

'Oh, la-di-da!'

'Me and my Susie go walkies down there,' said Mrs Cawthorne, prodding her guide dog with her white stick. 'She's not bothered about saunas.'

'It's a right of way!' came a chorus of protest.

'You'll have access,' Sugden explained.

'In fact,' Jeremiah Scrape broke in, 'there's no such right of way in the definitive map.'

'Then put it on.'

'You all know,' Jeremiah went on, 'that under the terms of the trust that we are required to manage the land and sell when it's no longer profitable. We have come to that stage now and the council has reached the conclusion that Mr Sugden's proposition is the best on offer and we have no hesitation in recommending it to you.' He buried his nose in a large air-force blue handkerchief and searched among his papers. Swire Sugden looked at his watch and glanced out of the window as if he was expecting something.

'How do we know you're telling the truth?'

'It should be here,' said Jeremiah, 'it's been locked safely away these thirty years or more.'

We sat holding our breath in the front row. We knew what he was looking for and it wasn't there. It was Elinor's turn now. She rose to her feet with her eyes blazing and walked to the centre of the stage.

'Is this what you want?' she asked, waving the envelope under his nose.

'Give me it back,' he said crossly as his face drained of colour. 'You've no right to it, thieving hounds.'

'Friends,' she continued turning her back on him, 'by a miracle the settlement has fallen into our hands and I can tell you that the late Lord Chatwin left everything to his son and heir.'

'Where is he though?'

'Fellow countrypersons, let me present to you Lord Chatwin of Spignel Meu, guardian of our heritage – Tumbleweed.'

Tumbleweed stood up and self-consciously acknowledged the cheers, sitting down again quickly. He would clearly rather have been bogwatching. Swire Sugden leaned over to whisper in Jeremiah's ear and then banged on the table for order.

'This is all most irregular and we shall be consulting our legal advisers,' Jeremiah Scrape announced.

'You've not heard the last of this,' Swire Sugden threatened as he stormed out of the church hall.

'Ladies and gentlemen, this will be our last meeting before the big day and I want to thank you all for your co-operation,' Mrs Grindlewood-

Gryke shouted above the noise. 'We still need volunteers. Some of you are still without your costumes so if you could all go down to the municipal tip and see if you can flush out any dustbin lids it would be a great help.'

'What do you think they're going to do?' Elinor inquired, nodding in the direction of the disappearing enemy.

'Just keep a tight hold on those documents,' Otley advised her. 'Possession is nine points of the law.'

I could envisage a long-drawn-out court case with us all ending up homeless and bankrupt, sleeping in cardboard boxes and begging for crumbs from the rich man's Scandinavian table, and I don't like raw herrings, yuk!

'I put it to you,' some old goat would bleat from under his wig, 'that these scheming, unprincipled charlatans, stopping at nothing to come by their ill-gotten gains, forged the very hand of a peer of the realm in a dastardly conspiracy to frustrate the worthy efforts of their local benefactor.'

'Don't call me a charlatan, you miserable old creep,' Otley would explode.

'Take him down!' the old fossil would splutter in a cloud of dust.

Come to think of it, I could go to Bowness-on-Windermere till he was released. It might not be so bad after all.

Tumbleweed had vanished leaving a bundle of pondweed under his chair but everybody else seemed reluctant to go and we stood about in groups while Aunt Bedelia and the ladies of the WI handed round cups of tea.

'Would you believe it!'

'They'll be finding Lord Lucan next!'

'They say he's in Australia disguised as a kangaroo.'

Suddenly the church bells started ringing 'Oranges and Lemons'! They were playing our tune, but wait a minute, they've never played that in Claro before. What could it mean?

'Quick, it must be the warning,' Otley shouted. 'Everybody out.'

We all rushed outside to find the bulldozers and an electric saw making for our oak tree. Swire Sugden sat smirking in his black Mercedes with two of his heavy mob standing by.

'Surround the tree and link arms,' Otley ordered. 'Elinor, you go home with the papers. We don't want anything to happen to them.'

We got to the tree before the bulldozers but the electric saw was perilously close.

'Go on, saw us in half then,' I said recklessly as the young man came nearer. He was a pleasant chap with blond curls and a Mickey Mouse tee shirt on. Just shows you can't go by appearances. I should have kept my mouth shut because he manoeuvred his machine until it was touching my midriff. Thank goodness for my spare tyre, I can afford to lose a bit of that. I shut my eyes.

'Does yer mother know yer out?' shouted one of the lads and then all at once they charged at him and manhandled him to the ground.

I felt at the torn threads in my blouse and looked at the grazed skin underneath and shuddered, but I was all right and so was the tree.

'You stupid nit,' Otley scolded. 'This isn't *The Paul Daniels Magic Show* where they get up and walk away.'

The bulldozers had turned round now and were heading for the bridge. It looked as if we had won this initial bout but men like Swire Sugden don't give up that easily. He drove up to us and wound the window down.

'Just you wait,' he said, 'I'll get you buggers.' He was a handsome chap in a sinister sort of way, Al Caponish with a dash of Dracula and a smidgen of Rambo thrown in, but he spoils himself being so nasty.

When they were well out of the way we made tracks for home and I looked foward to a quiet evening. A bite to eat, some relaxing television, an hour with Dorothy Wordsworth and so to bed.

'Coming down the pub for a little aperitif?' Otley inquired.

'I've got my dandelion wine.' I reminded him and he went out banging the door behind him. Oh well, I can go and see Tony now. I left Bedelia watching the box and climbed wearily up the rickety stairs. I took a swig of wine and collapsed on to the bed fully dressed.

> *The Roman army's a greedy lot,*
> *Stuck their fingers in the old jam pot,*
> *I tiddly-i-ty*
> *Pom pom.*

It's only the ragamuffins chasing Caesar down the Fosse Way. I don't know where Tony's got to. He said he was coming for some gnocchi tonight. Might as well write my letters.

At the Villa Claro
AD *60*

Dear Buddy,

No, the Romans are not blind, they'll see you coming if you go charging down to Colchester, go round the back and sneak up on them. Them funny statues they make with no eyes in and titchy little things are so we won't know what they're really like. Know what I mean?

My people have just finished their knitting and a thousand dishcloths are on their way to you. Do use them for mopping up the blood on the new road. That dalmatica that Tony sent is for you to wear, it's not a pudding cloth for making spotted dick in.

Nutty's gone up north for more smelly Brits but I'm not leaving my lovely villa and my roses so it's civil war. He's abducted me six times and Nero had to send the lads to rescue me.

Fancy the governor turning up after all this time! Did you say he was on his way to Mesopotamia? Give him a new head if you can't find any legs to fit. He sounds a bit miffed, you'll have to put him in your other saddle-bag to keep your husband company that's all. Men! they're never satisfied!

Nero sends his luv, you know he's coming over here to give us a turn this winter. He says will you show him how to make a snowman?

All my luv,
Carrie Brigantum

They've gone now and it's nice and peaceful just lying here doing nothing. How I wish all this was over and I could get back to my humdrum routine. But a promise is a promise and we have to pursue this thing to the bitter end. Otley, I know, will never give up. He's forgotten what it is to sit and hold hands among the buttercups. A miracle is called for, but miracles do happen and we just need to find the villa, that's all.

Twenty-Six

'It's time we had a talk,' Otley said the next morning.
  'What about?' I asked as I stirred up the tea-bags.
  'I'm not giving you a divorce so you needn't think I am.'
  'I don't want a divorce.'
  'Well, what do you want then?'
  'I just want to be able to do what I like.'
  'As if you were a person?'
  'Yes.'
  'What d'you mean, do what you like?'
We've had this conversation so many times. I mean like royalty do, pretend to be married but do their own thing on the quiet. Take Henry I, for example, the king who never smiled again, our teacher told us, after he had lost his only son and heir, in the White Ship: then they found he had twenty-four little baskets scattered all round the country. All I want to do is read Dorothy Wordsworth's *Journals* instead of cleaning the oven, then pop over to see Tony now and again.
  'We can still be friends,' I explained, 'and I'll co-operate on all ecological projects of this nature.'
  'Oh, thank you very much!'
  'The planet comes first and we really must subordinate our own basic urges to the greater good of all mankind.'
  'What's that supposed to mean?'
  '*That* burns up too much of our energy. It won't make any difference, I still care for you as a very dear friend and human being.'
  'You mean like Heloise cared for Abelard when he had his balls cut off? Blow that for a lark!'
  He always has to go and lower the tone of a conversation. It was his idea in the first place to try celibacy when the Hare Krishna lot came

round ten years ago with their gongs. Now I've got used to it he's changed his mind.

I helped Aunt Bedelia to clear the breakfast things away and get her dandelions ready. I had lost my heart to the little, golden flowers that brightened the meadows like a thousand suns. Unwelcomed, unwanted, despised and dug out, they had added a new dimension to my life, given me another self and I wanted never to go from Claro.

Suddenly there was a commotion outside as Nigel and Elinor hurtled up the garden path and through the front door.

'They've been in the night and dug it up!' Elinor panted.

'Who has?'

'Them, the bulldozers. They've gone over the excavations and into the meadow – '

'We've not been down there yet,' said Nigel, 'but we can see from the tower.'

We tore after them down the hill, nimble-footed Elinor and Nigel in their jogging suits, Otley in his army camouflage, myself in old faded jeans and Aunt Bedelia puffing behind in a blue and white apron and still holding the tea-towel.

'I don't believe it!' Nigel exclaimed. 'Look what they've unearthed!'

'I told you, it's my villa!'

'Don't start that nonsense again or they'll carry you off to the funny farm,' Otley said wearily.

'Look, there's the dining-room with the tiled floor. It's got crabs and fish and ducks, and that scorch mark is where Nutty set fire to Tony's hat.'

'Give over.'

We climbed down into the massive hole to get a closer look. Part of a wall painting here, a bit of a fresco there. Corridors, ante-rooms, kitchen, a flue still intact, a corner of the verandah and traces of the garden path down to the river.

'It's impossible,' said Nigel, 'there can't be a villa here.'

'I knew she was on this wavelength,' Elinor said excitedly, 'I believed her right from the start.'

'We'll get the council here. When they see it they'll stop any development,' Nigel said, turning some knuckle-bones over in his hands.

'Buddy sent us those,' I told him, 'for my birthday in AD 57.'

'Well I never!' Bedelia said. 'You don't look that old.'

It was such an important discovery that the Mayor and Corporation were persuaded to inspect it the following afternoon and the whole village turned out to wait for them. If all else failed I would have to write to the Pope.

Dear Pontiff,
  I appeal to you as an honorary Roman to nip over here in your Popemobile and put a stop to this wanton destruction. You know the Goths and Vandals you had a while back? Well we've got them here now and they're after building a den of iniquity on top of your Imperial Roman artefacts.
  I know you like hiking because I saw a photo of you in your little bum-freezers, so we'll take you up on the moors and then call at Harry Ramsden's for some fish 'n' chips. It'll be a change from going round blessing everybody.
  Well Karol I have to go now, see you on the balcony at Easter and watch out for those pigeons. Kind regards to the papal dunces.
      Your obedient vassal,
      Madonna Craven
PS If you can't get over yourself can you send Maradona? he'd be a handy chap to have around.

'Quick, they're coming!' Otley shouted as he raced towards the bridge. I did my best to catch up – if only I were Flo-Jo. A procession of black-clad dignitaries streamed down the road like a column of soldier ants and came to a halt on the bridge. Then there was a crunching and a snapping sound as the bridge crumbled and deposited its burden into the fast-flowing Wharfe. The Mayor and Corporation flapped about like mud skippers and some were swirled round by the eddies and then flung on to sprawling tree roots where they hung about like wet washing. We couldn't help laughing.

'Oh dear!' said Aunt Bedelia, wiping her eyes on the tea-towel. 'Don't they look comical in their best suits an' all.'

Always ready for a dip I leapt into the water and grabbed hold of an elderly lady with neat little curls and bifocals on the end of her nose. I pulled her to the side where Otley dragged her up the bank and began to dust her down as if she were not wet but dirty.

'Come on in,' I called, 'the water's lovely.'

Suddenly the river was full of plunging bodies going to the rescue, barking dogs and screaming girls mingling their cries with the masterful ones of the menfolk.

'Let go of his tie, Shirley, you'll strangle him!'

'I'm drowning, Darren. I've got my foot trapped under a lump of concrete!'

'Well, let go of his tie and grab hold of his ears!'

I could have sworn I caught a glimpse of Swire Sugden through the haze on the opposite side. He seemed to be smiling and then he was gone. The Mayor was struggling to free his chain of office from the overhanging branch of a fragile alder. Any second now it would break and throw him back into the river. Otley and I held on to him while Nigel searched for a large piece of wood to haul him out with, and in the meantime we had a close-up of the lush vegetation of the riverside: buttercups, forget-me-nots, dog roses and honeysuckle and the shy little water avens modestly hiding its peach-coloured face.

'Well, I never knew there was such a thing,' the Mayor spluttered.

'Quick, there's a kingfisher!' Otley said excitedly.

'Where?'

'Too late you've missed it.'

'I can smell aniseed balls,' the Mayor exclaimed. 'It's a long time since I had any of those.'

'That's the sweet cicely,' I said, pointing out the clumps of lacy white florets and feathery leaves.

'I've lost touch with mother nature these days.'

'I expect you only know about rateable values an' that.'

'Yes,' he sighed.

When Nigel came back he lay down on his stomach and held out a big stick which the Mayor clutched and Otley and I pushed him from the back until we got him out none the worse for his adventure.

'I quite enjoyed that,' he said.

Somebody had lit a bonfire and we sat round it chatting until we had dried our clothes. There were some bruised shins and sprained ankles, black eyes and a few cuts and grazes but nothing you wouldn't get on a rugby field, although a couple of old ladies were taken off home by ambulance with attacks of the vapours.

'Now then,' the Mayor said, 'where's this Roman villa?'

We led the bedraggled procession through the meadow and up to the dig where Nigel's mature students were hard at work sifting, sorting and cataloguing. We tumbled down into the hole like so many Alices and gazed in wonder around us. Jet beads, bone needles and pins and spoons, bronze horse-trappings and a tile of the IXth Legion lay on a stone table with a collection of coins and a few pieces of gold jewellery.

'Of course, this villa has no right to be here,' Nigel told them, 'but since it is we must save it for future generations to enjoy.'

'Have you found any skeletons?' asked one of the lads from the nail factory. 'Sir Mortimer Wheeler found one with a spear in his back.'

'Not yet.'

'Who lived here then?'

'Mrs Craven can tell you more about it,' Nigel went on. 'She is a sensitive and claims to be able to regress to the Roman era.'

'Don't say anything,' Otley whispered, 'they'll think you're mad.'

'It was built by the Romans for our Yorkshire lass Cartimandua –'

'Shh!'

'She traded with them in an attempt to bring some prosperity to the region –'

'May, shut up.'

'But Venutius opposed her and civil war broke out with husband and wife leading the warring factions.'

'We know all that, don't we?' came a voice from the back.

'You didn't know he was a drunken sot who beat her up on a Saturday night, did you?' I blurted out. 'And you didn't know he gave all her housekeeping money to the Druids – '

'You'll have to excuse my wife, she's not very well,' Otley broke in.

'This is all very interestin',' said the Mayor, 'but I can't say one way or t'other, it'll have to be discussed in council and there's yon bridge to be seen to now. I understand that Mr Sugden's going to law about it.'

'It could drag on for months,' I protested, 'years even.'

He shrugged his shoulders and clambered out of the hole with his retinue following on behind. They brushed themselves down and advanced towards the bridge then came to a sudden stop.

'Nah then, how are we goin' to get across this bloody river?' the Mayor inquired.

It looked as if we had painted ourselves into a corner and I was on the verge of giving up and going home when Jake trundled up with his totter's cart and his little skewbald pony. I didn't know he was interested in ancient history.

It was like a scene from the French Revolution with the gypsy ruffian and a bog-ridden Tumbleweed perched at the front and Swire Sugden trussed like an oven-ready chicken at the back, his hair singed, his face streaked with smut and his natty gents' suiting in disarray.

'Whoa there, lass,' said Jake as they came to a halt. 'Oi! Over here! Old Sugden's got something to say to you lot.'

The Mayor and Corporation made their way back and grouped themselves round the cart, glad that somebody else was making the decisions. Mr Sugden got to his feet when his bonds were cut and straightened his tie before he spoke.

'I'm withdrawing my plans and will not be taking legal proceedings after all. Lord Chatwin 'ere has the whiphand, an' I'm not throwing good money after bad, that's all I've got to say.'

'Now Lord Chatwin wants a word,' Jake said, giving him a nudge.

'I'm prepared to sell to Mr Sugden if he agrees to my conditions.'

'And what are they?' asked Sugden, interested in spite of himself.

'That you rebuild the villa as a health farm and hydro, we recognize the need to bring money to the area; establish a nature trail with two rangers, me and Jake, and you can have your holiday village if you reconstruct the marching camp and put some huts up there with thatched roofs like an old British hill fort.'

'It's worth thinking about.'

'And there's one other thing,' Tumbleweed said, addressing the Mayor, 'the gypsies want a proper site with lavatories and rubbish collection.'

'You can say that again,' came a voice from the crowd.

'It'll have to go before t' planning committee,' the Mayor said, 'but as you're all in agreement I'll do what I can.'

Jake ferried them across the ford on his cart with horse and master enjoying a paddle. Cries of 'and don't forget the bridge' pursued Swire Sugden as he wended his way home.

'Well done!' I said when Jake came back. 'You must have thrown the book at him, getting him to change his mind like that.'

'There's times when you have to take the law into your own hands,' Tumbleweed laughed, 'nothing to do with books.'

'Aye,' said Jake, 'I 'swore I'd get him one day – I strung 'im up on yon old oak and lit a bonfire under 'im.'

What a happy band we were that evening. Now we could prepare for the Jubilee without a care in the world. Nigel and Elinor practised the tango to work up some more passion. Bomp, bomp, bomp, bomp – dip – tara, ra, ra, ra. She had her bodystocking on again; I don't know what Napoleon would say. They are to attend the banquet as Antony and Cleopatra and hoped to outdo Taylor and Burton. Aunt Bedelia and I were trying to watch *Brookside*, but it was an impossible mix, like tripe and onions with Bolognese sauce, so when Otley went down to the pub to see the lads I strolled down to the villa. My beautiful villa – when it has been built I shall take my holidays there, no airport delays and no traffic jams, just taking tea with my little finger up and Dorothy Wordsworth on my lap. I shall tell Otley I'm in Majorca.

After walking round the dining-room with my memories I sat down at the stone table. It was here that Tony gave me my ring and told me that my funghi marinati was the best he'd ever had in spite of him getting an earful of it. Here's the chap on the white horse again, he never loses his feathers. Something seems to have upset him.

'That man in the Third Gauls, get a move on! Just because you eat blasted snails doesn't mean you've got to behave like one!' Here's the cavalry behind him, he's having a go at them now.

'First Thracian archers, halt! How many times have I told you to dismount before letting go of your arrows? My hat's like a flamin' pin-cushion.'

At the Villa Claro
AD 60

Dear Nero,

A thousand salutes O Caesar and may Jupiter smile on you at the Neronian Games. It can't be easy playing the lyre, singing, dancing and doing handstands simultaneously in the chariot race, and yes I do think it wise to have an enema the night before.

There's a shipload of dishcloths coming over COD, with a little bit of imagination they can be transformed into fig-leaves. I couldn't get Nutty to wear that flowered frock you gave him, he's dead ignorant and I wish you'd send the lads to sort him out again. Oh, by the way, we've got another one of your statues with no eyes in and everybody's saying it's made you go blind, know what I mean? take no notice luv they're only jealous. It's unfortunate your big end's gone just as we've run out of lanolin, will axle grease do?

> *Tony and I plan to marry when all this is sorted out and he has promised me Nutty's head for a garden ornament, he says it will be very effective with parsley sprouting from its orifices.*
>
> *What a good idea to build us a new housing estate so that we can pay property tax! We haven't quite got the hang of it, square houses and straight roads, with our little round huts and coracles we can only go round in circles. Luv to all down there in the Eternal City and be assured I turn a deaf ear to the rumours that it is a cesspit.*
>
> *Your faithful ally,
Carrie Brigantum*
>
> *PS Hopping across Africa reciting the Iliad is a gutsy thing to do.*

The scene faded and I lay there in a limbo land between that world and this. My eyes began to flicker open as a hand grasped my shoulder.

'May, wake up, it's raining!' Otley said as he helped me to my feet.

'Oh, my head!' I moaned.

He hauled me up from the bowels of the villa, took off his jacket and placed it tenderly round my shoulders. He needn't think I'm going roller-skating.

'It's all over now. You've proved your point,' Otley went on. 'No need for any more of this nonsense.'

'It's a part of my life, and I'm never going to give it up,' I said as we hurried up through the copse.

'You won't have time for all this stuff when we get home again, what with the oven to clean and everything,' he persisted.

'I can do my regressing when you go fishing,' I suggested.

'Fair enough,' he said.

Later on, after a warm bath and enveloped in one of Aunt Bedelia's flannelette nightgowns, I began to relax and look forward to the Jubilee. Otley made me some hot milk and honey and helped himself to a cheese and pickle sandwich and a mug of strong coffee. He has a cast-iron stomach.

'Are you all right down there?' Aunt Bedelia called.

'Yes, thank you, Aunt Bedelia,' I said.

'You needn't say "Aunt Bedelia" every time,' Otley reminded me. 'Like a tiny tot; you're grown up now.'

'I told you, I'm going down again. It's more fun,' I said.

'You're still my May!' Otley said, holding me close and nibbling my ear in a way that drives me wild. My hand shook, spilling my hot milk all down my flannelette frills, and before long they were lying in a heap at my feet.

I think I'm going to lose my virginity again for the jubilee.

Twenty-Seven

Jubilee day dawned with little puffs of warm air carrying the dandelion clocks hither and thither and turning the leaves on the trees inside out.

'It's going to rain,' said Otley, trying his hearth rug on and picking up his dustbin lid. 'How do I look?'

He had a rubber knife and cudgel and a hairy chest from the joke shop but something was not quite right.

'It's your bald head!' squealed Aunt Bedelia.

When he was fitted with one of Elinor's wigs he was more the part.

'You'd never get a bald Ancient Briton, would you?' she said.

'That's because they didn't live long enough,' he explained.

I wore the shantung tea-gown and a gold circlet round my forehead to make it clear that I'm the Queen.

'She didn't dress like that,' Otley protested. 'She wore winter woollies and moth-eaten old rabbit skins.'

'Nero sent me them.'

'Look, May,' he said, 'if you're not careful you'll end up at the funny farm the way you're going on.'

'So what!'

'What would you rather do, watch colour television with me or an old black and white set with the Monster Raving Loony Party?'

'I'd rather go to bed and read.'

Elinor was stunning as the Queen of the Nile, her long black hair smoothed out with wet-look gel, a gold and green silk robe and chunky turquoise earrings and bangles from Star of the East down the market; and how handsome was Nigel in his mini-skirt, feathers and horse brasses. Children and dogs followed them wherever they ventured.

We helped Mrs Grindlewood-Gryke and the WI set out their stalls with goodies. Some members were dressed as native Britons and others as Roman matrons.

'No orgies now!' cautioned the honourable lady.

The meadow began to mushroom with tents and huts and the street theatre erupted into an explosion of living history, the performers flinging themselves to the ground and then leaping into the air as and when the idea occurred and making funny faces all the while.

A steady stream of sightseers made their way along the river to see the villa where they were shown round by the WEA class decked out as praetorian guards and vestal virgins.

Now here's Mike with Jilly's Jazz Band. They might have made an effort to get the right costumes. Parti-coloured hose with cap and bells were not worn until the Middle Ages, and, fetching though Jilly's wimple is, she's going to get caught up in the blackberry bushes before the day is out. I must have a word with them.

'Hello, Mike! Yoohoo!'

He's not seen me, they've gone straight past, he has not yet come to terms with the fact that his mummy's a queen. I've got to go on the gate now so I haven't time to run after them.

There's the Watling Street Guard lads – I think they're all there: Judd, Jack, Freddie, Bob, Mickey, Jimmy, Ted, Gordon, Chas and Harry.

'Oi oi, can anybody come?'

'Left right, left right!'

'Cor, look at that!'

'Does yer mother know yer out?'

'Gerremoff!'

They've marched straight into the vestal virgins' changing tent.

'Aye aye, don't do anything I wouldn't do!'

'Come up an' see me sometime.'

'Oo-la-la!'

There's a bus pulling up at the stop proclaiming 'Lightwater Valley, Soopa Loopa'. I hope they won't be too disappointed when they get off.

'This isn't Lightwater Valley,' came an aggrieved voice.

'We don't go to Lightwater Valley,' said an equally affronted bus driver. 'All change!'

'What's this ticket for then?'

'That's a Metro Saverstrip. You can go anywhere with that.'

'I know, but we didn't want to come here.'

'I wanna ride on the Soopa Loopa,' sobbed a little boy, tugging at his mother's skirt.

'Shut yer racket, Jason, or yer can't watch that man with the big fat belly on *Sumo*.'

'Where's Michael Jackson?' a toddler screamed in the mêlée.

'Where can I go with this then?'

'That's a NightRider. Can't use it during the day.'

'And this?'

'You can go as far as Burnley if you're old or disabled.'

'I don't want to go to Burnley.'

The besieged driver revved up his engine in a threatening manner and berated his passengers.

'I'm not waiting all day for you to make your minds up. Either get off here or stay on and go back home again.'

Suddenly they all surged towards me and flung their coins into the canvas sheet I was guarding and one old codger decided to go home.

'We can have a paddle,' somebody said.

'I wanna go on the Soopa Loopa,' little Jason wailed.

'Shurrup!' his mother said, giving his behind a whack.

There would be the ox-roasting at midday and then a demonstration of marching by the lads followed by skirmishing with the Ancient Britons. I had not seen Otley for some time and climbed up on the wall for a better view. Already there was the smell of roast beef and the white-coated cooks stood by with their carving knives waiting to hack the poor beast up and put him between a thousand Yorkshire teacakes.

The scene lay before me like the field of a medieval tourney: banners and bunting and ladies in jewel-bright colours. Jake and Tumbleweed led a group of ecologically aware senior citizens up to the bog, taking the newly established nature trail through the woods. A queue had formed by the table holding the teacakes and a crowd gathered to watch the animal sacrifice slowly rotating on a giant spit. That looks like Otley standing behind the teacakes. I'll go over and have a word with him.

I pushed my way through the munching hordes, ice-cream, gingerbread men, toffee apples and potato crisps parted to let me pass. Jilly's Jazz Band trod the riverside path playing 'My Old Man's a Dustman' and pursued by barking dogs. I waved but they took no notice.

'Would you like some help?' I asked as Otley and his supervisor, Mr Hawksworth, began slicing up the teacakes.

'You can put the mustard on,' said Mr Hawksworth putting an economy size container in front of me.

'Can I put it on the teacakes?'

'No, you put it on the meat.'

'I don't eat meat, I shall be sick.'

'Well, you asked if you could help.'

'I didn't know I had to put it on the meat – '

'You'll have to excuse my wife, she's not well,' Otley broke in.

Soon the carvers were busy and the mound of teacakes began to go down, but not everyone was pleased with what they were given.

'Can I have horseradish sauce instead?'

'Where d'you think you are, the Ritz?'

'Haven't you got any HP sauce?'

'No, we haven't got any HP sauce, this isn't Tesco's.'

'Mum always puts tomato ketchup on.'

'Well you'd better go home then and get your tomato ketchup.'

'Oh dear! I prefer salad with mine.'

'There's plenty o' rabbit food round here, help yourself.'

'I never eat white bread. Haven't you got any stoneground wholemeal teacakes?' inquired a health-conscious optimist.

'You should 'ave brought yer own, shouldn't yer?'

After an hour or two of observing the various shapes and sizes of mouths crammed with teacake the novelty began to wear off and I felt a bilious attack coming on.

'Sit down, I'll get you a cup of tea,' said Otley.

When he came back we sat down on the grass and had a breather while Mr Sykes, the butcher, and his assistants went on carving. I averted my eyes.

'That looks like Jeremiah Scrape,' Otley said. 'What's he up to?'

I looked in the direction he was pointing – Roman villa, vestal virgins' tent, WI stalls with Aunt Bedelia and Mrs Cartwright frantically buttering and jamming home-made scones, street theatre, Punch and Judy, and there's old Jeremiah just passing the jazz band with his fingers in his ears. He seems to be heading this way. I hope Swire Sugden hasn't changed his mind.

'Make out we haven't seen him,' Otley said as he pretended to be searching for something in the grass.

Jeremiah was wearing his pin-stripes with the seat shiny from decades of polishing the council furniture with his bottom. He blew his inquisitive nose on a large handkerchief and produced a notebook and pencil which he pointed at the butcher.

'Nah then Mr Sykes,' he said officiously. 'You didn't get a permit for this, did you?'

'For what?'

'For cutting animals up and disposing of them in a public place.'

'I'm not disposing of it, we're eating it.'

'Same thing as far as council's concerned,' Jeremiah said, writing in his book.

'We've always done ox-roasting – my father and grandfather before me – anybody can tell you.'

'Council's turned a blind eye to it previously but I'm in charge now and I'm booking you under the Fireworks and Public Entertainments byelaw.'

'What you on about? We haven't got any fireworks.'

'Strewing guts about is the same as letting squibs off in a public venue, all comes under Fireworks byelaw.'

'I'm not strewin' guts about,' Mr Sykes protested.

'What's all that offal and stuff in your dustbin then?' Jeremiah countered. 'Refuse collectors reported it.'

'Well, you don't think I'm going to keep it in the fridge, do you?'

'No, but you left it out in the street.'

'It's my dustbin, isn't it?'

'Causing a stink on the Queen's highway,' said Jeremiah, riffling through the pages of his book, 'an offence against society.'

'Sod off,' Mr Sykes exploded, 'you bat-faced old creep.'

'Yeah!' came a chorus of voices and suddenly Jeremiah Scrape was manhandled down to the river and thrown in, notebook and all. When he struggled out he espied a happy couple engaged in skinny-dipping in the shelter of an overhanging sycamore and went on his way muttering something like 'without the benefit of suitable drawers'.

'This way for the skirmishing!' Mr Ridgeway called.

'We're on, we're on!' Otley cried as the Ancient Britons and the Watling Street Guard assembled to receive their marching orders.

'Oi, oi, how's yer father?'

Jostling, raspberrying and treading on each other's toes, they crowded round their officer to hear what he had to say.

'Romans line up at the camp and Brits over there in the woods,' Nigel instructed. 'And we all converge down in the meadow where the skirmishing will take place. Jazz band will split up into two so both sides have got musical support.'

'We're not lurking!'

'Nobody'll see us.'

'Fair's fair!'

I found myself a nice bit of grass with a backrest against a tree trunk and waited for the show to begin. The crowd began to gather.

'I wanna go on the Soopa Loopa,' hollered little Jason.

'Shut yer gob, the Romans are comin',' his mummy said, thrusting an orange drink-on-a-stick into his gaping mouth.

Presently the Watling Street Guard came over the hill to the strains of 'Viva España' and soon we were all singing away.

'Tarra, rah, España.'

Tramp, tramp, tramp.

Jilly and the band in mini-skirts and sandals led the patrol, Nigel came next wearing a fireman's helmet and carrying a stuffed bird on a stick, then the lads in a variety of truncated nightgowns and horse brasses jangled their way down the hill. The band had done a quick change!

Soon the marching changed to slithering as the patrol hit a scree that propelled them forward as if they were on ball-bearings and they came tumbling headlong to the bottom.

'Watling Street Guard, halt!' Nigel shouted frantically.

The musicians were knocked over like a row of skittles and all came to rest higgledy-piggledy as they were stopped in their tracks by a magnificent horse chestnut tree.

'As you know,' said Nigel, with great presence of mind, 'the Romans introduced the chestnut into Britain – not this one, though, it was the other one.'

'Which one?'

'The sweet chestnut. They ground the nuts into flour.'

'Didn't the Roman army use conkers in their catapults?'

'No,' said Nigel, 'they used boulders in their ballistas.'

While the Romans were dusting themselves down and rearranging their feathers and mini-skirts, the lurking Brits emerged from the woods and advanced in a rabble brandishing their rolling pins. A great cheer went up from the crowd as Otley approached daubed with my blue eye shadow and making threatening gestures in the direction of the enemy.

'Erewiggo, erewiggo, erewiggo,' chanted the yobs.

'I thought we were marching, not lurking,' the lads complained.

'Get stuck in!'

'Never mind abaht the fancy stuff!'

'Away the lads!' Otley called as he charged at the Romans.

What a racket ensued! Catcalls and guffaws from the spectators, battle-cries from the combatants and a clashing of dustbin lids together with the strains of 'Any Old Iron' and 'Viva España'. Then when it was realized that things had taken a turn for the worse and somebody was going to get killed the vicar stepped in and bought them all ice-creams.

Girls gathered round the Watling Street Guard demanding their torn mini-skirts back and a little posse of skinheads formed in front of the Brits shouting: 'Give 'em a knuckle samwidge, mate,' 'Yeah, put the boot in'.

I felt a migraine coming on and made my way to the villa for some peace and quiet. I kept waving to Mike but he took no notice, and if I hang about here Otley will only ask me to fetch him a slice of ox and then I shall be sick.

The vestal virgins had gone for a tea break and I sat down thankfully in the cool of the ruins and closed my eyes. I'm going paddling today with Tony. Nero wants a big river pearl to go in his belly-button, he says he can't see the other one for fluff. Who's this coming?

'Second Asturians – you 'orrible little men – halt!'

'Can we 'ave our castanets back, sir?'

'No, you can't 'ave your castanets back. Them Brits can 'ear us comin' a mile off what with your stampin' and clackin' and oléin'. We didn't build this road for you to dance a bloody fandango on.'

There they go paso dobleing all over my rose garden, I'm fed up.

At the Villa Claro
AD 61

Dear Buddy,

Fancy flogging you just because you sliced the legs off the general. And that officer, luv, I said he was a legate from the Balearics not leg him one in the bollocks but it's a mistake anybody could have made. I don't know what they'll do to you either. Why don't you come up here for a week or two and I'll show you how to knit a string bag to put hubby in then you can hang him up with the onions.

Men! I'm sick of the lot of them. I know how you feel, they're all or nothing. There's Tony never out of the bath and Nutty never in it, one stinks like a knocking shop the other like a nest of polecats; I'm beginning to wonder how they'd look on the mantelpiece but don't let on I said so!

We can go down to Aquae Sulis for a bit of steaming an' that, you need to get away funny time of the moon coming up, know what I mean? Whatever you do don't go charging down to Colchester they'll have your guts for garters. Oh dear! Tony's here for his gnocchi.

Your luving friend,
Carrie Brigantum

PS I told Nero you'd meet him at Dover but I should leave your chariot behind he might not understand if you cut him in two, he's funny that way.

I opened my eyes to the sound of yet more crashing of dustbin lids, gales of laughter and the occasional scream coming from behind the bushes. A good time was being had by all. But I'd had my fill of merrymaking and decided to stay put a while until my headache eased. It was nice and cool here in the bowels of the earth and the sounds muffled as if from the bottom of a swimming pool.

I looked forward to the banquet and wondered idly whether Swire Sugden would turn up and spoil it. So far everything had gone our way, but it was hard to believe that the wily old campaigner would not have a few more tricks up his sleeve. The thought occurred to me that if he had it would mean our staying on at Claro, and I didn't want to go home anyway.

Perhaps Otley would clean the oven and water the busy Lizzies and leave me here. But now we are one again he'll expect his own personal maid, cook and bottle-washer. Baldrics! I'm going to sleep!

Twenty-Eight

All was quiet when I awoke and everyone had vanished as if in a dream. Then I remembered they would be getting ready for the Roman banquet later on in the evening. They shouldn't leave all this stuff unguarded – and what's that envelope over by the pile of coins? It wasn't there when I came.

Dear Mrs Craven,
 Sorry I have to miss the orgy. Had the most exciting offer to do another dig at Isurium Brigantum, your cantonal capital, it's a dream come true if you'll pardon the expression. Could this be your ring? it was found down by the river with an ear-pick and a stiletto. Happy dandelion days and many of them. Arrivederci.

Nigel

It is, it is! My little band of Welsh gold with the tiniest of freshwater pearls, no good for belly-buttons so I kept it; and I remember Tony poking the funghi marinati out of his ears with this pick.

The evening sky was darkening as I made my way up to Claro. It was airless and humid with a threat of thunder in the heavy sulphur-coloured clouds. Aunt Bedelia stood at the gate with her arms akimbo, then Otley and Elinor joined her. Where had I been to? The dandelion quiche was curling up at the edges and the semolina pudding congealed into a wodge you could use as Polyfilla.

'I fell asleep in the villa.'

'You know I got injured in the skirmishing? My old war wound – I'm going home to see Dr Moss tomorrow,' Otley said in an offended tone.

'It's your own fault,' I said peevishly. 'You leapt right into the middle of the Watling Street Guard with your bad leg.'

'I didn't know they were making a tortoise, did I?'

We relaxed for an hour with a cup of tea and Otley switched the magic box on to see what the world was up to. The Tour de France flashed before our eyes in a kaleidoscope of green jerseys, yellow jerseys, black bottoms and a pink-spotted 'King of the Mountains'; close-ups of whirring wheels and legs working like the pistons of diesel engines, induction, compression, power and exhaust. Then the long-distance shots of the pack streaming down the highway like white corpuscles along an artery.

'It's as good as *The Living Body*, isn't it?' said Elinor.

'That reminds me, I mustn't forget the black pudding for tonight,' Bedelia said as yet another shiny black behind came up on the screen.

Mrs Grindlewood-Gryke had ordered most of the stuff from a local catering firm and all we had to do was add the finishing touches to make it look Roman. We had Trimalchio's feast to go on, described by Nero's mate Petronius, so we had an idea of what they ate, and let me say that it was as much of a surprise to find they had sausages and black pudding as it was to find out they had concrete.

Aunt Bedelia had been busy for days shaping sausage meat into pigs' testicles and dormice. For hedgehogs we just stuck cocktail sticks into the dormice. The long trestle tables were set out in the meadow and garden lights strung out in the trees, and soon the diners began to arrive. The lads from the nail factory were still wearing their helmets.

Mrs Grindlewood-Gryke had spared no expense to feed the multitude. There was turkey and chicken, lamb and pork; a variety of fish, sausages, salads, jacket potatoes; jellies, trifle, cakes and enough sticky buns to satisfy a Billy Bunter. Ginger beer, cider, real ale and plonk.

Here and there a Roman dish, cabbage cooked with leeks, stuffed dates, tripe in ginger sauce, yuk! I'm not sitting there, I'll have the cabbage. We had done our best and we lacked the peacocks, the ostriches, the slaves and the pack of hounds but nobody seemed to be worried.

'Friends, Romans and countrypersons,' Elinor said, 'we want to thank you all for your support in these last few difficult weeks. Thanks to your determination we have achieved our object –'

'Hear! hear!'

'Up the 'Ammers!'

'The meadow, the woods and the old oak will still be here for our children and grandchildren to enjoy.'

'Hooray!'

'We shall nevah surrendah!' came a Churchillian voice from the lads.

'And let's have a round of applause for Mrs Grindlewood-Gryke who has provided this splendid feast for us. Thank you, Mollie.'

When the thumping and cheering had died away Mrs Grindlewood-Gryke rose to her feet fingering her pearls and smoothing down the flounces of her garden party frock.

'As you can see we are talking sub rosa,' she said pointing to the wild roses above our heads, 'so I am about to let you into a secret. Lord Chatwin and I are going to be married.' She turned to Tumbleweed on her right. 'It is leap year and I lost no time in popping the question as I think he is the right man to lead Claro and Grindlewood Park into the twenty-first century.'

'Aye aye!'

'Don't do anything I wouldn't do!'

'And I can assure you that he *is* my old friend Spiggy Meu. He has proved it beyond the shadow of a doubt. Now eat up and don't forget to take your litter home with you.'

The next half-hour or so passed quietly but for the sound of happy munching and quaffing. Elinor looked lost without Nigel to tango with. Perhaps Otley could step in there and give me a chance to get to know Mistress Wordsworth.

'Not with this leg,' he said. 'She's too enthusiastic.'

'It'll be nice in the Martello tower.'

'You're trying to get me off with her,' he said. 'You don't care about me, do you?'

'Of course I care about you – you're my husband, aren't you? You just get on my wick at times, that's all.'

'You'll feel different when we get home.'

'Mr Craven,' I said sternly.

'Yes, Mrs Craven?'

'I'm not going home.'

'Oh, don't start all that guff about being a person again.'

The little puffs of wind playing with the leaves were getting stronger now, shaking the petals from the wild roses and throwing them at the diners as if they were confetti.

'Look! We're married to Claro!' Mollie squealed in delight.

Thunder rumbled in the distance and then rolled away again over the hills. What a relief! It was a lovely night and nobody wanted to go home.

'With a bit of luck it'll stay over in Manchester,' Otley said.

'Who's this coming?' Elinor said, pointing to a figure marching towards us along the riverside.

'Well, I'll be blowed! It looks like Julius Caesar.'

'It's Swire Sugden!'

'Can't be, not dressed up like that!'

'It is, though.'

Sugden approached with his horse brasses jangling and his kilt lifting in the breeze revealing his Union Jack boxer shorts. He came to a halt on a little knoll and flung out his arms in a dramatic gesture.

'"Now is the winter of our discontent –"' he began.

'That's *Richard III*,' Miss Briggs, the schoolmarm, called.

Sugden took a deep breath and started again.

'"To be or not to be –"'

'And that's *Hamlet, Prince of Denmark*.'

'"Once more unto the breach, dear friends –"'

'*Henry V*.'

'Look, I'm not an educated man, I came here to show my solidarity and things are going to be different from now on.'

'Beware the ides of March, Mr Sugden.'

'Aye, that's right, lass.'

He came down from the knoll and seemed to be searching for somebody. I hid behind Otley hoping it wasn't me.

'There you are, Mrs Craven,' he said advancing towards me. 'What was in that bottle I found in the bathroom?'

'That you were going to show the police?'

'Aye,' he said with his chins juddering like a jelly.

'I told you, it was dandelion wine, Aunt Bedelia made it.'

'I slipped it in my pocket and forgot about it till one day when I was down at yon ford and I took a swig and, by God, it's potent.'

'Did you see things?'

'I did that! It was as if I were back in Roman times. Then Julius Caesar comes up and I knew what he were going to say before he said it.'

'As if he was your alter ego?'

'Or *doppelgänger*, summat like that.'

We got talking and strolled along the riverside path too engrossed to hear the rumble of thunder getting nearer, or note the wind getting up to a blustery gale.

'I was a decent bloke and I never had syphilis neither,' Mr Sugden explained, 'I had lead poisoning, that's why I went bald.'

'I know, it's all that lead piping you used.'

'An' it were just the same then. It didn't matter what you were buildin' they didn't want it.'

'They weren't used to square houses,' I explained.

'We tried to install modern conveniences but they'd rather have typhoid than aqueducts.'

'I know.'

'And them Druids were disgusting with their tatty beards and dirty finger-nails –'

'Sacrificing babies an' that,' I broke in.

'We used rabbits,' he said.

It was nice to talk over old times and Swire Sugden assured me that in future he would get a consensus before sending in the bulldozers. His life had taken on a new dimension. It wasn't just here and now, he was part of the past and he was going to sign up for the WEA history and archaeology classes.

'It's boring being trapped in your body, isn't it, when you can be a time traveller?' I enthused.

'I always used to like Doctor Who,' he said.

We turned back to retrace our steps as a clap of thunder echoed through the valley and the wild wind battered the trees. Everybody rushed to clear the remains of the banquet away, filling their carrier bags with chicken legs, sausages and currant buns, the lads from the nail factory draining the glasses and bottles in a last minute celebration.

'Hey up, there's some more 'ere,' said Mickey, with a bottle in one hand and a hunk of meat in the other.

'That's right, don't leave it for the rats,' Mrs Grindlewood-Gryke called. 'Old Jeremiah will be round here in the morning.'

The gale flushed out litter left from the afternoon's festivities and soon the meadow was full of Brits and Romans chasing frantically after paper cups and plates, ice-cream cartons, streamers and sad deflated balloons. Kilts and togas and hearth rugs were flicked up to reveal Y-fronts and boxer shorts in red, white and blue stripes; green and yellow spots; black and white snatches of music, 'God Save the Queen' and 'Maybe it's because I'm a Londoner'; and wasn't that young Burt the body-builder with his packed lunch in a posing-pouch?

'Well, I never!' said Aunt Bedelia stalking off with her skirt up over her head showing her fleecy-lined Directoire knickers.

'Quick! Catch that,' Elinor called as she ran after a greasy, paper napkin, her gold satin pleats swirling around making her look like a giant sunflower. Oh dear! I think she's forgotten something.

A van stood by to take the bottles up to the municipal bottle bank, another for the cans and a red plastic hippopotamus with its mouth wide open waited to receive the litter. 'Please leave this field as you would wish to find it,' it said.

'I want nothing left here that David Bellamy wouldn't approve of,' Mrs Grindlewood-Gryke ordered as the wind whisked her flounces up to display her silk Marks & Spencer camiknicks with elasticated waist and cotton-lined double gusset.

'Where have you been to?' Otley asked as I ran to the hippopotamus clutching an armful of debris.

'I was talking to Mr Sugden. He's a reformed character. We ran back when the gale blew up.'

'I know. We could see all your bloomers,' he said accusingly.

After a struggle with the wind we managed to get the meadow looking neat and tidy, tables were loaded on to a dumper and the villagers made for home with their booty.

Suddenly there was a flash of lightning and a roll of thunder and the heavens burst sending us scuttling into the woods for shelter, but it wasn't long before the rain got through and drenched us with miniature Niagaras that came cascading down from the broad leaves.

'We might as well go home as stand here,' Otley said.

'Run for the tower,' Elinor said. 'It's nearer.'

We didn't so much run as squelch, slosh and slither up to the marching camp with the electric storm raging about us. One step forward and two steps back.

'My poor little dandelions,' Aunt Bedelia lamented. 'They don't like rain.' The water flattened her curls and ran in a river over her spectacles and off the end of her nose. She slipped into a ditch and we pulled her out gasping for breath. 'They shut their eyes, little poppets, and hang their heads till it's all over.'

'They've gotta have rain or they won't grow,' said Elinor angrily.

'We know that but they don't,' Bedelia spluttered through the wet.

As we struggled up the hill with brambles and goose-grass snatching at our clothes there was an almighty clap of thunder together with a flash of lightning that seemed to strike the Jubilee Tower.

'It's a thunderbolt!'

'It's hit the tower!'

'Quick!' screamed Elinor. 'My books! My souvenirs!'

Smoke was rising from the top of the tower when we fell into the round kitchen exhausted. I sank into a squashy chair not caring whether we were on fire or not, it had to get through the water first. Elinor grabbed a fire extinguisher and dashed up to her den.

Otley threw us a large towel each and some dry clothes which we changed into like embarrassed children on the beach, then we had a mug of cocoa and a gingerbread man with currant eyes and chocolate buttons down his front. We would have to stay here the night.

'I'll take Elinor some cocoa up,' Otley said. 'See if she's put the fire out and done anything about that Martello tower holiday.'

'It'll do you good to get away. I'll stay here another week or two till you come back,' I called after him. I can get on with Dorothy Wordsworth. I'm anxious to know how they got on in the woods because Otley's always nice going in and nasty when we're coming out.

Otley came tearing back down the stairs white as a sheet and put the mug of cocoa down on the table.

'She's gone!'

'I told you,' Aunt Bedelia said, 'she's always doing that.'

'Hadn't we better call the police?'

'No, she'll come back when she's ready.'

The next morning we went down to the cottage, the sun shone and the trees sparkled with diamond necklaces. It put Otley in a romantic mood and he suggested going to Margate for a second honeymoon.

'I'm staying here.'

'We can go Olde Tyme Dancing again.'

'No!' I said stamping my foot. 'Not with your filthy mouth.'

'We'll stay in bed all day and go out all night like you said.'

'I've changed my mind.'

'We've got to go home. That oven's disgusting, I'll go and get the car, no need to hang about here now.'

'I like it here.'

I kept out of his way while he fussed about with the old banger and went to get some petrol. Bedelia was busy roasting dandelion roots, I thanked her for having us and gave her the royal wave. I am a queen after all. I hoped she would ask me to stay.

'May, can you give me a hand with this,' Otley called out.

I went to see what he wanted and before I knew it I was bundled into the car and we were on our way home. We passed Swire Sugden out for a walk and when he saw us he held out his arms and mouthed a farewell.

'What's he saying?' I asked.

'I dunno,' Otley said. 'He's shouting "Carrie" or something.'